"You'll kill me, will you?" One Eye sneered, rising to face him. "You'll kill One Eye? If One Eye were that easy to kill, he'd never have survived kithood." He spat at Clear Sky, pointing with his tail at the wound along his face. "Keep that to remember me by," he snarled.

As the rogue slunk away into the forest, Clear Sky felt his legs trembling. He sank to the ground, taking in huge gulps of air. He felt so utterly defeated, as though he would never be able to get up again.

I've made a terrible mistake. . . .

WARRIORS

THE PROPHECIES BEGIN

Book One: Into the Wild

Book Two: Fire and Ice

Book Three: Forest of Secrets

Book Four: Rising Storm

Book Five: A Dangerous Path

Book Six: The Darkest Hour

THE NEW PROPHECY

Book One: Midnight

Book Two: Moonrise

Book Three: Dawn

Book Four: Starlight

Book Five: Twilight

Book Six: Sunset

POWER OF THREE

Book One: The Sight

Book Two: Dark River

Book Three: Outcast

Book Four: Eclipse

Book Five: Long Shadows

Book Six: Sunrise

OMEN OF THE STARS

Book One: The Fourth Apprentice

Book Two: Fading Echoes

Book Three: Night Whispers

Book Four: Sign of the Moon

Book Five: The Forgotten Warrior

Book Six: The Last Hope

EXPLORE THE WARRIORS WORLD

MANGA

The Lost Warrior

Warrior's Refuge

Warrior's Return

The Rise of Scourge

Tigerstar and Sasha #1: Into the Woods

Tigerstar and Sasha #2: Escape from the Forest

Tigerstar and Sasha #3: Return to the Clans

Ravenpaw's Path #1: Shattered Peace

Ravenpaw's Path #2: A Clan in Need

Ravenpaw's Path #3: The Heart of a Warrior

SkyClan and the Stranger #1: The Rescue

SkyClan and the Stranger #2: Beyond the Code

SkyClan and the Stranger #3: After the Flood

NOVELLAS

Hollyleaf's Story

Mistystar's Omen

Cloudstar's Journey

Tigerclaw's Fury

Leafpool's Wish

Dovewing's Silence

Mapleshade's Vengeance

Goosefeather's Curse

Ravenpaw's Farewell

ALSO BY ERIN HUNTER

SEEKERS

RETURN TO THE WILD

MANGA

SURVIVORS

DAWN OF THE CLANS

WARRIORS

THE BLAZING STAR

ERIN HUNTER

HARPER

An Imprint of HarperCollinsPublishers

With special thanks to Cherith Baldry

The Blazing Star
Copyright © 2014 by Working Partners Limited
Series created by Working Partners Limited
Map art © 2016 by Dave Stevenson
Interior art © 2016 by Allen Douglas

Library of Congress Cataloging-in-Publication Data
Hunter, Erin.
    The Blazing Star / Erin Hunter. — First edition.
        pages   cm. — (Warriors. Dawn of the clans ; #4)
    Summary: After facing their first battle, the remaining mountain
cats must seek the Blazing Star in order to survive a new threat: a deadly
disease sweeping through their territory.
    ISBN 978-0-06-241003-0 (pbk.)
    [1. Cats—Fiction.   2.   Diseases—Fiction.   3.   Survival—Fiction.
4. Fantasy.]   I. Title.
PZ7.H916625Bl 2014   2013047960
[Fic]—dc23   CIP
                                                                  AC

Typography by Hilary Zarycky
16 17 18 19 20   CG/OPM   10 9 8 7 6 5 4 3 2 1
❖
First paperback edition, 2016

To Roberta

ALLEGIANCES

CLEAR SKY'S CAMP

LEADER

CLEAR SKY—light gray tom with blue eyes

LEAF—black-and-white tom

PETAL—small yellow tabby she-cat with green eyes

QUICK WATER—gray-and-white she-cat

NETTLE—gray tom

SNAKE—gray tom

THORN—mangy tom with splotchy fur

KITS

BIRCH—brown-and-white tom

ALDER—gray-and-white she-kit

TALL SHADOW'S CAMP

LEADER

TALL SHADOW—black, thick-furred she-cat with green eyes

GRAY WING—sleek, dark gray tom with golden eyes

JAGGED PEAK—small gray tabby tom with blue eyes

DAPPLED PELT—delicate tortoiseshell she-cat with golden eyes

SHATTERED ICE—gray-and-white tom with green eyes

CLOUD SPOTS—long-furred black tom with white ears, white chest, and two white paws

WIND RUNNER—wiry brown she-cat with yellow eyes

GORSE FUR—thin, gray tabby tom

THUNDER—orange tom with amber eyes and big white paws

LIGHTNING TAIL—black tom

ACORN FUR—chestnut brown she-cat

KITS

OWL EYES—gray tom

PEBBLE HEART—dark gray tabby tom with amber eyes

SPARROW FUR—tortoiseshell she-kit

MORNING WHISKER—tiny she-kit

MOTHFLIGHT—she-kit with green eyes

DUST MUZZLE—gray tom-kit

RIVER RIPPLE'S CAMP

LEADER

RIVER RIPPLE—silver long-furred tom

NIGHT—black she-cat

DEW—she-cat with a short, thick gray coat and bright blue eyes

ROGUE CATS

HOLLY—she-cat with prickly, bushy fur

MOUSE EAR—tom with ears the size of a mouse's, missing part of one ear

MUD PAWS—tom with four black paws

STAR FLOWER—golden she-cat with green eyes

ONE EYE—mangy tom with knotted fur and one eye

HIGHSTONES

THUNDERPATH

TALL SHADOW'S
CAMP

THE FOUR TREES

FALLS

RIVER

RIVER RIPPLE'S
CAMP

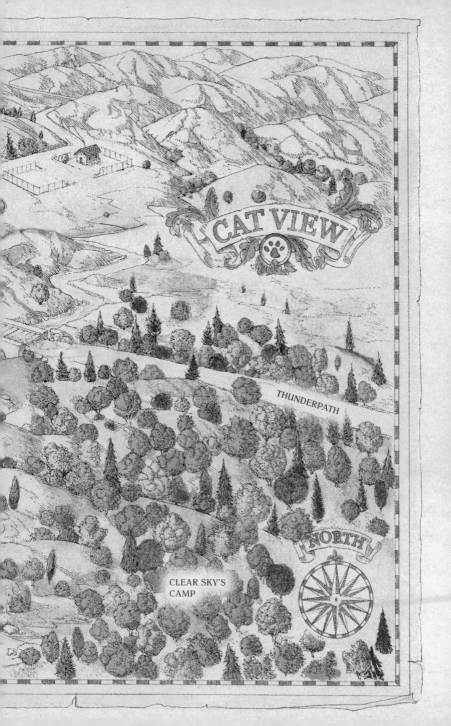

PROLOGUE

Gray Wing crouched at the top of the hollow, the faint sounds of his sleeping denmates just barely reaching his ears. The fat, white circle of the moon floated above his head, casting a frosty light over the moorland grass.

A gentle breeze ruffled Gray Wing's pelt. His eyes grew heavy, and he opened his jaws wide in a yawn.

He was sitting in the cave behind the waterfall. The gushing cascade glittered in the moonlight, and tiny specks of silver whirled across the walls and floor of the cavern. *I'm back in our mountain cave!* he thought. *It's been so many moons since we left!*

Movement beside the far wall caught Gray Wing's gaze. Stoneteller, the Tribe's Healer, was pacing toward the tunnel at the back of the cave, which led to her den. Her paw steps were unsteady with age, her body scrawny and her pelt thin. *She's so old,* Gray Wing thought. *I can't count how many seasons she's seen.*

Gray Wing glanced around. He saw his mother, Quiet Rain, curled up in her sleeping hollow, and the rest of his Tribemates were asleep too.

There's Dewy Leaf . . . oh, she's had her kits! Three of them, and they look so strong and healthy. And there's Snow Hare. She used to tell such wonderful stories.

Curiosity swept over Gray Wing. When he lived in the cave he had never entered the Healer's private den. *But I'm dreaming!* he realized. *Maybe I can follow her now, and she'll never know.* He rose to his paws and padded after her.

But Stoneteller had vanished by the time Gray Wing reached the mouth of the tunnel. All he could see was a faint silver glow at the far end. Ignoring the prickling of his pelt, he slipped softly down the dark passage toward the light.

As he approached the end of the tunnel Gray Wing crept forward more cautiously and stretched his head into Stoneteller's cave. He stifled a gasp as he gazed around.

The cave was much smaller than the one where the Tribe lived. Moonlight flooded through a jagged hole far above, washing everything with a frosty light. Stoneteller sat with her back to Gray Wing, gazing upward.

Pointed stones stretched down from the roof of the cave, and more of them grew up from the floor. Several met in the middle, so that it seemed as if the Tribe's Healer was sitting in a forest of stone trees. Ripples of water trickling down the stones shone in the moonlight and gathered in pools on the floor.

Fascinated, Gray Wing crept into the cave, drawing closer to Stoneteller as quietly as if he was stalking a piece of prey. He was sure that he hadn't made a sound, but before he could dart out of the way, Stoneteller extended a paw to halt him. Gray Wing yowled in alarm.

This is a dream, he told himself. *How can Stoneteller know I'm here?*

"Why are you following me?" Stoneteller asked. Her voice was gentle, though she didn't turn to look at Gray Wing.

His ears flattened in mingled fear and embarrassment. He had no idea how to respond. "I don't mean any harm," he protested. "I . . . er . . . I just wanted to . . ." His voice trailed off and he gazed up at Stoneteller, bracing himself for a sharp rebuke.

Sighing, Stoneteller drew her paw back. "You came here because I invited you," she meowed, her voice full of wisdom. "I *allowed* you to follow me. I called you here."

Every hair on Gray Wing's pelt prickled with amazement and he raked his claws across the hard, damp floor. "You can do that?" he whispered. "Even though I live so far away?"

Stoneteller looked at him for the first time. "Part of your heart will *always* belong here."

Gray Wing knew that was true. Though life in the mountains had been harsh and cold, sometimes he still longed for the thunder of the waterfall and the sharp peaks outlined against the sky. *And I still miss the cats I left behind . . . especially Quiet Rain.*

"Then why—" he began.

"Be quiet," Stoneteller mewed.

Her trembling whiskers were angled toward a spider spinning its web in the silvery moonlight. Gray Wing spotted some flies caught at the edge of the net; the spider was making her slow way over to them, the shining strands quivering with her movement.

Gray Wing stifled a *mrrow* of laughter. *That's going to be one fat spider very soon.*

With a sudden flash of movement Stoneteller leaped up and raked her claws through the web, shredding it into scraps. Gray Wing let out a gasp as the spider hurtled down. Instantly it sent out a strand of web, halting its fall so it could lower itself slowly to the ground. It scuttled out of sight, its home destroyed.

"Why did you do that?" Gray Wing asked, staring at Stone-teller.

The Healer returned his stare. "Never mind that," she meowed. "What did the spider do?"

That's a really dumb question, Gray Wing thought. *But I can't tell Stoneteller that!* "Well, the spider saved herself," he replied.

"Yes, it did," Stoneteller agreed. "And what will she do now?"

What is this? Gray Wing asked himself, beginning to feel irritated. *I'm not some kit who needs to be taught how to groom myself!* Taking a deep breath, he answered, "She'll build a new web."

"That's right," Stoneteller mewed. "Wisdom and a long life come from being flexible. One day soon, you will need to be just as flexible. You will have to be strong for yourself, and for other cats. You already know that life is hard. It's about to become harder."

Apprehension thrilled through Gray Wing from ears to tail-tip. He let out a snort of surprise and distress. "Can't you tell me more than that?" he demanded. "Can't you be more specific?"

Stoneteller's voice softened and she dipped her head sympathetically. "It's not for me to plan out your future, Gray Wing. I can only give you guidance. You must make your own decisions, but you will need to be strong—stronger than ever before."

She glanced over Gray Wing's shoulder. Turning his head to follow her gaze, Gray Wing seemed to see all the way down the tunnel to where his mother, Quiet Rain, was still asleep in her hollow. A deep ache awoke in his heart. *It's been so long since I left her in the mountains. So long since I felt the soft touch of her fur.*

"Make your mother proud," Stoneteller instructed. "Remember who you are and where you come from. I'm telling you these things because I know you're strong enough to listen. A great destiny awaits you and your friends, Gray Wing—but it won't wait forever. . . ."

CHAPTER 1

❧

"It's time to bury our dead," Tall Shadow declared.

The black she-cat's words dragged Thunder's attention back to the death and devastation all around him.

Everywhere beneath the branches of the four oak trees the moonlight showed him pools of drying blood and tufts of torn-out fur. Cats lay on their sides in the trampled grass, their eyes open and their faces frozen in expressions of pain or shock. The anger that had made them fight had vanished like mist under the morning sun. Now every cat looked vulnerable, the living as well as the dead.

Thunder caught the flapping of a black wing from the corner of his line of vision, and turned to spot a crow as it alighted on a low branch. Its tiny, bright eyes flicked greedily from cat to cat. A shudder ran through Thunder from ears to tail-tip, and his fur bristled.

Tall Shadow is right. No cat should be left here as food for scavengers, not when they've given their lives in such a bloody battle.

He felt as if he were carrying a heavy, wet rock in his chest in place of his heart—somehow, he knew that everything had been leading up to this terrible battle: No matter what any cat could do, *nothing* could have stopped it. Cat against cat, claw against teeth—all because of arguments over territory. A vision of blood splashing against bark flashed behind his eyes and he shuddered. Spirit-cats had come to visit them in a vision, to tell them that fighting must stop. *I want it to,* Thunder thought now. *But how do we claw our way back to peace?*

Thunder struggled to find meaning in this devastation, but it was like groping blindly through thick fog. *Now we've all seen that fighting tooth and claw over territory brings nothing but death and destruction, pain and grief.* Thunder wondered whether the cats they had lost today had died so that could be understood.

"There are so many," Thunder meowed as he moved forward to stand beside Tall Shadow, picking his way carefully among the bodies. "How can we protect them?"

Tall Shadow stretched out one foreleg, and thoughtfully slid out her claws. "This is what spilled blood," she responded. "And this is what will make things right."

Make things right? Thunder thought, bewildered. He knew what the she-cat meant, but almost unbearable pain pierced him at her words. *What could possibly make things right?*

"However long it takes," Tall Shadow went on, "we will make a hole in the ground, big enough for all our fallen friends to lie in together. In life, they were torn apart; in death, they will be united."

Thunder felt every hair on his pelt prickle at the words Tall Shadow had chosen. *Unite. That was what the spirit-cats told us at the end of the battle. Unite or die.* "Yes, this is what we should do," he mewed hoarsely.

Gray Wing, Wind Runner, and River Ripple gathered around, murmuring their agreement.

"It will take a lot of effort from every cat," Gray Wing warned them.

"Then we must make that effort," Tall Shadow insisted. "Only the earth will be able to protect our fallen denmates from crows and foxes."

As she and the other cats began to scrape at the ground, Thunder noticed that his father, Clear Sky, was standing silently a couple of fox-lengths away. He looked reluctant to step forward and join in.

Thunder padded over to him, reflecting that it was not so long ago he and his father had been fighting to the death. At his approach, Clear Sky dipped his head, deep shame in his blue eyes. "I caused this," he rasped, as if he was fighting the urge to wail aloud. "It was my anger that created the chaos, my anger that brought these cats into the battle that killed them. *So many of them* . . ." he added in a whisper.

Memories crowded into Thunder's mind: Clear Sky's first rejection of him when he was a kit; their long estrangement, followed by Thunder's shock at his father's harsh methods when he tried to live with him in the forest; their arguments and their latest parting when Thunder's paws couldn't walk his father's path any longer.

But in spite of all that, Thunder was unable to repress a surge of sympathy. "Come on," he mewed encouragingly. "Let's do right by those cats who sacrificed themselves."

When Clear Sky did not protest, Thunder led him across

to the others, who had already begun to dig in the shadow of the four trees. No cat spoke as they scraped and clawed at the ground, the hole growing bigger and bigger.

Already tired from the battle, Thunder felt his legs begin to ache as his paws grew black with dirt, and his vision blurred from exhaustion. Yet he forced himself to go on. The harsh caw of a crow sounded somewhere overhead, and he found himself digging even faster.

At last Tall Shadow stood back, shaking off the earth that clung to her paws. "That should be big enough," she panted. "Now let's bring our friends over here."

Most of the cats divided into pairs, gripping the dead cats with their jaws and dragging their limp, lifeless bodies over to the grave. But Thunder found himself alone, standing over the body of Hawk Swoop. Her orange tabby fur was clotted with blood, and a cruel gash gaped in her throat.

Thunder felt sharp claws clenching around his heart as he remembered how Hawk Swoop had cared for him when Gray Wing first brought him to the hollow after he had been driven out of the forest by his father. His shoulder fur bristled as his gaze scoured the clearing and alighted on Clear Sky; he was padding up to the body of Rainswept Flower, whose life Clear Sky had taken just before the battle began.

They knew each other since they were both kits, Thunder thought, revulsion welling up inside him.

Then he heard his father's voice, a low, grief-stricken murmur. "I'm so sorry."

Clear Sky was truly mourning his dead friend.

The guilt will hurt him more than any cat's claw ever could.

His heart still weighing heavy in his chest, Thunder dipped his head to take Hawk Swoop's scruff in his jaws. Her fur was soaked with the taste of death, and he had to fight hard not to recoil. Her body was limp and heavy now that the life had run out of her. *I can see why the other cats worked in pairs,* Thunder thought as he tugged her toward the hole.

Before he had gone many paw steps, he caught a flash of black fur. He turned his head to see Lightning Tail, with his sister, Acorn Fur, hovering behind him.

"Please let us help," Lightning Tail meowed.

Thunder nodded, knowing how right it was that the two younger cats should help to bury their mother.

The black tom gripped Hawk Swoop's tail, his green eyes filled with sorrow as his teeth met in her orange tabby fur. Acorn Fur worked her shoulder underneath her mother's belly. With their help, Hawk Swoop's body suddenly seemed lighter, and in only a few heartbeats Thunder, Lightning Tail, and Acorn Fur carried her to the edge of the grave.

Panting as he recovered from the effort, Thunder took a step back. Lightning Tail and Acorn Fur stood over their mother's body, their heads drooping and their shoulders sagging. Exchanging a grief-stricken glance, they put their noses to the ground and pushed Hawk Swoop into the hole. At the last moment their eyes closed as if they couldn't bear to see her tumble and flop onto the pile of bodies.

"No day could ever be worse than this one."

The raspy, wheezing voice startled Thunder, who whipped

around to see Gray Wing. Beyond him, through the trees that still bore their last few ragged leaves, Thunder could see the line of the moor, bare and bleak under the frosty sky.

"The days ahead can only be better," the gray tom mewed.

Thunder straightened up, raising his head with an instinctive pride. *Gray Wing is right,* he thought determinedly. *We'll make sure we never feel grief like this again.*

"Hawk Swoop, I'll never forget you." Lightning Tail spoke from the edge of the grave, his voice throbbing with sorrow.

"Neither will I," Acorn Fur added. "We'll both miss you so much."

At their words, other cats gathered around the hole to gaze down at their fallen friends.

Shattered Ice crouched at the side of the grave, his gaze fixed on his friend Jackdaw's Cry. "We'll never dig out tunnels together again," he mewed in a voice rough with grief. "The hollow won't be the same without you."

"But you have not died in vain," Cloud Spots added, standing so close to Shattered Ice that their pelts brushed. "None of you have. We shall learn from this terrible day, we promise you."

More cats took up his words, raising their voices in wails of anguish. "We promise! We promise!"

As the yowling died away, Thunder drew back from the graveside, and found himself beside Tall Shadow. As if something invisible was tugging at their paws, River Ripple and Wind Runner padded up to join them.

A couple of heartbeats later, Clear Sky drew closer with

reluctant paw steps. His eyes seemed fixed, as if he was staring at something very far away, looking through the other cats at a vision they could not grasp. He halted a little way from the other four, who stood in a line facing the rest of the survivors.

We look like we're guarding the grave, Thunder thought.

Gray Wing limped to his littermate and sat beside him, though Clear Sky kept his distance from Thunder and the others.

"Listen to me, all of you!" Tall Shadow yowled, her gaze raking across the huddle of grief-stricken cats. "This must *never* happen again. We should listen to the cats in the stars, to the warning they gave us. From now on we have to work together peacefully, and at the next full moon we must return to this clearing to hear more messages from the spirit-cats."

"Yes!" Clear Sky's voice was a shaken purr. "At last there are cats who will tell us what we have to do."

Sudden understanding flashed into Thunder's mind like the dazzle of sunlight on water.

"So *that's* why you've been so protective and so hostile!" Gray Wing turned to his brother, his gaze full of compassion. "All this time your responsibilities have been too much for you. You tried to do the right thing, but you asked too much of yourself."

Clear Sky turned his head away in shame. "I'm so sorry. . . ."

For the first time in many days, Thunder felt hope stirring inside him. *Clear Sky will get guidance from the spirit-cats now, so maybe . . .* Then he shook his head. *Nothing will make me believe that these cats needed to die.*

Tall Shadow cleared her throat loudly, interrupting his thoughts. "If I can be allowed to finish what I was saying . . ." She paused as the other cats dipped their heads in acknowledgment, then continued, "I want a promise that all cats will respect one another. No more fighting over territory and prey. Too much has happened, and all of us need time to recover. Indeed, I believe that any cat who needs help should receive it: whoever the cat, and wherever they've chosen to live. Do you agree?"

As she finished speaking, Tall Shadow looked at Gray Wing, whose gaze immediately flicked to Thunder.

"My young kin proved himself in the battle," Gray Wing meowed. "Tall Shadow, he is the one you should look to in times like this."

Tall Shadow looked puzzled. "To Thunder?"

"Yes," Gray Wing replied, bowing his head. "I need to think about what's happened, and what the future will hold. Thunder should take his rightful place as leader with you and Clear Sky and River Ripple."

A storm of anxiety broke inside Thunder. Gray Wing had been like a father to him. Now it sounded as though he was distancing himself. Gray Wing was crouching down as if he was overcome by grief, as well as weakened by his illness.

Knowing that the time for reluctance or modesty was far behind him, Thunder turned to Tall Shadow. *These cats need me now.*

"Yes, we should help any cat in trouble," he replied.

A *mrrow* of agreement came from Wind Runner, while

River Ripple dipped his head. "I will help any cat I can," he responded, surprising Thunder with the depth of feeling in his voice. It was the first time River Ripple had lost his usual calm detachment. *And he wasn't really close to any of the cats who died today,* Thunder thought, impressed.

He turned to his father. "Clear Sky, do you agree?"

Clear Sky was once again gazing into the distance at something that only he could see. He started slightly at the sound of Thunder's voice. "Yes—yes, I agree," he mewed.

Thunder wished that his father seemed more committed to the decisions that the rest of them were making, but he told himself that Clear Sky was probably shaken up by the terrible events of the night.

Just like the rest of us.

CHAPTER 2

❧

"Now it's time for all of us to go home," Tall Shadow announced. "To the forest, or the hollow on the moor. Every cat is free to choose."

"I don't live in either camp," River Ripple put in. "But any cat is welcome to come with me to my island home."

Thunder watched as the cats padded to and fro, still looking uneasy. Gradually they began to gather into two groups, one around Tall Shadow, Wind Runner, and Thunder, the other around Clear Sky.

Acorn Fur was drifting closer to the cats who surrounded Clear Sky, and Thunder's pelt prickled apprehensively at the sight. He took a step forward, but before he could do any more Lightning Tail was beside him, his green eyes wide with shock as he gazed at his sister.

"She can't be thinking of leaving us!" he exclaimed.

Acorn Fur must have heard him, or spotted the two toms watching her, because she came padding over to them. "I'm not sure I want to go back to the hollow," she meowed, blinking apologetically. "Too much has happened. I'd keep expecting to see Hawk Swoop and Jackdaw's Cry. . . ." Her voice trailed off with a choking sound.

As she spoke, Clear Sky emerged from his group of cats and came to join them. "I'll happily take Acorn Fur with me into the forest," he declared. "If that's what she wants."

Acorn Fur didn't respond, just stared mutely at the ground. With an unpleasant jolt, Thunder realized that was exactly what she wanted. *And there's nothing I can do about it. We've all agreed to live in peace with one another. Besides,* he added to himself, *what Tall Shadow said is true: Every cat should be allowed to choose where they want to live.*

He drew a long sigh. Once again it was clear that nothing would ever be the same.

But Lightning Tail clearly wasn't able to accept that. "How can you leave me?" he yowled at his littermate.

"I won't be far away." Acorn Fur brushed her brother's shoulder with her tail. "The forest is very close. Would you like to come with me?" She gazed at him hopefully.

Lightning Tail hesitated for a heartbeat, opened his mouth as if to reply, but then looked away, as if unable to find the words. He gave a sad shake of his head.

A great surge of warmth and affection swept through Thunder for his loyal friend. He stepped up to Lightning Tail and pressed his muzzle gently into the younger cat's flank. "Acorn Fur is right," he mewed. "She won't be far away. And if the battle has proved one thing, it's this: We shouldn't think of ourselves as two separate groups, but one big group, split into two."

Lightning Tail gave a nod of understanding, but he still didn't look happy.

Of course he isn't, Thunder thought. *I'll make sure to look after him in the future.*

The two groups gradually drew away from each other, one toward the moor, the other up the slope that led farther into the forest. Only River Ripple didn't move. He gave a twitch of his ears as Thunder faced him with a questioning look.

"I'm happy that you seem to have settled your differences," the silver-furred tom began.

His words pierced Thunder, as if a different cat was calling to him from among the trees. *I've always felt more comfortable in the forest,* he reflected, remembering how natural it had felt to stalk prey in the undergrowth. He could see that other cats, too, seemed to be pondering River Ripple's words. *But it looks like I belong on the moor, for now. Gray Wing and Lightning Tail both need me to take care of them.*

Dipping his head in a polite farewell to River Ripple, Thunder padded over to Tall Shadow and Wind Runner. Clear Sky approached them, embarrassment in his eyes.

"I suppose this is good-bye, for now," he meowed awkwardly. "But you're all welcome to visit, anytime you want. No more guards on the borders. I promise."

Tall Shadow acknowledged his words with a stiff nod. "We'll meet here again at the next full moon," she announced. "Then we'll see how we're all getting on."

Clear Sky murmured agreement and returned to his own cats, leading them up the slope and into the shadow of the trees. Thunder watched them go until the last tail-tip had vanished into the undergrowth.

"Come on," Tall Shadow mewed, gesturing to her own

group with a swish of her tail. "Let's go home."

But will it still feel like home, Thunder wondered sadly, *with so many of us gone?*

He took the lead as the cats headed toward the moor. In spite of all their promises, he still felt uneasy. They might have made peace with Clear Sky's group, but he couldn't help wondering how long it would last.

Dawn light slipped through the branches, growing stronger as they neared the edge of the forest. Their progress was slow as they limped painfully through ferns and around bramble thickets, weakened by their wounds and their grief. Gray Wing wheezed with every breath he took.

If anything attacks us now, we're crow-food, Thunder thought, worrying that the scent of blood might attract predators.

As if his fear had called it up, he heard a rustling in the undergrowth a few paw steps ahead. He froze, raising his tail in a signal for the others to halt. Tasting the air, he wondered what might be lying in wait for them. There was no scent of fox or badger, but whatever was lurking in the bushes was too big to be prey.

"Who's there?" Thunder called, making his voice sound loud and commanding. "Show yourselves!"

After a moment's pause three cats emerged from underneath a holly bush. They all looked wiry and half-starved, and a faint, rank smell came from them. They held their tails low, and their pelts bristled with nerves.

Thunder let his gaze travel over the three cats as they stood in front of him, half cowering and half-defiant. Two of them were toms: One had pale brown fur except for four black paws; the other was a big tabby with unusually small ears. The she-cat had bushy fur that stuck up in prickles. Thunder relaxed slightly. Even in their present injured state, he couldn't see this sorry collection giving them much trouble.

The she-cat was first to step forward. "We saw the battle, and heard what you said afterward," she began, meeting Thunder's gaze. "We wondered if your group would have room for three more cats."

Tall Shadow padded forward to stand beside Thunder. "You were wise not to get involved in the fight. But who are you?" she asked.

"I'm called Holly," the she-cat replied. "These are Mud Paws and Mouse Ear."

The tabby tom ducked his head, looking shyly amused. "Can you guess how we got our names?" he asked.

Won over by their friendly tone, Thunder couldn't resist replying. "Mud Paws is easy," he meowed. "That cat has black rings of fur around all his paws, as if he's been padding through a muddy field."

Lightning Tail was curiously circling around the big tabby.

"You must be Mouse Ear because your ears are the size of a mouse's," Lightning Tail announced at last.

"What?" Mouse Ear faced Lightning Tail with his lips drawn back in the beginning of a snarl. Lightning Tail braced himself, as though ready for an attack.

Thunder took a pace forward, but Holly raised her tail to stop him. "It's okay," she reassured him. "Mouse Ear may look like a big bully, but underneath that tough shell he has a soft heart."

"Unlike you!" Mouse Ear retorted, backing away from Lightning Tail.

Holly's spine stiffened and her neck fur began to bristle.

Thunder let out a *mrrow* of laughter. "I get it. Holly! You're as prickly as that bush you were hiding under. Am I right?"

Mud Paws and Mouse Ear shared an amused glance as Holly raked the ground with her forepaws in irritation. "Maybe . . ." she admitted, glaring at her two friends.

Rays of sunlight were piercing through the leaves as the sun rose higher, and Thunder felt a wave of exhaustion sweeping over him. He needed to get back to the hollow and sleep. *For days and days.*

"Why do you want to join us?" Tall Shadow asked the three strangers. "You say you heard the cries and yowls of battle. Can't you see that we're injured? It will be no easy life with us. You may end up helping to tend the wounded."

The three cats exchanged glances. Then Mouse Ear stepped forward. "Yes, we saw the fight last night and we can see now how you've suffered. But why should that mean we don't want to share a home with you? We respect you for your bravery."

Thunder's pelt burned with shame to think that there had been witnesses to the horrors of the battle. He didn't feel brave at all.

"We think you're all very brave," Mouse Ear went on. "We like living on the moor, but it's hard when it's just the three of us. And we think that you could benefit from having us around. I can fight off just about any cat. I even got the better of a badger once! And Holly is really good at sensing whether cats can be trusted."

"It's true," Holly put in. "When you're hard to please, like me, you definitely get the sense of which cats deserve the benefit of the doubt. And Mud Paws is an excellent stalker. Those paws will take him anywhere, as silently as a spirit-cat."

"Spirit-cats?" Tall Shadow asked, pawing the ground. "What do you mean?"

Mouse Ear looked confused. "It's just an expression we have," he explained. "There aren't really spirit-cats living here. That would be too weird," he finished with a pretend shudder.

Thunder took care not to catch Tall Shadow's eye. *So these cats didn't witness everything that went on last night. They didn't see the spirit-cats.*

Exhaustion rolled over him again like a dark cloud. All he wanted was to curl up in his nest. He could hear approving murmurs from his denmates, and see some of them nodding. "Come on, then," he said to the three strangers. "You can accompany us."

With a sweep of his tail he signaled his cats to get moving again. His limbs aching, every paw step an effort, he led the newcomers across the moor to the hollow.

CHAPTER 3

Gray Wing stood beneath the spreading branches of the four oaks, his gaze fixed on the earth that covered the cats who had fallen in battle. Though almost a moon had passed since then, he could still hear the yowls of defiance and the screeches of pain, as if that terrible struggle would never stop. The taste of blood remained in his throat, as if he had been jerked back into that dreadful time. But already the ground had settled, and grass had even begun to grow again in the bare earth.

In the future, no cat will have any idea that this is a burial place, he thought sorrowfully. *But I'll never forget. And I'll make sure that the others remember these fallen cats . . . and Turtle Tail, too. She should not have died alone in the Twolegplace.*

Slowly Gray Wing began to groom himself; licking one forepaw and drawing it over his ears. His wounds had healed and his breathing was almost back to normal, yet he knew that nothing would ever erase the scars in his heart.

"So much has changed," he sighed aloud, "inside and out."

Gray Wing felt that he couldn't even lead a hungry cat to a pile of prey, much less take responsibility for their whole group. He knew some of his denmates would be glad to see him take up the leadership again, but nothing was further from his thoughts. *Not without Turtle Tail's support,* he sighed inwardly.

Gray Wing pricked his ears at the sound of paw steps padding up behind him. Without turning his head, he knew that a cat had come to sit beside him.

"I never thought I'd see such death here." Gray Wing recognized the voice of the loner, River Ripple. "This is my first time back since the battle."

Gray Wing nodded his head in acknowledgment, his dark memories threatening to overwhelm him. He remembered the hopes he and his denmates had shared when they set out from the mountains, looking for a better home. His body shivered at the painful realization that the journey had led so many of them to their deaths. *Turtle Tail, Bright Stream, Moon Shadow* . . . and that wasn't all. Rainswept Flower, Hawk Swoop, Falling Feather, Jackdaw's Cry—all gone.

"By next greenleaf," River Ripple went on, his voice gentle, "this grave will be covered in wildflowers. You should not keep returning, day after day."

Greenleaf . . . Gray Wing was momentarily puzzled. *Ah, that's the rogue cats' name for the warm season.* Recently the mountain cats and their descendants had begun using these terms, too. Gray Wing twitched his whiskers. "How do you know what I'm doing?" he asked. "I thought you said you hadn't been back here until now?"

River Ripple let out a soft *mrrow* of laughter. "Oh, Gray Wing, have you learned nothing? I may be a loner, but I know

more than any cat. I see what you all do and where you go."
Gray Wing felt the brief touch of a tail-tip on his shoulder.
"Stop tormenting yourself," River Ripple went on. "There's
nothing for you here. Go back to the cats who love you."

Gray Wing felt his throat tighten and when he managed
to speak his voice was wet and raspy. "I can't bear to think of
them, all alone."

"But they're not alone," River Ripple told him. "Didn't you
see them among the spirit-cats? They're not buried beneath
the earth; they're running with the stars." He gave Gray Wing
a gentle nudge. "Stop fretting—do you think your old friends
are hanging around here, waiting for you to visit? Of course
they're not. You must think of the living . . . *they're* the cats who
need you now."

Gray Wing turned to face River Ripple, knowing that he
was right. Something within him calmed. "Thank you for
being so kind," he mewed, touching noses with the silver-
furred tom. "Are you sure you won't come to live with the rest
of us in the hollow?"

River Ripple shook his head. "Thanks, but no."

"Okay," Gray Wing meowed. "But will we see you back
here when we meet again?"

"Yes, I'll come," River Ripple answered. "I'll be too curious to stay away. And in the meantime, if I catch you here
again, I'll be demanding the prey from your next hunt!"

In response, Gray Wing leaped away, racing through the
trees toward the hollow. "You'd have to catch me first!" he
called back over his shoulder.

* * *

When Gray Wing reached the edge of the hollow, he spotted Thunder at the far side, near the rock where Tall Shadow kept watch. Mouse Ear and Mud Paws were with him.

As he padded toward them, Gray Wing realized that Thunder was teaching the former rogues how to use the rabbit burrows when they were hunting. "Jump out like this!" he instructed, pushing off with his hind legs into a massive leap from a crouching start.

Gray Wing watched, the sight calling up the memory of when he was training Thunder, along with Acorn Fur and Lightning Tail. *I still can't believe Acorn Fur lives with Clear Sky now,* Gray Wing thought sadly. He forced his mind into a happier path, recalling earlier practices—how Thunder used to trip over his large, white paws when he was a kit.

Not anymore.

Gray Wing let out a purr of satisfaction. Thunder had grown into a formidable cat. *He's come a long way. I can step back and know the group is safe.*

A scamper of paw steps distracted Gray Wing from his thoughts as Sparrow Fur and Owl Eyes rushed past him, eager to join the training session.

"Hey! You know better than that!" Thunder called sharply as they tumbled into the group.

Sparrow Fur had barreled straight against Mouse Ear, who stared down at her in shock and snarled, "Get off my paws, midget!"

The young she-cat's eyes sparkled and she gave Mouse Ear

a teasing nip on the back of the leg before she jumped back. Mouse Ear let out a growl and batted at her, but his paw barely skimmed her fur, and his claws were sheathed.

"Annoying furball!" he muttered.

Thunder rolled his eyes. "This is a training session, not a wrestling match," he meowed, giving Sparrow Fur a hard stare. "Now concentrate! Let's see your pouncing again. See that stone over there? Pretend it's a mouse!" He watched approvingly as all the cats crouched and then leaped for the imaginary prey.

"Oh, stop whining and just do it! You'd think you didn't have paws at all!"

Gray Wing jumped with shock as the mocking voice interrupted the training session. It was coming from just outside the hollow, and for a moment he couldn't identify the cat who had spoken. Slightly disturbed, he climbed the slope again.

Beyond the camp Gray Wing spotted Jagged Peak, halfway up one of the twisted thorn trees that grew nearby. He was clinging to a branch, his claws sunk deeply into the bark, his eyes wide with apprehension.

Holly stood at the other side of a narrow gully that became a stream after heavy rain. She was looking up at Jagged Peak with a smirk on her face.

"Come on!" she repeated. "Just jump! I'm not standing here all morning listening to you complain."

Gray Wing felt his heart begin to beat faster and his shoulder fur bristle as he started toward them. *What is Holly doing? Jagged Peak can't make that jump!*

"You should talk!" Jagged Peak retorted to the she-cat. "After the way you've been whining about having to share prey!"

Gray Wing halted as his younger brother hurled himself out of the tree, easily clearing the gully and landing beside Holly with a thump.

"See, I did it," he meowed, giving her a smug look. "Happy now?"

A half-stifled *mrrow* of laughter sounded behind Gray Wing, who turned to see Cloud Spots padding up to him.

"It's not funny!" Gray Wing snapped. "That new rogue is picking on Jagged Peak. Someone needs to teach her . . ." His voice trailed off as he noticed the amusement glimmering in Cloud Spots's eyes.

"Stay out of it," Cloud Spots advised him. "I don't believe it's what you think it is. Besides, Jagged Peak can take care of himself."

Can he? Gray Wing asked himself. Ever since his younger brother was injured falling out of a tree he had always assumed that Jagged Peak *couldn't* take care of himself. *Have I been unfair to him?*

Leaving Holly and Jagged Peak to their own peculiar kind of training, Gray Wing headed back into the hollow, to where Thunder and his cats were still practicing their pounces. Before he reached them, Pebble Heart appeared out of their den, and padded up to walk alongside him.

Since he was a young kit, the tabby tom had shown healing skills, sometimes mysteriously knowing how to treat illnesses without being told. He had strange dreams, too: Gray Wing's pelt prickled as he remembered Pebble Heart telling him about a dream of cats screeching and clawing at one another—a vision of the battle before it took place.

Since Turtle Tail's death, Gray Wing sensed that something had changed deep inside Pebble Heart. He seemed more thoughtful and focused. After the battle he had helped to take care of the wounded, showing infinite patience and the authority of a much older cat. Gray Wing had the feeling that the little tom's paws might be small now, but the steps he was destined to take would be big.

A surge of warmth swelled up inside Gray Wing's chest and, for once, it was nothing to do with his breathing problems. *I promise I'll be a good father to all three of these kits. I'll do my very best for them.*

"Have you had any more dreams?" he asked Pebble Heart.

"No . . ." Pebble Heart replied hesitantly.

But Gray Wing felt certain that his adopted son wasn't telling him everything. Sadness and anger mingled in his heart. *Surely if there's any cat he can trust, it's me?* But then he reminded himself that Pebble Heart would share his secrets when the time was right. Nothing would be gained by nagging him.

Gray Wing comforted himself with the thought that he had allowed Thunder to find his own path. *And look at him now—teaching the younger cats and the rogues. He's every bit a leader!*

"Okay, keep practicing," Thunder told the other cats, before breaking away and padding up to Gray Wing. "Did you see Clear Sky or any of the others while you were out?" he asked.

"Only River Ripple," Gray Wing replied.

Since the battle, the moorland cats had seen Clear Sky and his followers from time to time. They had shared a few polite words, and even prey, then gone their separate ways. It was a relief that the territory borders weren't being jealously guarded, but Gray Wing couldn't help feeling that things could be better. Stiff politeness was all very well, but it was a far cry from the close friendship they had felt for one another on their journey out of the mountains.

"It's not long before the next meeting at the four trees," Thunder went on. "Do you think the spirit-cats will appear again?"

"I'm not sure." Gray Wing thought for a moment, then added, "But we all agreed to meet there at the next full moon, to see how we're getting on, so we need to do that, spirit-cats or no spirit-cats. Unite or die: That's what we said we'd do."

CHAPTER 4

❧

The icy glow of the full moon poured down upon the four oak trees. The leaves rustled in a gentle breeze, casting dappled patterns of light and shadow on the great rock.

Beneath the trees, the clearing was alive with cats. Gray Wing spotted Acorn Fur bounding eagerly forward to nuzzle Lightning Tail, who covered her ears with affectionate licks. Nearby Dappled Pelt and Quick Water touched noses, then settled down for a long chat. Gray Wing caught a snatch of conversation between Shattered Ice and Petal.

"... you and the other rabbit-chasers," the yellow tabby she-cat meowed good-humoredly. "Why don't you learn to stalk?"

"Why don't *you* learn to run?" Shattered Ice retorted, giving her a friendly nudge.

Gray Wing watched with hope in his heart. "Most of these cats haven't seen one another since last full moon, when we were fighting," he murmured to Thunder and Tall Shadow, who were standing on either side of him. "And now look at them! Maybe the peace really will last."

Tall Shadow blinked, looking on with mild surprise as Cloud Spots and Leaf touched noses and settled down side by side, their pelts brushing. "Perhaps the worst is behind us," she agreed.

"And we can start making plans for the future," Thunder put in.

Clear Sky padded over to join them. Relief flooded over Gray Wing to see his brother looking relaxed and friendly. *For so long, all he cared about was protecting his territory. A few moons ago, he wouldn't even share prey with me. But we all learned lessons when our friends died.*

"It's good to see you," Clear Sky mewed, dipping his head to the moorland cats. His gaze traveled across the mingling groups, and he added, "Do you think the spirit-cats will be pleased with us?"

"I hope so," Gray Wing replied. "We've done nothing wrong. And yet . . . somehow, things don't seem quite complete." He couldn't explain the emptiness he felt any more clearly. *Surely there's more to uniting than just not battling one another?*

Gradually the babble of talk died away and the cats gazed up expectantly at the dark sky. But all they could see were stars and the cold circle of the moon.

What do we do if the spirit-cats don't come? Gray Wing wondered.

His belly cramped with tension as a confused murmur came from a little group of cats off to one side of the hollow. *Please, not another attack!*

Then the group of cats parted and River Ripple brushed between them and padded up to Gray Wing. His perfectly groomed pelt shone silver in the moonlight.

"Greetings," Gray Wing purred, amusement bubbling up

inside him. "I don't have any prey to share, you know."

River Ripple dipped his head, his eyes glinting with humor. "I wouldn't miss this meeting," he mewed. "I remember how scared you all were, the last time the spirit-cats appeared."

"But it doesn't look like they're going to show up tonight," Wind Runner murmured sadly.

"I think they will," River Ripple responded confidently. "Just wait."

As if his words were a signal, a mist began to rise from the ground, chilly with the promise of leaf-fall. It swirled around the waiting cats, rose to cover the four great oak trees, and finally blotted out the moon and the stars.

Gray Wing found himself standing in the midst of a silver-gray cloud, so thick he couldn't even see the cats standing next to him. Nervous meows came from close by, and his own pelt was prickling as he tried to push down his fear.

Gradually the cloud began to fade until Gray Wing could make out the shapes of his denmates, standing within a fuzzy ring of light that encircled the whole clearing. Then as the last of the mist cleared away, he saw that the light came from the spirit-cats, sitting all around as if they were still alive.

Gray Wing had to blink as he looked at their brightness, but he recognized them instantly: the cats who had died since they left the mountains. *Bright Stream, Shaded Moss, Moon Shadow . . . and Turtle Tail!* He felt just as shaken as he had the first time they appeared.

The shining form of Rainswept Flower rose to her paws and took a step forward. As she did so, Gray Wing noticed that Clear Sky had turned his head aside in shame, as if he couldn't bear to look at the cat whose life he had taken before the battle had even begun.

"You have done well to observe peace since the last full moon," Rainswept Flower meowed. "And yet the claw still blights the forest."

Gray Wing and the other living cats exchanged confused glances.

"How can that be?" Tall Shadow asked. "We haven't fought since . . ." Her voice trailed off, as if she could hardly bear to finish her own sentence. "Since the battle here."

"Unless cats have been fighting in secret?" Wind Runner snapped, gazing around with suspicion in her eyes.

"No, that's ridiculous!" Gray Wing protested. "We would know!"

Turtle Tail padded forward to stand beside Rainswept Flower. "You will realize what it means, in time," she assured them.

Gray Wing's heart filled with sorrow as he gazed at his dead mate. Her pelt shone with starlight; she was even more beautiful than he remembered. It hurt him more than any claw to hold her gaze, and his voice shook as he asked, "Can't you just explain? Won't that save time and bloodshed?"

Turtle Tail blinked sadly. "Cats can fight and fight and fight," she mewed. "But sometimes even the sharpest claw cannot make a wound."

Gray Wing let out a frustrated growl. "What does that *mean*?"

He turned his head as he spotted movement to one side, and saw River Ripple padding closer to the two starry she-cats with a whisk of his tail.

"If something is *meant* to happen, it will," he pointed out calmly. "And no cat's will is strong enough to stop it from happening."

A chorused purr of approval rose from the spirit-cats. "River Ripple is clever," Shaded Moss meowed with an approving blink of his deep green eyes. "You should listen to him."

"Yes, I agree with what he said," Thunder added eagerly, a glow of understanding in his eyes. "I felt that after the battle—like everything that had happened up until then was leading us to that moment, to that fight."

Gray Wing felt his chest tighten at his young kin's words. He turned in an anxious circle, his gaze raking the assembly of the spirit-cats as he tried to read something in their impassive expressions. "But *why* did it have to happen?" he asked. "Why was it unchangeable? I remember how I made the decision to leave the mountains, to settle in the hollow, to raise Thunder as my own. I *made* those choices."

Turtle Tail gazed at him sympathetically. "Did you?" she asked gently. "Or did you follow an errant brother out of the mountains?"

Gray Wing's chest felt like it had been filled with ice. It was a feeling of helplessness. *She's right—it* wasn't *my decision to leave the mountains,* he realized. *If Jagged Peak hadn't decided to run away and follow the cats who left, Quiet Rain would never have insisted that I follow him to make sure he came to no harm. Everything that happened after that wouldn't have happened if Quiet Rain hadn't pleaded with me. . . .*

"Gray Wing, you mustn't worry," Turtle Tail meowed. "I know you don't like feeling powerless, but you were brought to this point for a reason."

Gray Wing turned his head away; gazing at the beautiful tortoiseshell she-cat was just too painful. "You were taken from me," he choked out. "What could have been the reason for *that*?"

He began to pace to and fro in agitation, until Tall Shadow stepped forward and intercepted him.

"Calm down," she ordered. "We're being told what to do."

Gray Wing took a deep breath, forcing himself to stand still again. "I want to be rid of these awful feelings," he hissed. "I thought the spirit-cats would help."

Before he had finished speaking, Storm bounded forward and faced him. "You and the other cats are getting all the help you need," she told him, her whiskers twitching impatiently. "All the help that we can give."

"That's right." Moon Shadow padded up to the side of his sister, Tall Shadow. "But there's still more work to be done. Only the Blazing Star can blunt the claw."

Frustrated by the constant hints and riddles, Gray Wing felt another angry yowl burning in his chest, but before he could utter a sound Bright Stream spoke, echoing Moon Shadow's words.

"Yes, the Blazing Star. To survive, you must grow and spread like the Blazing Star."

To survive? Gray Wing thought, bewildered.

"Aren't we surviving already?" Thunder called out.

"Is the peace going to be broken so soon?" Wind Runner demanded.

Desperate yowling rose up from the other living cats, as they hurled more questions at the spirit-cats. But there was no reply. Instead another mist rose from the ground and drifted around the oak trees, blotting out the starry forms. When it faded, they were gone.

Gray Wing stepped forward to where Turtle Tail had been standing, but she had left no mark or scent of her presence. The rest of the spirit-cats had left no trace, either. If it weren't for the tightness of his chest and the burning ache of grief in his throat, he would have thought he was dreaming again.

But I know I wasn't. The spirit-cats were real—and so was their advice. To survive you must grow and spread like the Blazing Star.

At least, he thought, his instincts had been right. He had felt that their troubles were not over, and the vague words of the starry cats seemed to confirm that more lay ahead.

He remembered the dream that kept coming to him ever since the battle, when Stoneteller had summoned him to her den and told him that he had to be strong.

Maybe this is what she meant. Our survival is going to come under threat, and we need to . . . to grow and spread like the Blazing Star. "Whatever that means," Gray Wing muttered aloud.

As he stood deep in thought the rest of the cats crept forward to gather around him, their voices hushed now.

"What could the Blazing Star be?" Dappled Pelt wondered.

"And how can we grow and spread like it?" Petal added,

glancing around as if she expected one of her denmates to come up with the answer.

Clear Sky shouldered his way to the front of the crowd to stand beside Gray Wing. "Maybe it's a battle tactic," he suggested.

"That doesn't make sense!" Tall Shadow argued, narrowing her eyes at Clear Sky. "There are no cats to fight anymore."

Wind Runner blinked, looking unusually hesitant. "What else could they have meant when they said that a 'claw still blights the forest'?"

"Maybe the claw isn't a real claw, but another riddle?"

Gray Wing froze as a new voice joined the conversation, strong and confident. He whipped around to see a strange she-cat who he was sure hadn't been there just a moment before. She gazed boldly into his eyes. Her fur was thick and golden, its tabby markings rippling over her body, except for her chest and paws, which were pure white.

"Where did you come from?" he asked. "Are you part of Clear Sky's group?"

The she-cat didn't reply, and Clear Sky wasn't taking any notice of her. "I wish the spirit-cats had been more help," he mewed with a lash of his tail; clearly he felt just as frustrated as Gray Wing.

Gray Wing saw River Ripple turning away and heading back the way he came with a nod of farewell.

"You're leaving already?" he asked, shocked.

"I can see which way this is going," River Ripple confirmed with a wry twist of his mouth. "I'm not sticking around for another night of bickering. If I happen to figure anything out, I'll come and find you."

Gray Wing watched as the silver-gray tom disappeared into the darkness. Thorn, Dew, and Nettle from Clear Sky's group were watching him too, and—to Gray Wing's surprise—so was Dappled Pelt, with something in her gaze that he couldn't quite account for.

Dragging his attention back to the debate over the spirit-cats' message, Gray Wing noticed that Thunder wasn't making any contribution. He was too busy looking at the strange she-cat who had just spoken, his whiskers twitching bashfully.

The she-cat padded over to him—her gaze fixed as if she saw no other cat—and stood in front of him, her tail flicking slowly to and fro.

"I've been dying to meet you," she purred. "I've heard so much about you on the moor: what a great leader and fighter you are."

As he listened, Thunder's chest puffed up with pride. He opened his jaws to speak, but nothing came out. It was as if he had no idea what to say.

The she-cat waited for a moment, then turned and padded away, glancing back to shoot a final glance at Thunder from luminous green eyes before she vanished into the undergrowth. Thunder couldn't tear his gaze away.

Gray Wing felt a rumble of laughter rising in his throat. *Thunder might be a big, strong leader of cats,* he thought, *but in other ways he's still very young.*

CHAPTER 5

❧

Clear Sky paused beneath an arching clump of ferns, and took in a
long breath of the cool morning air. Since the first visit from
the spirit-cats, there was no need to patrol his boundaries anymore, but he enjoyed the peace and quiet of the forest in the
dim light of dawn. And since the second visit from the spirit-
cats the night before, he wanted time to ponder their message.

The Blazing Star. Could it be the sun? Clear Sky wondered, padding onward through the undergrowth, the dew-laden grasses
brushing his pelt. *But no—how could any cat use the sun as a weapon?*

Deep in thought, he didn't realize at first how far his paws
were taking him, until he caught a familiar acrid tang at the
back of his throat, and heard a distant rumble.

The Thunderpath!

Clear Sky halted, then turned back toward his own camp,
his fur bristling. *I certainly don't want to go there!*

The harsh reek of monsters faded, but Clear Sky's nose
twitched as he picked up another scent. There was a cat in the
forest—one he didn't recognize—and as the scent gradually
strengthened he realized it was drawing closer to him.

Every hair on Clear Sky's pelt prickled with suspicion. *Is this a sneak attack?* But the strange cat was moving too clumsily for that; Clear Sky could see the tops of the ferns waving as the cat blundered forward, making no attempt at quiet.

Clear Sky hesitated a heartbeat longer, then leaped up into the nearest tree and crouched on a low branch, half-hidden by a clump of leaves.

A moment later a ginger tom emerged from the under-growth and started sniffing around the roots of the tree. Now that he was so close, Clear Sky's belly turned over at the stench that was rising from him.

A kittypet—and one he had seen before, slinking through the forest with some kits.

Clear Sky waited until the tom turned to pad away, then rose to his paws and took a pace farther along the branch, into the open. "You again! What do you want here?" he demanded.

The kittypet reared back in alarm, then crouched to the ground, laying his ears back. "My name is Tom. I—I don't mean any harm," he stammered. "I've been wandering around in the forest for a while, and I noticed the cats are forming into . . . groups."

Clear Sky twitched his ears. "And?"

"I like the sound of that," Tom went on. "Cats working together, helping each other to find shelter and prey. It's got to be much better than working alone, scrounging for scraps while hoping it doesn't rain too hard. I was wondering if . . . well, if your group might have room for one more?"

Clear Sky studied the ginger tom closely. He wasn't entirely convinced by the kittypet's speech or his cringing manner. "I can see the marks on your neck where you wore your Twoleg collar," he meowed. "And your round belly. You must have had a few *easy* meals lately."

Tom gave his chest fur a couple of quick licks. "I once lived with Twolegs," he admitted reluctantly. "But I've since returned to the wild."

"Returned?" Clear Sky challenged him.

Tom rolled his eyes. "All right, not 'returned' exactly. This is my first time living in the wild. But it feels like I'm returning . . . to my *real* home."

Clear Sky let out a snort of laughter. "Oh, I feel *so* sorry for you! It must have been hard, living in the warm and dry of a Twoleg den when your spirit was craving the cold, wet, and hunger of the wild!"

Studying Tom afresh, Clear Sky noticed that his pelt did look a bit ragged in places. Though he still had the stench of Twolegs on him, it was believable that he had been living like a real cat for a little while. But Clear Sky was still reluctant to take in a kittypet, especially when he remembered what had happened with Bumble.

Leaping to the ground, Clear Sky kept a wary distance from Tom while padding around him to size him up.

"So can I come and live with you?" Tom asked. "I've heard about your survival tactics, and I think I could work the same way."

Instantly suspicious, Clear Sky narrowed his eyes as he gazed at Tom. "What have you heard?" he demanded sharply.

Tom hesitated, as if he sensed Clear Sky's tension. "Well . . . that you make tough decisions when it's necessary."

"Times have changed," Clear Sky responded, wondering if

Tom was referring to his behavior before the battle. "All the cats live peacefully now. Really, there's no particular reason to join a group of cats. You should be able to survive pretty well on your own."

Tom twitched his ears. "True," he mewed. "But I can also bring benefits to your group."

"What would those be, exactly?" Clear Sky asked, his interest piqued. What could a kittypet offer *real* cats?

"I may not be as skilled at hunting as you," the ginger tom replied. "But I can learn quickly. And I have my own ways of fighting." He studied his paws, and Clear Sky couldn't decide if he looked modest or guilty. "I know how to fight with cunning," he added.

"Do you mean fight dirty?" Clear Sky asked sharply.

Tom didn't reply. Instead he looked up at Clear Sky with wide, pleading eyes. "There is much that I can teach you, I promise. Won't you take me in?" he begged.

Guilt throbbed through Clear Sky. Facing the truth about himself, he knew that he had caused so much unhappiness in the past. *Perhaps it's time to make amends.*

"Okay," he meowed. "You can come back to the camp with me, if you think you can prove yourself. But I'm warning you: We can't support any cat who doesn't contribute."

Tom puffed out his chest, his expression suddenly proud and happy. "You won't regret this," he promised. "We won't let you down."

Clear Sky, who had turned away and taken a couple of paw steps back toward his camp, halted and turned back again. "'We'?" *I agreed to take in one cat,* he thought, his pelt beginning to prickle with anger. *Is this ginger flea-pelt trying to cheat me?*

Tom let out a pleased *mrrow*. "I have a friend with me."

As he spoke, there was a loud rattling of twigs and leaves from up above and another cat landed on the ground. Clear Sky fought the urge to leap away, his pelt crawling at the thought that the newcomer had been lurking in the very tree where he had hidden to keep an eye on Tom—and he'd had no idea the cat was there.

They must have been following me. They arranged this meeting!

Sizing up the new arrival, Clear Sky realized that he had never seen a rogue like this before. The fur that covered his scrawny body was knotted and his claws were broken. One eye was missing, and in the one that remained was a look that was pure wild. He paid no attention to Clear Sky, but circled on the spot, hissing and spitting as if he was facing a whole group of enemy cats.

"This is One Eye," Tom announced proudly. "He's the bravest rogue cat in the whole forest." When Clear Sky didn't respond, Tom added, "He may look like a sick, skinny old thing on his last legs, but he's the perfect addition to your group. You won't have to worry about being attacked with him around. I invited him here today—"

Tom broke off with a screech of pain as One Eye pounced onto his back, digging his jagged claws in. Jerking away, he turned a shocked stare on One Eye as the rogue jumped down again. "What was that for?" he asked.

"I can speak for myself!" One Eye hissed.

Clear Sky thought that Tom was right to look shocked. *What is he thinking, hanging around like this?*

Tom sat down and started to groom his pelt, his pride clearly ruffled. Meanwhile, Clear Sky watched One Eye as he circled languidly, his tail high in the air. He was becoming more and more intrigued to hear what the rogue had to say for himself.

"I remember this forest when all the trees were saplings," One Eye began. "I lived here before any of your group were even born."

So how old is he? Clear Sky asked himself. *If he's as old as these trees, he should hardly be able to walk!*

While Clear Sky was trying to decide how to respond, One Eye whipped around and confronted him. "Are you the leader, then?" he asked.

Surprised by the direct question, Clear Sky raked the ground with his forepaws. "Well . . . of this part of the forest, yes."

"Then you're the cat I want to speak to," One Eye continued. "Tom's told me all about you. I'm here to offer my services to your group of cats, and trust me, this is *not* an offer that you want to turn down."

Momentarily stunned, Clear Sky was acutely aware that he had to take control of this situation. "What do you think you can bring to my group?" he asked.

One Eye looked thoughtful for a moment. Before he could reply, the sound of fluttering wings in the tree above distracted all three cats. A plump pigeon had alighted on the lowest branch.

"Excuse me," the mangy rogue drawled.

With a massive leap he hurled himself into the tree,

his claws sinking into the body of the pigeon. It struggled wildly, its feathers falling like snow, then went limp. One Eye thumped back to the ground and dropped the prey at Clear Sky's paws as if shaking dirt from his fur.

"Will that do?" he asked.

Clear Sky gazed down at the dead bird, impressed in spite of himself.

"I'll show you my hunting and fighting techniques anytime you like," One Eye offered.

"We don't need to learn any fighting techniques," Clear Sky retorted sharply. "Just the hunting skills will do." For a few heartbeats he hesitated, then added, "Have either of you ever heard of the Blazing Star?"

One Eye and Tom glanced at each other. Tom shook his head, but after a moment One Eye muttered, "It could be a plant."

It could be anything, Clear Sky thought, disappointed not to have discovered any useful information. *I guess it was a bit of a long shot.*

"Okay. You can follow me back to camp," he meowed to One Eye and Tom, some instinct telling him it was better to have these cats as friends rather than enemies.

But as Clear Sky turned to head toward home, One Eye padded ahead of him, leading the way as if he already knew where the camp was. The pigeon dangling from his jaws, Tom brought up the rear.

Why do I feel as though they always knew they'd be coming back with me? Clear Sky thought. There was more to these cats than they were letting on.

CHAPTER 6

🍀

A stiff breeze was blowing, whipping dead leaves from the trees. *Leaf-fall is nearly on us,* Clear Sky thought as he headed along his border with Tom and One Eye by his side. Acorn Fur padded in their paw steps a couple of tail-lengths behind.

Privately Clear Sky held on to his reservations about admitting the mangy rogue and smelly kittypet to his group. But he had to admit that, so far, they were contributing. One Eye was a ruthless hunter, and was helping to keep the cats well fed—even if most of them were still a little wary of him.

They'll probably get used to him in time, Clear Sky told himself. *And isn't it better to have a cat like One Eye by my side rather than wandering free?*

The sound of crackling behind him made Clear Sky halt and turn, his shoulder fur beginning to bristle at possible danger. The sound reminded him too clearly of the flames that had devoured the forest. *I don't want to go through anything like that again.*

Then he spotted Acorn Fur rolling around in a hollow of dead leaves, batting at them with all four paws. He rolled his eyes. *Well, she's hardly more than a kit. . . .*

"Acorn Fur—" he began.

"Stop messing about," Tom interrupted with a snarl. "I'm starving, and I haven't eaten since morning."

Acorn Fur clambered out of the hollow, a hurt look in her eyes as she shook scraps of leaf off her fur. "Sorry," she muttered.

Clear Sky glanced across at Tom, seeing that his belly had shrunk in the few days since he joined the group. *And a good thing too!*

"In the forest we only eat when there's food available," he meowed gently. "It's something we must all get used to. I remember when—"

"Don't tell me *again* about how you were all starving in the mountains," Tom interrupted again. "I've heard that story too many times!"

"I never asked you to join the group," Clear Sky retorted, his voice rough with the beginnings of a snarl. "You can leave anytime you like."

Tom looked like he was about to start arguing, but clearly had the sense to keep his jaws shut. Clear Sky relaxed, glad that the confrontation was over.

Her paws pattering on the dead leaves, Acorn Fur bounded up and brushed her pelt against his. She seemed ready to do the same to Tom, then halted, her nose wrinkling slightly.

"I'm sorry if I messed up," she mewed. "I don't want to start a fight. The last moon has been so great."

"True," Clear Sky murmured. Now that normal life had replaced the constant skirmishing, it had been a relief to sleep through the night and wake up refreshed. He suppressed a shiver at the thought of the nightmares that had plagued his rest for so long. He'd been so worried about protecting his cats and their territory, ensuring that every cat had enough to eat. It hadn't been easy. It would be good now to share prey and territories, to pull together.

As the patrol set out again, a rustling sounded from the edge of the forest. Instantly One Eye whirled in the direction of the noise. "Get off our territory!" he snarled. "Whoever you are."

"Hey, wait!" Clear Sky meowed. "We don't have trespassers now!"

But he was too late. While he was still speaking, Tom charged off toward the sound, his fur bristling up like a hedgehog's spines. Clear Sky raced after him, with Acorn Fur dashing alongside, eager to help. One Eye trailed after them as if he had lost interest.

"Stay out of the way!" Clear Sky ordered Acorn Fur as he threw himself in front of Tom.

The kittypet was facing a dangerous-looking tabby tom, muscular, with small ears, like a mouse's. Tom was snarling and flourishing his claws, but it was obvious to Clear Sky that he had no idea how to fight.

"Back off, unless you want your ears shredded!" Clear Sky snapped at Tom, pushing him away.

He was vaguely aware of other voices calling at a distance, and a few heartbeats later Gray Wing and Thunder emerged from the undergrowth, their eyes wide as they padded up to the group of cats.

"Okay, Mouse Ear, keep calm," Gray Wing meowed, brushing the tabby tom's shoulder with his tail. "It was all a misunderstanding. There's no need to fight."

Meanwhile Thunder was gazing curiously at One Eye. "Who is this?" he asked.

"A new friend," Clear Sky replied, dipping his head to his son. "His name is One Eye. He joined my group a few sunrises ago. And this—" he began, stretching a paw out toward Tom.

"You don't need to tell us." Clear Sky was startled to hear the growl in Gray Wing's voice—his brother was usually the calmest of cats. "We know all about Tom."

"How?" Clear Sky asked, surprised.

"Clear Sky, you've taken in the kittypet who stole Turtle Tail's kits," Gray Wing told him. "You do remember Turtle Tail, don't you?"

Guilt stabbed into Clear Sky. "Those were Turtle Tail's kits? I didn't know!" *I should have tried to stop him from taking them,* he thought.

As quickly as it came, the guilt disappeared, replaced by fury. *How dare Gray Wing humiliate me like this in front of Tom and One Eye! I've worked so hard to keep the new rules we agreed with the spirit-cats.*

"I thought all the old grudges had been put behind us after the battle," he meowed stiffly. "Isn't that what every cat agreed? Gray Wing, I would have thought that you of all cats would be fair and open-minded about these things. After all," he continued, letting anger guide his words, "you've relied on Thunder to lead your group now that you're no longer up to the task. Thunder would have been within his rights to drive you out and leave you to fend for yourself—a broken cat. You should count yourself lucky!"

"That's not how we do things!" Thunder protested.

Gray Wing stayed silent. Clear Sky knew that he had touched a nerve, and he could see the hurt in his brother's eyes. Instantly he regretted losing his temper. Pacing forward, he touched noses with his brother. "Not that it would ever come to that," he purred. "I would *always* give you a home."

"Yes!" Acorn Fur gave an excited little bounce. "Come and live with us, Gray Wing!"

Clear Sky spotted Thunder cringing at the young she-cat's eager words. *That wasn't what we needed to hear right now,* he thought. "That's enough," he told Acorn Fur sternly. "Gray Wing has a perfectly good home of his own."

As silence fell, Clear Sky realized that Tom and the big tabby were still facing each other, glaring aggressively, their neck fur standing on end.

"Calm yourself, Mouse Ear," Thunder hissed at the tabby as he stepped between the two of them.

The tabby obediently backed off, and Thunder turned to Tom. "I think we've met before," he mewed.

Clear Sky spotted a flash of anger in Tom's eyes, before it turned to amusement. "I believe we have," he agreed. "In fact, I believe you stole my kits from me. How are they? I hope they don't wake up in the night crying for their dead mother?"

"That's enough," Clear Sky snapped at Tom, shocked by the kittypet's cruel words. He turned to the other cats and added with a glance at Mouse Ear, "We're all bringing new cats into our groups. Let's just accept this is the way things have to be for now. Thunder, Tom may have been a kittypet, but you should trust that your father knows a good fighter when he meets one."

"Fighter?" Thunder's tone was sharp. "What do you need a fighter for?"

"It would be a foolish cat who wasn't prepared to defend himself," Clear Sky replied. "Dogs, badgers, rogue cats, Twolegs . . . Who knows where the next danger will come from? And there is *always* a next danger," he continued, pleased to see that Thunder couldn't hold his gaze. "Isn't that why the spiritcats came back, to advise us on how to *survive*? You train your cats in fighting techniques, right?"

Thunder's gaze was fixed on his paws. "We train cats in *hunting* techniques. We don't need anything else."

Gray Wing padded closer to his young kin, standing beside him. "Any cat has the instincts to use claws in a fight," he told his brother. "But *hunting* . . . Now, that takes patience and learning. Thunder is doing the right thing."

He turned, and with Thunder at his side headed toward the moors. After one last glare in Tom's direction, Mouse Ear followed.

"Good-bye!" Clear Sky called out uncertainly.

Mouse Ear was the only cat to look back. "You're a fool," he meowed to Clear Sky. "I've known One Eye for a long time— and he's not to be trusted. You'll live to regret taking him in."

Clear Sky didn't respond. Stiffly he turned away, signaling with a wave of his tail for his cats to follow him on the way back to their camp. He had to make a conscious effort to keep his shoulder fur lying flat.

No ex-rogue is going to tell me what to do!

CHAPTER 7

On the way back to camp with Gray Wing and Mouse Ear, Thunder pondered whether they could trust Clear Sky. He was worried by the importance his father put on training to fight. *He can talk about dogs and badgers until his fur falls off,* Thunder thought. *But I can't shake the feeling that he intends to fight other cats.*

When he arrived back at the camp, he saw Owl Eyes, Sparrow Fur, and Pebble Heart batting a ball of moss to one another at the edge of the hollow. From her place on the rock, Tall Shadow kept watch over them.

I don't think I could ever have Tall Shadow's patience, Thunder thought. *But maybe that's why we make a good team.* He didn't always agree with the black she-cat, but he valued her wisdom and experience. *And Wind Runner has stopped pushing herself forward since she had her kits. That makes life a lot easier.* All the same, he wished that Gray Wing had never wanted to give up the leadership.

"I wonder if Tall Shadow has spotted Tom or One Eye while she's been up on that rock," Gray Wing muttered, as if he had sensed some of what was going through Thunder's mind.

"We've *got* to tell every cat that One Eye has joined up with

Clear Sky," Mouse Ear put in. "Mud Paws and Holly know him too, and they'll certainly have something to say!"

While the tabby tom was speaking, Pebble Heart broke away from his littermates and raced over to Thunder and the others. "Is everything all right?" he asked anxiously.

Has he picked up that we're worried? Thunder wondered.

"Everything is fine, little one," Gray Wing mewed reassuringly.

Though he said nothing, Thunder asked himself whether they ought to be more open with Pebble Heart. It was clear that he had talents that were beyond most cats—maybe they should encourage him to use them.

Gray Wing bounded across the hollow and leaped up onto Tall Shadow's rock, leaning close to whisper in her ear.

"Let all cats gather together beside the rock!" she called out immediately.

Thunder and Mouse Ear collected Owl Eyes, Sparrow Fur, and Pebble Heart and headed down into the camp, finding a place to sit close to the rock. Lightning Tail joined them; Cloud Spots and Dappled Pelt settled nearby, while Jagged Peak limped up with Holly and Mud Paws. Wind Runner and Gorse Fur sat at the entrance to their den while their kits wrestled happily in front of them.

Gray Wing's glance traveled across the camp as the rest of the cats gathered around. "Clear Sky has some new cats in his group," he announced.

"So what?" Jagged Peak asked with a dismissive flick of his tail. "We've got three new cats ourselves."

Mouse Ear rose to his paws and dipped his head respectfully to Gray Wing and Tall Shadow. "The problem is," he explained, "that Clear Sky's new cats are a rogue and a kittypet. And the rogue in particular is an old enemy of ours. . . ."

Holly sprang to her paws, her spiky fur seeming even more bristly than usual. "Not One Eye?" she snarled.

Mouse Ear nodded.

"I thought he lived on the other side of the Thunderpath," Mud Paws meowed. "What's he doing over here?"

"It can't be anything good. That cat is bad news," Holly hissed. "He's a dreadful bully—a thief, a scavenger. He manipulates other cats and stirs up trouble. Has Clear Sky gone mad?"

Thunder noticed that Jagged Peak was shifting closer to Holly, his eyes shining with admiration. "I think you must be a very wise cat," Jagged Peak murmured, "to have such insight."

Holly gave him a swift glance, surprised and pleased. Thunder had to stifle a *mrrow* of laughter. *She's certainly brave,* he thought. *Maybe that's what Jagged Peak likes about her.*

On top of the rock, Tall Shadow turned to look at Gray Wing. "Clear Sky is your brother," she meowed. "What do you think about this development?"

Thunder knew what he thought: that Clear Sky must have bees in his brain to introduce troublemakers into his group. But he stayed silent to listen to what Gray Wing would say.

As Gray Wing stepped forward, Thunder heard the quiet rattle of his breathing. *His health is still poor,* he thought anxiously. *And fighting in that huge battle can't have helped.* He knew that

Pebble Heart had worked hard with Dappled Pelt and Cloud Spots to heal their denmates' injuries, but Thunder didn't think there was anything that any cat could do to heal the injury to his lungs that Gray Wing had suffered in the forest fire.

"I'm sure Clear Sky thinks he's doing the right thing," Gray Wing began.

Tall Shadow let out a derisive snort. "Clear Sky *always* thinks he's doing the right thing," she pointed out. "He thought he was doing the right thing when he started guarding his borders, and look where that got us."

Thunder couldn't hide his surprise that Tall Shadow had interrupted so quickly after inviting Gray Wing to speak. But the black she-cat herself seemed to realize that she had made a mistake.

"I'm sorry," she mewed, dipping her head to Gray Wing. "I haven't been myself since our last visit to the four trees. I can't stop thinking about the Blazing Star and what the spirit-cats' message might mean." She shook her head impatiently. "It's keeping me awake at night."

Gray Wing touched Tall Shadow lightly on the shoulder with the tip of his tail. "That's okay," he reassured her. "It worries me, too. As for Clear Sky, I'm sure he knows he did wrong leading up to the battle, and he's full of regret. He won't want to stir up trouble again, but we have to be realistic. Clear Sky is a cat who will always try to protect his home, and he'll go to great lengths to do that. He's taken on some pretty unpleasant cats: One Eye . . . and Tom, who stole Turtle Tail's kits—"

He broke off as yowls of protest broke out from the cats sitting around. Thunder felt a huge bubble of anger swelling inside him. He couldn't control it; leaping to his paws, he glared around him, his neck fur bristling and his tail lashing as the words seemed to explode from him:

"We need to start fight training!" Thunder declared. "Clear Sky's cats are doing just that, and so should we—especially with dangerous cats like Tom and One Eye to deal with."

Several other cats yowled their agreement, but Thunder noticed that Sparrow Fur and Owl Eyes were exchanging looks of distress.

"Do they mean our father?" Sparrow Fur asked indignantly. "I don't know if he's dangerous, but I'm sure he's not evil."

Thunder wasn't surprised that the kits should feel curiosity about their father, and maybe even a trace of loyalty. But he didn't have time to speak to them; as the yowling died away, Gray Wing had begun to respond.

"Harmony and peace are good," he meowed. "But I've been thinking this over, and I'm afraid we're being stupid to ignore what might happen. We don't intend to attack any cat, but we should be prepared. Even if the threat doesn't come from One Eye and Tom, there are other dangers out there."

"Dogs, foxes . . ." Jagged Peak interrupted.

"Exactly," Gray Wing responded. "Leaf-fall is here, and before we know it, leaf-bare will be upon us. And with leaf-bare come desperate, hungry animals. So is it agreed? We will live in peace, but we train for battle—battle we hope we never see."

The cats' angry yowling gave way to murmurs of excitement.

Lightning Tail sprang up beside Thunder, his whiskers twitching eagerly. "I'll help you with the training, Thunder," he promised.

"I'll help, too," Holly put in. "I know a few moves that can deal with cats like One Eye."

"Will you train me too?" Jagged Peak asked, limping forward hopefully.

Thunder was about to protest that Jagged Peak's damaged leg would hinder him, but Holly spoke before he could.

"Of course I'll train you," she responded smoothly. "Every cat has it in them to become a fighter."

Owl Eyes and Sparrow Fur exchanged an excited glance. "Even kits?" Sparrow Fur asked.

"Especially kits," Holly replied. "Suppose enemies attacked the camp? You would need to be able to defend yourselves. There's no time to lose."

Together with Holly and Lightning Tail, Thunder led all the cats who were willing to fight out of the hollow, where he found a clear space for training. He felt a thrill of hope. *Yes, Clear Sky is taking in some untrustworthy cats. But the need to train has united us here in the hollow, and that's got to be a good thing. The spirit-cats told us to unite or die. Whatever dangers await us, we will be ready!*

As he waited for all the cats to arrive, Thunder heard Sparrow Fur speaking just behind him, her voice full of anxiety. "Why do all the cats think that Tom is our enemy?"

Glancing over his shoulder, Thunder saw that all three kits were clustered around Gray Wing, who seemed stumped for a reply.

"Well . . ." he began.

"He's our *father*!" Owl Eyes interrupted. "And if they don't want him around, then maybe they don't want us, either."

"There's no need to worry about that," Gray Wing meowed. "All three of you have a lot to contribute to our group. It doesn't matter what your father did."

"But we don't *know* what he did," Sparrow Fur objected. In a lower voice she added, "One day, I'm going to find him, and learn the truth for myself."

Holly moved into the center of the training area, and the rest of the cats formed a ragged circle around her. Gray Wing looked relieved as the kits stopped questioning him.

"I'm going to show you how to fool your attacker by rolling out of the way," Holly announced. "Look, throw yourself to one side like this." She demonstrated the move, letting her legs skid out from under her and ending up on her back with her paws in the air. "Lie on your back and let them see your belly."

"But . . . doesn't that put you in danger?" Owl Eyes asked. He glanced around nervously as he realized that all the older cats were listening to him. "Gray Wing told us you should never expose your soft belly to an attacker."

"True," Holly meowed, her eyes gleaming. "But the point is to make your opponent *think* that's what you're doing. As they launch into an attack, you kick out with your back legs and stun them—like this." She let fly with a powerful kick from her back legs.

"Wow!" exclaimed Shattered Ice. "That's great! What do you do next?"

"Leap to your paws," Holly replied, doing so. "Then pounce on their back. They won't know what's happening, and you can rake your claws down their side and bite their tail at the same time. I've defeated cats in moments with this move."

Thunder's pelt prickled with excitement from ears to tail-tip. He slid out his claws, imagining himself sinking them into One Eye or Tom. Then he winced as he remembered the reek of blood and the shrieks of the cats who died in the battle at the four trees.

"Even Jagged Peak could do this," Holly continued. "Actu-ally, especially Jagged Peak. With his limp, attacking cats will think he's vulnerable. If he lies on his back and shows his belly, it will make them overconfident. But you can still leap, even with three legs—can't you, Jagged Peak?"

Jagged Peak gave a vigorous nod, his eyes glowing with pleasure at Holly's confidence in him.

"Come on, then," Holly mewed. "Let's practice together. The rest of you, divide into pairs and do the same. But, remember—no claws!"

Thunder watched as Shattered Ice padded up to Owl Eyes. "Come on, young one," the gray-and-white tom meowed. "See if you can trick me."

Owl Eyes flung himself enthusiastically into the exercise, though Thunder was glad to see that Shattered Ice was being gentle with his smaller opponent.

Feeling a touch on his shoulder, Thunder turned to see Lightning Tail. "Get out of our camp, filthy invader!" his friend snarled, though his eyes were sparkling with amuse-ment.

"Who're you calling filthy?" Thunder retorted.

Lightning Tail batted at him with his claws sheathed, and Thunder immediately fell to the ground and rolled over. "Got you!" Lightning Tail exclaimed. "You must find it *so* hard, being so big and all. Don't you trip over those massive paws?"

"Try me!" Thunder meowed.

As Lightning Tail leaped at him, Thunder brought up his hind legs as Holly had shown them, and gave Lightning Tail a hard blow in his chest, throwing him to the ground. While Lightning Tail was struggling to get up, Thunder launched himself onto his back. "See?" he growled into his friend's ear. "I can move as fast as any cat."

He leaped away, and Lightning Tail gave his pelt a shake, panting hard and scattering the bits of debris that had clung to his fur. While he was recovering, Thunder glanced around to see that Gray Wing was sparring with Tall Shadow, and Mouse Ear was training with Pebble Heart.

Mouse Ear is trying too hard not to hurt him, Thunder thought. *They'll never get the move right that way.*

Before he could make any suggestions, Pebble Heart let out a wail of distress. Mouse Ear sprang back, his eyes wide with alarm. "I didn't touch him!" he exclaimed as all the cats raced over to see what was happening.

Then Thunder noticed Mud Paws. He had been standing nearby, watching the other cats train, but now he was crouched over something small on the ground, his whiskers trembling. Curious, Thunder padded up to him and saw that he was staring at the body of a mouse.

Owl Eyes padded up, then halted, clawing at the ground with anxiety. "Pebble Heart—do you know what's wrong?" he asked.

Pebble Heart crept up, his pelt fluffed up with apprehension, and Thunder realized that the small cat had sensed something amiss before any cat had spotted the mouse. He gave the body a quick sniff, then backed away again, his eyes wide and scared.

Thunder peered over Pebble Heart's shoulder, examining the body closely for the first time. The mouse's belly was horribly swollen and there were flecks of white foam around its mouth. Its eyes, open wide in death, were oozing pus, and there was an open sore on its tail.

"Get back, all of you!" Thunder ordered.

"Sickness," Pebble Heart murmured, looking up at him. "Sickness too powerful for healing herbs."

Thunder nodded. "Go back to the hollow," he told the other cats, who had retreated a few paw steps and stood waiting with bristling fur and quivering whiskers. "Gray Wing and I will dispose of the mouse. And warn the others not to eat any prey that looks like this," he called after them as they turned to go.

"Have you ever seen this sort of thing before?" Thunder asked with a questioning glance at Gray Wing.

Gray Wing shook his head. "Never—not even in the mountains," he replied. "We need to get rid of this prey to make sure no cat eats it. No—don't touch it!" he added as Thunder stretched out a paw.

Together the two cats collected fallen leaves from the thorn trees and wrapped them around the mouse, careful not to let their paws come into contact with its corpse. Then, still with the greatest care, they rolled it toward a pile of rocks.

Thunder wrinkled his nose at the faint stench that rose from the dead animal. "What *is* that?" he muttered. "It's worse than the smell of death."

At last Thunder and Gray Wing managed to shove the mouse's body into a crack between two rocks, and piled more and more pebbles on top of it until the stench was gone.

"Done!" Gray Wing exclaimed, settling back on his haunches. "And now we'd better find a stream to wash our paws . . . just in case." He let out a long sigh. "This is not a good sign."

CHAPTER 8
❧

When they returned to the hollow, Gray Wing found the other cats anxiously watching for them. He leaped up onto the rock beside Tall Shadow, and told his denmates about the mouse they'd found and how he and Thunder had disposed of it.

"What are we going to do?" Wind Runner asked, encircling her kits with her tail and drawing them protectively toward her. "What if there are more sick mice?"

Even in the midst of his worry, Gray Wing couldn't help thinking about how much Wind Runner had changed. Ever since one of her litter, Emberkit, had died soon after being born, she had been extra careful with the others. *And who can blame her?*

But that wasn't the only change. Since the battle she had been more reserved, and Gray Wing wondered whether her ambitions for leadership had waned, or whether they had simply changed direction. *She's more focused on Gorse Fur and the kits now,* he thought, *instead of trying to tell other cats what to do.*

"We have to be on our guard when we're hunting," Tall Shadow replied. "If there's any chance that the prey is ill, you mustn't attack. And certainly don't bring anything doubtful back into the camp."

"Why do we have to be so cautious?" Mud Paws asked.

Tall Shadow leaned closer to Gray Wing, murmuring into his ear: "Should we tell the three newcomers about the spirit-cats? Will they even believe us?"

Gray Wing wasn't sure. "They say they saw the battle. I don't know what else they saw. I know that we don't want to frighten them with stories about ghost cats and messages from the sky," he responded. "But I trust them and, sooner or later, some cat will tell them anyway. I think we should share what we know with them."

Tall Shadow hesitated briefly, then gave a nod.

"We recently received a warning," Gray Wing began, clearing his throat.

Instantly Holly leaped to her paws. "What kind of warning?" she demanded. "If it was from that nasty cat One Eye, we'll—"

"No," Gray Wing interrupted. "It was from some . . . distant friends."

"Do you mean traveling cats?" Mouse Ear asked, sounding puzzled.

"Not exactly," Gray Wing mewed. *These cats are going to think I have bees in my brain!* "It's complicated," he went on, eager to get to the end of the explanation as quickly as possible. "Just after the battle—before we met you—the . . . *spirits* of the cats who died appeared to us."

A squeak of amazement came from Sparrow Fur. She and her two littermates hadn't been in the battle or the later meeting, and now they were drinking in every word Gray Wing spoke, their eyes wide and excited.

"Spirit-cats?" Mud Paws gaped with astonishment, exchanging glances with his two friends. "Are you sure you weren't . . . well . . . a bit *confused* after all that fighting?"

Gray Wing shook his head. "Every cat who was there saw them and heard them. The spirit-cats told us to unite or die. They also told us to meet them again by the four trees at the next full moon."

"So that's where you all went the other night," Holly meowed. "I thought you'd just gone out on patrol."

"Yes," Gray Wing continued. "Perhaps we should have told you, but . . . We saw the spirit-cats again, and that's when they gave us the warning. They told us that a claw still blights the forest. To survive, we must grow and spread like the Blazing Star."

Holly let out a snort of disgust. "Your spirit friends certainly like being vague, don't they?" she mewed tartly. "What in the world is that message supposed to mean?"

"The claw might be the sickness that killed the mouse," Cloud Spots murmured thoughtfully.

"And the Blazing Star," Mouse Ear repeated. "Isn't that some kind of five-petaled plant?"

"What plant?" Gray Wing asked. "Where—?"

His voice was drowned out as excitement flared up among the listening cats at Mouse Ear's suggestion, and they crowded around, eagerly offering their own ideas.

"I think it means we should go back to the mountains," Tall

Shadow meowed. "A plant like that grows there."

Gray Wing stared at the black she-cat, hardly able to believe he had heard those words from her. *After all we've been through!* But he had no chance to object, because all his denmates were calling out their own explanations.

"I think it means we should follow a shooting star to a new territory!" Owl Eyes squealed, jumping up and down in excitement.

His sister, Sparrow Fur, gave him a shove. "When was the last time we saw a shooting star, mouse-brain?"

"A blaze . . ." Wind Runner murmured anxiously. "I'm afraid that might mean another fire somewhere. We could end up racing away from it, splitting up forever." Bending over her kits, she drew them closer, covering their ears with licks. "I won't let that happen," she promised.

Gorse Fur pressed himself to her side. "Whatever comes, we'll stay together."

"Wait!" Jagged Peak added his voice to the rising clamor. "Maybe it has to do with the plant Mouse Ear just mentioned. He said it has five petals, right? I think I remember seeing it in the mountains, too. Maybe we need to divide into—"

"That's enough," Gray Wing interrupted, becoming flustered by all the different ideas. "Have you all been quietly hatching your own explanations? You haven't been discussing this with any other cat at all? No wonder you're coming to such ridiculous conclusions!"

The other cats were silent, looking up at him with disconcerted expressions, as if they didn't know what was making him so irritable. Jagged Peak in particular looked hurt.

Well, I'm sorry, Gray Wing thought. *But they have to learn that panic and wild speculation will get us nowhere.*

"We all need to calm down," he meowed. "Now, Mouse Ear, where exactly is this plant—the 'Blazing Star'—growing? If we can find it and bring it back to camp, maybe it will give us a clue about what the spirit-cats were telling us. One thing at a time, okay?"

The cats muttered their agreement, though Gray Wing could see that they still weren't happy with him. *But that's fine, as long as we can work this out.*

"We found the Blazing Star growing on the other side of the Thunderpath," Mouse Ear told the others.

"You mean we've got to cross it?" Shattered Ice asked doubtfully. "I don't like the sound of that."

Gray Wing didn't like it, either, remembering the problems they had experienced on their journey, including the death of Shaded Moss under the paws of a monster.

"We used to go across all the time," Mud Paws mewed reassuringly. "It's not dangerous if you know how."

"I think we should give it a try," Tall Shadow decided. "I'm willing to lead a patrol over there and bring some of the plant back."

Renewed excitement stirred among the cats now that they had a plan. But Gray Wing saw that Jagged Peak was still looking hurt. A brief pang of guilt clawed at him: he hadn't allowed Jagged Peak to express his idea.

I still treat him like the careless kit I left the mountains to chase, he thought. *Maybe I need to start taking him more seriously.*

Holly leaned toward Jagged Peak and whispered something in his ear. Jagged Peak's eyes widened and he let out a *mrrow* of laughter.

Holly managed to cheer him up, Gray Wing thought, impressed in spite of himself. *She's good for Jagged Peak; there's no denying it. I just hope she doesn't push him too far. . . .*

CHAPTER 9

❧

Tall Shadow narrowed her eyes as she glanced up at the sun. "If we go now, we should make it back before nightfall," she meowed.

The days are getting shorter. Thunder's pads prickled with dread. *And the nights are getting colder. Soon leaf-bare will be upon us.*

But he pushed the thought away. Around him, his denmates were like a nest of bees, buzzing with curiosity.

"Come on!" Dappled Pelt meowed eagerly. "We've got to find this plant right away."

"Yes, I'm sure it's the answer!" Gorse Fur agreed.

Cloud Spots nodded thoughtfully. "It might even protect us against the sickness."

"Okay, let's go." Tall Shadow beckoned Mud Paws, Holly, and Mouse Ear with a wave of her tail.

Thunder followed them as they climbed the slope out of the hollow, and realized that most of his denmates were crowding after him. Tall Shadow halted and turned to face them.

"Wait a moment." Her voice was frustrated and her tail-tip twitched. "Not *every* cat can come. We can't leave the camp unprotected, can we? And how many cats does it take to pick a flower?"

"Why can't we come?" Shattered Ice asked.

Immediately arguments started to break out, some cats agreeing with Tall Shadow that only a small patrol was needed, while others were insisting on their right to join in.

"That's enough!" Thunder meowed, stepping forward. "I'll go with Tall Shadow," he continued decisively. "And we'll need at least one of our new members to show us the way."

Holly, Mud Paws, and Mouse Ear glanced at one another. "I don't mind staying," Holly murmured.

"Okay, I'll go," Mouse Ear offered.

"Perhaps I should go, too," Gray Wing added, padding up to Thunder's side.

Thunder turned to his kin, noticing the signs of strain and weariness in the older cat's face. "No, you stay and rest," he meowed. "It's been a long day, and you're not really needed for this." He saw sadness flash into Gray Wing's eyes, and quickly added, "Besides, a reliable cat should be left in charge of the camp—a cat we can all trust."

Gray Wing looked unconvinced, but dipped his head in agreement. "Very well," he mewed, turning away before Thunder could say any more.

Realizing there was no more he could do to reassure Gray Wing, Thunder headed after Tall Shadow, only to find Pebble Heart blocking his way.

"I want to go," the kit pleaded, his eyes wide and anxious. "I know herbs, and maybe I can help."

Thunder's first instinct was to refuse. *We don't want kits distracting us.* But then he reminded himself that Pebble Heart was no ordinary kit. *There must be a special reason that he wants to come.*

Thunder glanced at Gray Wing, who gave a nod. He turned back to Pebble Heart. "If Gray Wing thinks it's a good idea, you can join us."

Mouse Ear took the lead as the cats loped in silence across the moor, heading for the forest near the edge of the Twoleg-place. Thunder kept an eye on Pebble Heart to make sure that the kit didn't fall behind.

He's so serious, so watchful. Why did he want to come on this trip? I know Gray Wing says he has dreams. . . .

"Do many rogues live on the other side of the Thunderpath, where the Blazing Star grows?" Tall Shadow asked Mouse Ear as they reached the edge of the forest.

"Not many," Mouse Ear replied. "It's wet and marshy over there, and few cats enjoy the feeling of mud on their paws . . . not even Mud Paws," he added with a snort of laughter.

"But you must have been—" Tall Shadow began, only to break off as a bundle of mangy fur erupted from a pile of dead leaves and brush, hurling itself on top of Thunder, striking out to claw him across the nose.

"I saw it first!" a raspy voice meowed.

Thunder recoiled, stunned at the speed of the attack, and swiped a paw over his stinging snout. When he recovered he saw One Eye standing in front of him, his tail lashing and his lips drawn back in a snarl. A dead bird lay at his paws.

"We're supposed to be at peace!" Thunder snapped, sliding out his claws as he braced himself for another attack. "I didn't even see your wretched bird!"

One Eye took a threatening pace forward.

"Get back!" The shrill screech came from Pebble Heart. "Every cat get back!"

A thrill of fear ran through Thunder at the urgency in the kit's voice. For the first time he looked closely at the bird and saw that its belly was swollen and some of its feathers were missing. Dried pus crusted the areas of exposed skin.

"Stop!" Pebble Heart squealed as One Eye stepped forward, about to sink his teeth into the prey.

Thunder sprang forward, barreling into the mangy tom, driving him back from the bird. One Eye fought back hard, digging his teeth into Thunder's neck.

"Get off!" Thunder mewed through gritted teeth. "I'm trying to save your miserable pelt!" He flung One Eye away, then pinned him down with both forepaws on his chest. The tom glared up at him with hatred in his one eye.

At last Tall Shadow realized what had frightened Pebble Heart. "The bird is sick!" she yowled. "Every cat stay away!"

While she was speaking, the undergrowth parted a few fox-lengths away, and Clear Sky appeared, followed by Petal and the two kits, Birch and Alder. "One Eye, what's going on here?" he asked with a rapid glance around at the other cats.

Thunder stepped back, allowing One Eye to get up, seeing recognition and then fear creep into his eye as he surveyed the dead bird. "Nothing," the rogue muttered, not meeting Clear Sky's gaze.

I'm not letting him get away with that! Thunder thought. Clearing his throat, he dipped his head toward his father. "Actually," he began, "One Eye attacked me for getting too close to his kill. I fought him off because the bird is sick. Whatever he says, I was trying to help."

Clear Sky narrowed his eyes. "Sick?"

"Yes, it—" Thunder broke off as the two kits bounded forward and peered curiously at the bird. "No!" he went on sharply, pushing them away with a gentle paw. "Stay back."

But Birch dodged around him, stretched out his neck, and touched the dead bird with his nose. "Yuck!" he exclaimed, his curiosity changing to disgust as he backed away. "It smells foul!"

Thunder let out a sigh and glanced at Clear Sky, who beckoned the kits with a jerk of his head. "Get back here *now*!" he mewed commandingly. There was concern in his eyes, which surprised Thunder—it was a look he hadn't seen from his father when *he* was a kit who needed him. He tried not to feel envious that Clear Sky cared for kits who weren't even his own.

The two kits bounced back to Petal, who gathered them close with her tail, and licked their ears affectionately.

Clear Sky padded forward and gave the bird a careful inspection, looking just as disgusted as the other cats.

"You've been in the forest a long time," he said to One Eye. "Have you seen this illness before?"

One Eye twitched his ears. "It's just sickness," he replied. "Sickness is part of life in the wild."

Thunder could see that Clear Sky wasn't satisfied with

One Eye's answer. His eyes looked apprehensive as he glanced back at the kits. Then he turned back toward the moorland cats. "What brings you here?" he asked.

Tall Shadow stepped forward. "We found out something about the Blazing Star," she explained. "It's a plant that grows on the other side of the Thunderpath, and we're going to get some, to see if it will help us to understand what the spirit-cats meant."

Clear Sky's whiskers quivered in annoyance. "You got a clue as to what the message meant, and you weren't going to tell me? Aren't we all in this together? *Unite or die*, remember?"

Shame swept over Thunder as his father spoke. He could see that Tall Shadow felt the same. How could it not have occurred to any cat to tell Clear Sky what they had discovered?

"We never meant to keep it from you," she assured Clear Sky. "We were just working quickly. But you're right. We should find the Blazing Star together."

Clear Sky gave a grim nod, obviously not appeased by the black she-cat's words. "Petal, take the kits back to camp," he ordered. "One Eye, you go too."

Petal turned away, leading her kits back into the undergrowth, but One Eye stood still, bristling. "I should come with you," he insisted. "You can't shoo me back to camp like some mewling kit!"

"You're not needed here," Clear Sky meowed firmly. "And part of living in a group is knowing your place. Do you understand, One Eye?"

Thunder was suddenly aware that the air was thickening

with tension as the two toms faced each other. The mangy rogue's single eye burned with hatred, and Thunder could tell from Clear Sky's tight voice and rigid stance that he wasn't confident, in spite of his show of authority.

But Clear Sky's gaze never wavered, and at last One Eye took a few paces back toward the camp. Thunder hoped that the confrontation was over, but as he and the others were turning to leave, One Eye halted and looked back over his shoulder.

"There's not much you could do to keep me from following," he hissed. "I may have only one eye, but it sees everything."

Before Clear Sky could respond, One Eye turned away again and vanished into the undergrowth.

For a moment Clear Sky seemed lost for words. Then Tall Shadow padded up to him and brushed her pelt against his. "We'd better get going," she mewed. "Daylight is short."

She took the lead again as they headed toward the Thunderpath. Mouse Ear walked beside Clear Sky, while Thunder brought up the rear with Pebble Heart, who still looked uneasy.

"Are you okay?" Thunder murmured.

The kit nodded. "I'm fine. I'm just worried about what is happening in the forest."

So are we all. . . . Thunder thought.

Before they had gone many paw steps, Mouse Ear turned to Clear Sky. "Now you must see what a mistake it was to let One Eye join your group," he meowed bluntly.

Clear Sky glared at him, the fur on his shoulders beginning

to fluff up. "I see no such thing," he retorted. "One Eye may be a bit strong-willed, but it will just take time for such an independent cat to adjust to living with many other cats." Thunder could see uncertainty in his father's eyes as he added with a show of confidence, "One Eye has given us invaluable fighting techniques, and that's what matters."

Tall Shadow, who had glanced back to listen to the exchange, had a knowing look in her eyes, but all she said was, "No more talking! We have to get a move on, if we want to get across the Thunderpath and back before it gets dark."

Already Thunder could pick out the acrid tang of monsters among the forest scents, and before long they emerged from the trees and stood on the narrow strip of grass that bordered the hard, black stone. A dead ash tree leaned over the grass, surrounded by a thicket of brambles.

Tall Shadow glanced carefully in both directions. "Okay, Thunder," she mewed. "You go across first."

"Wait!" Mouse Ear flicked out his tail to halt Thunder. "You haven't felt the Thunderpath yet."

Tall Shadow gave him a puzzled look. "What do you mean?"

"Like this." Mouse Ear cautiously placed one paw on the black surface and twitched his ears. "No rumbles," he reported. "It's safe for us all to cross."

Thunder exchanged a surprised glance with Tall Shadow and Clear Sky. "I suppose there's a lot we can learn from the rogues," Clear Sky commented.

"So let's do it," Mouse Ear urged, tapping his paw impatiently. "The monsters won't wait for us forever."

Without hesitation he bounded across the Thunderpath, with Tall Shadow and Clear Sky hard on his paws. Thunder noticed that Pebble Heart was looking apprehensive, and touched him reassuringly on the shoulder with his tail-tip. "Come on," he encouraged the kit. "We'll cross together."

Pebble Heart looked up at him, eyes wide. "I never thought a Thunderpath could be so *big*! It's nothing like the ones in the Twolegplace."

"So you'll have a great story to tell Sparrow Fur and Owl Eyes," Thunder responded.

Taking a deep breath, the kit sprang forward. Thunder kept pace with him, and the two of them arrived safely beside Tall Shadow and the others. A moment later a monster swept past, its unnaturally bright red pelt glittering in the sun.

"Monsters can go that fast?" Pebble Heart exclaimed, his chest swelling with pride now that he had made the crossing. "Amazing!"

Mouse Ear took the lead again as the cats headed away from the Thunderpath. Thunder began to pick up a different scent, of mud and water and rich, growing things. His nose twitched. *That must be the marsh. Give me the moor or the forest any day!*

Eventually Mouse Ear halted at the top of a shallow slope that led down to a wide stretch of stagnant water dotted with tussocks of grass. Clumps of reeds clattered together as they swayed in the breeze. A dragonfly hovered above the surface of the water, its body a bright, iridescent blue. As Thunder watched, a frog leaped from the bank nearby with a loud *plop*;

ripples spread out from the spot where it disappeared.

Tall Shadow was gazing across the marsh too, looking transfixed. A faint purr came from her throat. Mouse Ear had to prod her to get her attention.

"This is what we've been looking for," he told her, pointing with one paw to a spot a little way up the slope.

Eagerly Thunder joined Tall Shadow and Clear Sky around the plant. "Oh . . . is that it?" he asked, slightly disappointed.

The Blazing Star was smaller than he had expected, with spiky leaves and yellow flowers whose five petals spread out separately. It didn't seem important enough to be the answer to the spirit-cats' riddle.

"Just a small, yellow flower, shaped like a star," Tall Shadow murmured.

"It looks like a paw with claws extended," Clear Sky commented, holding up his own paw to demonstrate. "Perhaps the spirit-cats meant that we need to fight. To defend our territory from . . ."

He left the thought unfinished.

"From who?" Mouse Ear asked, his challenging tone attracting the gaze of every cat.

Tall Shadow shook her head. "The spirit-cats did not tell us to fight. They said we should grow and spread like the Blazing Star." She thought for a moment, then added, "All these flowers bend toward the sun. Perhaps they meant that we should follow the sun. Move again—follow the sun even farther than before?"

"No," Clear Sky meowed with a whisk of his tail. "We've

made that journey already. I believe *this* is where we're supposed to be."

Thunder stared thoughtfully at the flower, waiting for an explanation to occur to him. *Why couldn't the spirit-cats be a bit clearer?*

"What do you think, Thunder?" Clear Sky asked him.

Thunder couldn't deny a secret spring of satisfaction growing in his chest, like water bubbling up between rocks. *My father wants my advice! How far we've come!*

"I'm not sure," he replied, unable to stop staring at the flower. *The petals spread from the center, each pointing in a different direction. . . .*

While he was still pondering, Thunder remembered Pebble Heart's presence. The kit was so quiet and serious that it was easy to forget he was there. "Do you have any ideas?" he asked, turning to Pebble Heart.

The little tom stared for a heartbeat longer, then backed away. "I—I don't know," he stammered. But he wouldn't meet Thunder's gaze and Thunder guessed he wasn't telling the full story. "I think things are about to change," Pebble Heart added in a small voice.

Tall Shadow's whiskers drooped. "It's time to go," she meowed. "Sunset is almost here." She bent her head and bit off a stem with two or three flowers on it. "I'll take this back and see if it gives any of the others some ideas."

Clear Sky nodded approvingly. "I'll take some too." He bit off one stem, then after a heartbeat's pause picked another. "And I'll take this to River Ripple," he added.

I should have thought of that! Thunder was annoyed with himself. *We're not doing a very good job of being united if we forget to tell Clear Sky or River Ripple about important stuff.*

Clear Sky took the lead as the patrol headed back toward the Thunderpath. This time, they all stood back to let Mouse Ear rest his paw on the black surface.

"Better wait," he warned them. "There's a monster coming."

Thunder looked up and down the Thunderpath, but he couldn't see any trace of a monster. *I wonder if this is some crazy rogue superstition?*

As he waited, he noticed that Tall Shadow was gazing back toward the marsh, a faraway look in her eyes. "Tall Shadow, are you okay?" he asked.

The black she-cat looked startled, almost as if Thunder had caught her doing something wrong.

"What are you looking at?" he asked.

Tall Shadow glanced back at the marsh, and her tail curled up happily. "It's just so beautiful here," she purred.

Beautiful? Has she got bees in her brain?

Thunder couldn't place the uncomfortable feeling that Tall Shadow's words gave him. He glanced at Pebble Heart to see how he felt about it, but once again the kit wouldn't meet his gaze.

A distant roar, growing rapidly louder, distracted Thunder. Looking along the Thunderpath he saw a huge monster bearing down on them on massive, black paws. The rattle and rumble of its passing seemed to shake his bones; wind buffeted their fur and almost carried them off their paws.

Thunder glanced at Mouse Ear, impressed. *He's not so crazy after all.*

Once the monster had passed, Mouse Ear tested the surface again, then gave a satisfied nod. "We can cross now," he mewed. "It's safe."

All five cats ran quickly across the Thunderpath. Once they reached the opposite side, Clear Sky dipped his head to the moorland cats.

"Good-bye for now," he murmured politely. "I'll be sure to let you know if we come up with any ideas about the Blazing Star."

Thunder called out a farewell as his father disappeared among the trees, then followed Tall Shadow as she headed back to their camp. Pebble Heart, growing tired now, lagged behind.

Mouse Ear's words repeated themselves in Thunder's mind as they crossed the moor.

We're safe. But for how long?

CHAPTER 10

The sun shone, but wind whistled through the branches of the trees, whirling dead leaves around Clear Sky. He sat on a hillock in a forest clearing, watching One Eye and Tom. They had gathered some of the other cats to train them in battle techniques.

"Quick Water, have you gone to sleep?" the former rogue snarled. "And you, Leaf? You're as slow as a dying snail!"

One Eye is harsh, Clear Sky thought, watching him give the unfortunate Leaf a cuff around the ear. *But he certainly can fight!*

Clear Sky and One Eye had never spoken again of the argument they had had in front of Thunder and Tall Shadow. Clear Sky didn't know for sure whether the rogue had followed him across the Thunderpath to find the Blazing Star.

I saw no sign that he did, Clear Sky tried to reassure himself. *But I wouldn't put it past him.* One Eye's challenge to his authority still rankled, although he kept telling himself what he had told Mouse Ear: It would take time for a lifelong rogue like One Eye to learn the rules of group living. Some flare-ups and squabbles were only natural. *But if it happens again . . .*

Focusing on the training, Clear Sky knew he couldn't argue with one fact: One Eye fought very sneakily, with techniques and tricks that Clear Sky himself had never dreamed of. Tom, too, was losing his kittypet softness and learning to use his claws. And kittypet or not, he was full of ideas on how to trick his opponents and defeat them.

"Now watch this," One Eye meowed, facing Thorn. "Fighting is about winning, right? And to win, you need to distract your enemy. Thorn, I'm coming at you. Fight me off!"

Thorn braced himself, letting out a fierce growl. One Eye crouched low to the ground, then leaped forward as if he was aiming for Thorn's neck. Thorn instinctively brought up his paws to fend him off. Swift as a striking snake, One Eye ducked underneath his legs and pushed him over, raking his paws across Thorn's soft belly. Then he stood back, waiting for the disconcerted tom to stand up again.

"If I'd been using my claws," One Eye rasped, "your belly would have been torn open."

Thorn clearly didn't know how to respond to this. One Eye let out an amused snort. "Next time, you *will* know what to do."

Thorn nodded, while nervous *mrrow*s of laughter came from the other cats who had watched the move.

Clear Sky twitched his tail in satisfaction. One Eye and Tom were giving his cats an advantage in battle that no other group would have. *That will matter someday,* he realized. None of his cats had been able to decide what the Blazing Star meant, and the future was still as dark to them as ever. But whatever the coming seasons held, being a skilled fighter could save a cat's life. *Not in battle,* he reminded himself, feeling slightly nauseous at the terrible memory. *Not unless we have no other choice.*

"What about hidden weapons?" Tom asked, stepping up beside One Eye.

The old rogue turned to him with an enthusiastic swish of his tail. "Yes, good thinking! In a forest like this, no cat needs to rely just on their claws and teeth. There are a lot of things that can inflict pain. Tom, why don't you go and look for a rock with a sharp edge."

Tom immediately whipped around and raced into the trees, his tail streaming out behind him.

Clear Sky was impressed. *I never thought of using rocks in battle.*

"Okay." One Eye turned back to the other cats. "Pair up, and I want to see you practicing that neck feint. Concentrate on speed. No claws . . . for now."

But before the training exercise could begin, a small cat emerged from the undergrowth at the edge of the clearing and ran toward the group. Startled, Clear Sky peered at the little tortoiseshell and recognized Sparrow Fur, one of Turtle Tail's kits who Gray Wing was raising. She had grown since he first saw her in Gray Wing's camp after the forest fire. *And even since Tom took her,* he added to himself, still feeling guilty for not recognizing her then.

"Are you doing fight training?" she asked eagerly as she pattered up to One Eye. "I came looking for Tom—he's my father, you know. He was just here. . . . Where did he go?" When no cat responded, she added, "Can I train with you? I think I'm a pretty good fighter, but there's always more to learn, isn't there?"

Without warning, One Eye pounced in front of Sparrow Fur, pushing one paw into her forehead.

"Ow!" Sparrow Fur yowled. "You don't have to use claws!"

One Eye didn't move. "*I* don't know you," he told her in a low snarl. "And that makes you my enemy."

"I'm not!" Sparrow Fur protested. "Tom's my father. And can you put your claws away, please? You're hurting me."

"If you love your father so much," One Eye replied calmly, "then you should come and join him in this group, shouldn't you? Until you do, you can't be one of us."

Clear Sky shifted his weight on the hillock, feeling a prickle of uncertainty in his pelt. The ghost cats had told them, *Unite or die.*

We aren't supposed to fight over territory anymore, he thought. But then he reflected that, in a way, One Eye was right. There were reasons that his group and the group in the moorland hollow had stayed separate. *And why should we share battle techniques with an outsider? No cat knows who our next enemy will be.*

Narrowing his eyes, he settled down on the hillock again to see how this encounter would play out.

Sparrow Fur's pelt was bristling in anger, and she arched her back. "You can't keep me from seeing my father," she meowed. "I'm not leaving until he comes back!" She swiped at One Eye's nose with her claws.

The rogue easily dodged the blow. "Either you can leave or you can fight me," he rasped. "Prove you're serious by taking me down—if you can—and you can stay."

"I'm a very good fighter!" Sparrow Fur retorted. "I fight

with my brothers all the time."

"I'm no kin of yours," One Eye mewed darkly. "Whether you survive this fight is no concern of mine. So will you leave? Or fight?"

Clear Sky could see the kit's frustration and uncertainty in her fluffed-up fur and twitching tail. *I know how she feels; she can't understand why a grown cat would be this mean to her.*

"All right," Sparrow Fur agreed, raising her head bravely. "If I have to prove how much I need to see my father, I *will* fight you!"

This is going too far, Clear Sky decided. Rising to his paws, he cleared his throat.

One Eye turned and gazed up at him, dark amusement smoldering in his eye. "The kits who live in these groups are so sheltered," he began. "In the wild, kits learn from birth how the real world works. If you challenge a cat, you must fight him. And if you made a mistake in challenging him, you learn."

Clear Sky could understand the logic of what One Eye was saying. *Sparrow Fur is a feisty little thing—maybe too feisty for her own good.* But his pelt still prickled uncomfortably, and he was not sure why he felt that way. *Has the forced peace of the last moon made me go soft? Or is it because she's sort of my brother's kit that I want to protect her?*

At last Clear Sky decided that One Eye was right. It was just for that kind of blunt, unattractive wisdom that he had allowed the rogue to join his group. *Sparrow Fur won't be forever harmed by a few scratches!* Nodding his head, he allowed the fight to begin.

Instantly Sparrow Fur hurled herself at One Eye, getting in a couple of stinging blows around his ears. Clear Sky stifled a *mrrow* of laughter. *Maybe she was right to challenge the old rogue! Perhaps she's a born fighter. . . .*

But within a heartbeat, the fight changed. One Eye swiped the little tortoiseshell across the shoulder. Clear Sky could see blood welling from the scratches as Sparrow Fur staggered and fell.

One Eye glanced across at Clear Sky, and gave him a nod. Clear Sky understood. *He's just teaching her a lesson. He'll back down now.* Every hair on Clear Sky's pelt was urging him to run down from the hillock and break up the fight. But he forced himself to stay where he was.

One Eye took a step back from the kit, lashing his tail as if challenging her to get up. Sparrow Fur struggled to her paws. She was clearly in pain, but she glared steadily at the rogue with fire in her eyes.

She's just like her mother, Clear Sky thought, remembering Turtle Tail in the mountains. *Determined to the last . . .*

With a howl of anger the kit leaped at One Eye, sinking her claws into his neck and back. Her hind paws barely touched the ground as she bit hard into his pelt and scrabbled to claw at his remaining eye. "I want to see my father!" she yowled.

Clear Sky could see the change come over the rogue cat in stiffening limbs and bristling pelt, but his own paws felt frozen to the hilltop, as if what he was seeing was some kind of dark dream.

One Eye threw the kit off his back effortlessly, then

pounced on top of her. He dug his teeth into her flank and twisted his head, tearing at her flesh. Sparrow Fur let out a wail, her soft, small paws batting helplessly at her attacker. Without mercy One Eye rolled her onto her back and tore into her white belly fur.

The other cats stood around watching, their eyes wide with horror, but clearly not daring to intervene because their leader had allowed the fight. Acorn Fur and Quick Water looked particularly distressed, both she-cats turning a pleading gaze toward Clear Sky.

Stunned at the vicious attack, Clear Sky realized that the rogue was about to kill the kit to teach her a lesson. *And I am letting it happen!*

At last he forced his paws to move, hurling down from the hillock and racing across the clearing. "Stop!" he yowled.

One Eye raised his head, baring teeth that were stained with Sparrow Fur's blood, one paw still pinning down her feebly twitching body. With horror, Clear Sky realized that he was too late. He was not going to reach Sparrow Fur before One Eye dealt the killing blow.

But at the same moment an orange blur came flying out of the trees and leaped on top of One Eye, knocking him several paces away and digging claws into the side of his head. One Eye screeched in protest.

Tom! Relief washed over Clear Sky as he recognized the former kittypet.

"Leave her alone!" Tom growled, attacking One Eye in a whirl of teeth and claws. "She's my kit!"

The two cats rolled over together on the ground, their paws locked around each other's bodies, their jaws snapping.

Clear Sky hardly spared them a glance. He halted beside Sparrow Fur, who lay bleeding in the grass where One Eye had left her. His belly heaved with a mixture of revulsion and pity. The tortoiseshell kit was unconscious, her chest barely moving to show that she was still alive. Terrible wounds gaped in her flanks and belly.

A *helpless kit!* Clear Sky thought, guilt surging through him like storm water. *What was I thinking?*

Desperately he turned toward the other cats who were still watching, transfixed with horror. "I need help," he mewed, his voice shaking. "Please. We need cobwebs to stop the bleeding."

Instantly the cats scattered into the undergrowth. Clear Sky felt a brief glow of gratitude that they didn't turn their backs on him after they had watched him allow the unequal fight to happen. But a heartbeat later he pushed the feeling away.

That's not important now. What matters is saving Sparrow Fur!

Clear Sky was vaguely aware that Tom and One Eye were still fighting somewhere on the other side of the clearing, but he couldn't bring himself to care. All his attention was on the injured kit.

Acorn Fur was the first cat to return with a thick pawful of cobwebs. She bent over her former denmate, gently licking the blood away from her wounds and pressing the cobwebs over them. They quickly soaked with blood, but when the other cats returned with more cobwebs, the bleeding was gradually brought under control. Sparrow Fur's breathing grew deeper and more regular, though she didn't open her eyes.

"Will she be okay now?" Acorn Fur asked anxiously.

Clear Sky heaved a huge sigh of relief. "I hope so," he replied. "But we need to get her back to camp and care for her."

He realized that the hissing and screeching from Tom and One Eye had died away to silence. *Good, the fight is over,* he thought. *Now I can deal with them both. . . .*

But when he glanced across at the other side of the clearing, his jaws gaped in shock. Tom lay with his legs splayed out and his eyes wide in a fixed stare. Blood clotted in his fur and on the grass around him. One Eye sat beside him, calmly licking his paws and cleaning blood off his whiskers.

"He fought well," he meowed, "for a kittypet."

Clear Sky heard gasps of horror from the other cats, feeling as though all the blood in his veins had turned to ice.

"Oh, no," Thorn muttered, sounding sick. "Tom didn't deserve to die like that."

"He was only defending his kit," Acorn Fur whispered.

With a massive effort, Clear Sky pulled himself together and gave his pelt a shake. "Carry Sparrow Fur back to camp as quickly as you can," he ordered. "Treat her like you would your own kit. And one of you should run ahead and tell Petal to make a soft nest out of moss."

Acorn Fur raced off at once, while Thorn and Leaf gently picked up Sparrow Fur's body, careful not to dislodge the cobwebs over her wounds. As they headed into the trees, Quick

Water padded just in front of them, carefully holding back branches and bramble tendrils so that they didn't catch on the kit's pelt.

Once they had gone, Clear Sky slowly padded across the clearing toward One Eye, who was still grooming himself, his gaze firmly fixed on his paw.

Clear Sky halted a few paw steps in front of the rogue, then discovered that he had no idea what he wanted to say. "What . . ." he managed to stammer.

One Eye looked up at him, the fur around his mouth spiky with drying blood. "Stupid kittypet," he rasped, his voice filled with contempt. "He should have known better than to challenge me. I've killed much tougher opponents than him."

"Like the kit?" Clear Sky asked, unable to find words strong enough to express his disgust with the rogue. "The helpless kit you practically tore apart, for fun?"

One Eye flicked his tail dismissively. "That kit was too proud," he mewed. "She didn't know when to give up. Now she's learned a valuable lesson."

Clear Sky's claws slid out, and his foreleg swiped a hard blow at the side of One Eye's head. The rogue dodged it with no trouble at all, giving Clear Sky a derisive look.

"You can't stop me from defending my honor," he told Clear Sky. "That's how it works in the real world."

Honor? Clear Sky thought. *This cat has no honor!*

He struck at One Eye again, but the rogue avoided that blow with as much ease as the first. "We have rules here!" Clear Sky hissed.

"Your so-called rules are a joke," One Eye snarled back. "No cat really cares about anything but himself. Pretending otherwise just causes heartache . . . and sickness."

Clear Sky's heart thumped uncomfortably. *Sickness?* "What do you know about the sickness?" he demanded.

One Eye gave the same dismissive flick of his tail.

"That bird was very ill," Clear Sky went on, his apprehension growing with every heartbeat. "Do you know more about it than you told us?"

"I know enough to tell you that some of the cats in your group are as good as dead."

He didn't know if One Eye's words were to be trusted, but felt his fur bristling along his back. "Which ones?" he demanded. "How do you know?"

One Eye flicked his tail again. "I could tell you, but I won't bother. I guess I only care about myself."

Clear Sky found the malevolence in his single eye sickening. A red mist clouded Clear Sky's vision. He pounced on One Eye, holding him down with both forepaws while he dug into the rogue's neck with his teeth. One Eye struggled, but rage gave Clear Sky new strength.

Every instinct was urging him to rip out the vile cat's throat and let his blood run out into the grass, but he knew that would be to lower himself to the same disgusting level. Instead he stood back, releasing One Eye. The rogue leaped up, smoothing one paw over his ears.

"Get out of here," Clear Sky ordered, forcing his voice to remain even as he spat out the words. "Do not come back. Or

I will kill you with my own claws."

As One Eye glared for a moment, Clear Sky realized something that had always bothered him about the rogue. His eye had no expression, just a malignant yellow glow.

"You'll kill *me*, will you?" the rogue asked. "Will you really?"

Clear Sky felt the blood pounding in his ears and braced himself, ready for battle. But One Eye turned away, heading for the edge of the clearing and into the trees.

Clear Sky took a deep breath. *One Eye has gone—and I feel like he's taken all of my honor with him.* He realized that he should have driven One Eye out after he challenged his authority in front of Tall Shadow and Thunder. *How will I ever explain what happened to my cats?*

Ready to despair, Clear Sky closed his eyes. A heartbeat later he felt a hard blow on his back, and let out a startled yowl. Claws dug into his back, and One Eye snaked a paw around Clear Sky's neck, aiming for his eye.

That's a move Tom came up with! Clear Sky thought, struggling frantically to throw One Eye off. Pain stabbed into his face as One Eye raked his claws over his cheek.

Clear Sky let himself go limp and collapsed to the ground, rolling over so that One Eye was underneath him. Then he wriggled around and swiped his claws across the rogue's shoulder, breaking his grip. Clear Sky sprang to his paws, panting.

"You'll kill me, will you?" One Eye sneered, rising to face him. "You'll kill One Eye? If One Eye were that easy to kill, he'd never have survived kithood." He spat at Clear Sky, pointing with his tail at the wound along his face. "Keep that to remember me by," he snarled.

As the rogue slunk away into the forest, Clear Sky felt his legs trembling. He sank to the ground, taking in huge gulps of air. He felt so utterly defeated, as though he would never be able to get up again.

I've made a terrible mistake. . . .

CHAPTER 11

Gray Wing woke up, blinking at the sunlight that streamed into his den. The kits who shared it with him were nowhere to be seen, their nests cold. *Where have they gone?* he wondered, struggling to his paws and trying to ignore the ache in his joints. *I hope they're not getting into any trouble.* He would never forget how Tom had taken the kits away, and how Turtle Tail had been killed when she went to look for them. *And now Tom's in the forest again....*

Leaving the den, Gray Wing saw that the sun was already high in the sky; it was a crisp, cold day with a hint of frost on the breeze. Tall Shadow was sitting on her rock keeping watch, as usual. Lightning Tail and Shattered Ice were returning from a hunting expedition, a rabbit dangling from each of their jaws, while the three newcomers were practicing their hunting moves in the middle of the clearing.

I must have slept in again, Gray Wing thought guiltily, remembering the days when he would always be the first cat to wake up.

An ear-splitting yowl roused Gray Wing from his memories. *That's Wind Runner!*

His pelt prickling with apprehension, Gray Wing turned toward Wind Runner's den, seeing that several cats were clustered around the entrance. His fear deepening, his heart beginning to pound, he raced over to join them.

Shouldering his way between Jagged Peak and Dappled Pelt, he saw that Wind Runner's kit Morning Whisker was lying on her side just inside the den, her belly horribly swollen. Blood was dribbling from her mouth and from sores beneath her fur. Nausea gripped Gray Wing's belly at the same time as deep compassion welled up inside him.

She has the sickness!

"I can't bear it!" Wind Runner whimpered. She was standing a couple of fox-lengths away, leaning on Gorse Fur for support. "I can't lose another kit! Why couldn't it be me instead?"

Then Gray Wing spotted Pebble Heart slipping into the den beside Morning Whisker and leaning over her, opening his jaws to push some chewed-up herb into the sick kit's mouth. Her littermates, Moth Flight and Dust Muzzle, watched anxiously from their mother's side.

Instinctively Gray Wing sprang forward and knocked Pebble Heart away from the struggling kit, spinning him around to face him. "What are you doing?" he demanded angrily. "Stay away from that kit! She's dying!"

Pebble Heart set the lump of chewed leaves down carefully. "I know," he replied. "I was helping to treat her. Cloud Spots says that tansy—"

"Where is Cloud Spots?" Gray Wing interrupted. "He

should be dealing with this, not a cat as young as you."

Pebble Heart rubbed his cheek affectionately against Gray Wing's shoulder. "Cloud Spots went to gather herbs. We've been using the tansy, and we've nearly finished what we had in our collection. We need more, so Cloud Spots left me in charge."

Gray Wing closed his eyes, feeling like a complete mouse-brain. "Oh . . . " he muttered. His instincts still screamed at him to keep Pebble Heart away from the sick cat, although he knew that that poor little Morning Whisker had no other hope. *Pebble Heart is special,* he reminded himself. *He has his own path to follow.*

"I'm going to give this tansy to Morning Whisker," Pebble Heart mewed, picking up the chewed-up lump and gently forcing it between her jaws. "Don't worry. Cloud Spots told me to be careful not to touch her sores or let her breathe on me."

As Gray Wing watched, Owl Eyes slipped up to his side and touched noses with him. "Morning Whisker will be okay, won't she?" he asked anxiously.

Gray Wing let out a long sigh. "I don't know." *There's so much I don't know these days. . . .*

Gray Wing padded over to Gorse Fur and Wind Runner, laying his tail comfortingly over the distraught she-cat's back. "Morning Whisker will be okay," he told her, wishing he believed his own words. "You mustn't lose hope."

Wind Runner broke off her pitiful yowling and sank to the ground. "That's easy for you to say," she whimpered. "All your kits are alive and healthy."

Gray Wing rested a paw on her shoulder. "My kits may be alive," he mewed gently, "but my mate is gone, and I know grief as well as you. You cannot let the misery overwhelm you. Your other kits still need you, and you must focus on helping them."

Wind Runner blinked and turned her head away, still trembling, but Gorse Fur gave Gray Wing a grateful nod. "We don't know what will happen," he murmured to his mate.

Gray Wing padded away, leaving the two cats to their suffering. Then he realized that one of his kits was still unaccounted for. Beckoning to Owl Eyes, he asked, "Where's Sparrow Fur?"

"She went to find our father," Owl Eyes replied.

Gray Wing flinched, though he tried to hide the pain he felt to hear one of the kits call Tom his father. *Even though it's true* . . . "Wait a moment," he meowed. "Why would she go off into the forest without telling me?"

Owl Eyes scrabbled at the ground with his forepaws, not meeting Gray Wing's gaze. "Jagged Peak said it was okay. Anyway, we're all one big group now, aren't we?"

"Sort of," Gray Wing responded, wincing as he realized he wasn't sure what the rules were anymore. He couldn't help thinking of Tom's treachery in the past—the way he had stolen the kits, and that he might have been involved in Turtle Tail's death.

"No, this isn't right," he growled, glancing around wildly. Fear surged over him as he imagined what Tom might do to Sparrow Fur, or what other dangers the kit might encounter alone in the forest without him or any of her denmates. *Foxes, dogs, Twolegs . . . she might meet any of them!* "We have to form a search party. We have to get her back."

He spotted Jagged Peak, who had joined Holly and the other newcomers, and beckoned him over with a commanding flick of his tail.

"What's wrong?" Jagged Peak asked as he limped up.

"Sparrow Fur—*my* kit—went off to find Tom the kittypet, and Owl Eyes said you gave her permission!"

Jagged Peak's eyes widened with surprise. "Yes, I did. Is there a problem?"

"A *problem?*" Gray Wing was stunned. "You *let* her go? She's just a kit!"

Jagged Peak began to look uncomfortable. "I'm sorry. I thought it would be okay. After all, he is their father. And she's not a tiny kit anymore."

Gray Wing had to admit that his brother was right. The kits were growing up. *And Sparrow Fur always knows what she wants, just like her mother.*

Gray Wing's heart pounded as he thought over what Jagged Peak had just told him. *It sounds so reasonable,* he thought. *And yet . . .* "They have no mother now," he meowed. "I'm all they have. I must protect her."

Jagged Peak twitched his whiskers to show he understood. "That's true," he responded gently. "But the kits are nearly grown. They aren't helpless anymore. They're old enough to make their own decisions, and all three of them *wanted* to train with Tom."

Gray Wing shook his head. "But what if . . . what if . . ."

"What if what?" Jagged Peak asked, amusement glimmering in his blue eyes. "You can't protect them forever. You can't protect any cat forever, Gray Wing, no matter how hard you try to. That's a lesson I must learn, too."

Gray Wing looked at him and wondered whether the young cat was talking about how Gray Wing had treated him. *It's true. I have* always tried to protect him. *But where's the harm in that?*

Then he turned his head to one side, realizing what his brother had said. "What do you mean?" he asked. "A lesson you must learn?"

Jagged Peak leaned in closer to Gray Wing, his whiskers quivering with excitement. "I've got news," he announced. "And I want you to be the first to hear it. It's very early yet, but I can't keep quiet any longer. I'm going to be a father! Soon I will have kits of my own!"

Gray Wing stepped back a pace and stared at him. In his mind, Jagged Peak was still the tiny kit who had run away from the mountain cave and needed looking after on the journey. *And now he's going to have his own kits!*

"With Holly?" he asked.

"Yes, of course with Holly," Jagged Peak responded. "We love each other. I've never felt this way before," he admitted shyly. "She challenges me, and we keep each other on our paw tips. I just hope I can be as good a father as you've been to Turtle Tail's kits."

Gray Wing hardly heard the last few words. He was staring at Jagged Peak, realizing that his brother looked happier than he ever had since they came from the mountains. His pelt and his eyes shone, and he barely limped anymore. It also seemed the confidence he once had, before his fall from the tree, was back.

I promised Quiet Rain I would take care of Jagged Peak, he thought ruefully. *And I've done my best to keep that promise. But by protecting him so fiercely, have I been holding him back?*

As Gray Wing was lost in thought, Thunder stalked into the camp with Cloud Spots just behind him. Both were carrying herbs. Gray Wing looked up and remembered that Pebble Heart had told him Cloud Spots had gone out foraging, but he hadn't realized that Thunder was with him.

I slept through all of this, and no cat thought to wake me.

Thunder and Cloud Spots bounded across the hollow, carrying the herbs to Wind Runner's den. Cloud Spots stayed to examine Morning Whisker, but Thunder padded back into the center of the camp and glanced around. "Let's gather around the lookout rock," he meowed to his denmates. "I have an announcement."

Gray Wing followed him and sat at the foot of the rock. While the rest of the cats gathered, Thunder leaped up beside Tall Shadow, waiting until every cat was assembled.

"We must be extra vigilant about the sickness," he began once his denmates were ready, his gaze troubled. "From now on, no cat is to touch Morning Whisker except for Cloud Spots and Pebble Heart—no, Wind Runner, not even you and Gorse Fur," he added as the tabby she-cat opened her jaws to protest.

Gray Wing could sense Wind Runner's grief and anger

as she gazed up at Thunder with a challenge in her eyes. But Gorse Fur touched his tail-tip to her shoulder and murmured something into her ear. Wind Runner gave a reluctant nod and seemed to relax.

"And we must all be careful when we're out hunting," Thunder went on. "No going after prey that's been near a sick animal. Better to go hungry than to bring illness back to the camp!" As the cats began to murmur among themselves, Thunder nodded, adding, "That's all," and jumped down from the rock.

Gray Wing caught his eye and beckoned him aside. "When did Morning Whisker become ill?" he asked.

"Just after moonhigh," Thunder replied. "You were sleeping soundly, Gray Wing, so no cat woke you. But listen," he added, looking troubled. "Cloud Spots has never seen this sickness before. We have no cure for it. And I'm so worried about Wind Runner—she's still grieving for the first kit she lost. What do you think I should do?"

Just give her time. Gray Wing was opening his jaws to reply when he realized that this was all wrong. Thunder should be working out what *he* wanted to do, not asking another cat for advice. "Uh . . . I'm probably the last cat you should ask," he stammered. "I'm still grieving, too."

Thunder brushed his tail along Gray Wing's flank. "I miss Turtle Tail," he murmured, then padded off to check on Morning Whisker.

Gray Wing watched him go, his pelt prickling like a whole nest of ants was crawling through it. *If I stay in Thunder's camp, and if I'm always here for Thunder to consult, will I be holding him back as a leader?*

Gray Wing sighed and turned away from the group of cats clustered once more around Wind Runner's den. He knew there was nothing he could do to help Morning Whisker, and he wanted to stay out of the grieving family's way. After a moment he began padding up the slope out of the hollow, wondering whether to go hunting.

But at the edge of the camp, Gray Wing halted. In the distance he spotted a cat heading straight toward him, racing across the moor with his belly brushing the grass and his tail streaming out behind him. As Gray Wing watched, he stumbled over a tussock of grass, rolled over, then kept running. Clearly some huge need was driving him.

Only Wind Runner has that speed . . . but it's not Wind Runner.

As the cat drew nearer, Gray Wing could see how dirty and disheveled he was, his fur clumped and stained. And for all his speed, he was limping on one paw, as if he had been in a fight.

Then recognition burst over Gray Wing like a shock of icy water.

Clear Sky!

CHAPTER 12

❧

Gray Wing sprang a few paces across the moor to meet his brother, who collapsed at his paws, panting. There were scratches across his face, his fur spiky where blood had dried. As Clear Sky struggled for breath, Gray Wing reflected on how strange it felt that he, who had suffered so much with his breathing since the forest fire, should be waiting for his strong, fit brother to be able to speak.

What happened to him?

Clear Sky looked up at Gray Wing, his eyes full of misery. "I've made a dreadful mistake!" he gasped. "I should never . . . I can't believe . . ."

"Just get it out!" Some cat snapped out these words from behind Gray Wing, surprising him. He turned to see that Jagged Peak had emerged from the hollow, with Holly just behind him. "What are you trying to tell us?"

A terrible sense of foreboding settled over Gray Wing, like a storm cloud heavy with rain. He could still hear Wind Runner's soft wailing from the other side of the camp.

"What's that?" Clear Sky asked, sitting up and angling his ears in that direction. "What's happened?"

"It's Wind Runner," Gray Wing explained. "Her kit Morning Whisker is very sick."

Clear Sky's shoulders sagged. "Then what I'm about to say will be even more difficult to hear. You have troubles enough without it."

Gray Wing's apprehension grew and he dug his claws into the ground. "Just tell me," he rasped.

"It's Sparrow Fur," Clear Sky began, as if he had to force each word out. Gray Wing felt his heart clench. *What's happened to my kit?* "One Eye attacked her, and when Tom tried to intervene, One Eye killed him." He shook his head helplessly. "I thought One Eye would help my group, teaching us his fighting moves, giving us a different way to see things—but now I realize there's something very wrong with him. He not only attacked a kit; he killed the cat who was supposed to be his friend."

Gray Wing could barely speak. "Sparrow Fur . . ." he choked out. "Is she dead?"

Clear Sky shook his head. "No. But she was very badly wounded."

Gray Wing immediately turned to look at Jagged Peak. He could see pain in his eyes, but it wasn't enough. Gray Wing wanted to hurt Jagged Peak the same way Clear Sky's news was hurting him.

Gray Wing lashed his tail at Holly, who'd drawn protectively close to Jagged Peak. "Leave us to talk about this in private," he snapped.

Holly opened her jaws to retort, then clearly thought better of it. She glanced questioningly at Jagged Peak, who gave a silent nod. After a brief hesitation Holly drew back a few paces and joined Mud Paws and Mouse Ear, who had heard the commotion and were watching from close by.

"I feel dreadful." Clear Sky's voice was breaking as he darted glances between Gray Wing and Jagged Peak. "This is all my fault."

Gray Wing tried in vain to stop his body from trembling, with rage as much as fear for the injured kit. He fixed an icy glance on Jagged Peak. "No," he told Clear Sky. "It's not all your fault. Our brother here is just as much to blame as you are."

Jagged Peak limped forward. "I am sorry, Gray Wing. I should have checked with you. But Sparrow Fur was so insistent," he mewed defensively.

"If Sparrow Fur *insisted* she wanted to leap into a swollen river, would you let her do *that*?" Gray Wing hissed at him. "If she *insisted* on eating one of those sick mice, would you encourage her? You're so sure that you're better now, that you deserve to be a father, but you let a young kit leave our camp, alone and unprotected. Now she's fighting for her life! You don't deserve to have kits of your own!"

At those words, Holly leaped forward and confronted Gray Wing nose to nose. "Don't you dare speak to Jagged Peak like that!" she snarled.

Too furious to respond, Gray Wing whirled away from her to face Jagged Peak. "Do you need your mate to stand up for you?" he asked mockingly. "I hope she's not depending on you for any help when she has her kits."

Hearing himself, Gray Wing felt his fur bristle with shame, but he was too angry to stop.

Then suddenly a paw came lashing out and caught him hard on the side of the jaw. *Jagged Peak is fighting back!* As he was wrestled to the ground, Gray Wing could feel hard muscles beneath the young cat's pelt. Injured leg or not, Jagged Peak had been training recently.

For a moment the brothers tussled together on the ground. Then Gray Wing felt a paw in his side, thrusting him away, and heard Clear Sky's voice. "Stop it, both of you! Do you think fighting helps?"

As Gray Wing staggered to his paws, he saw Holly watching all three of them, cold fury brewing in her eyes. "Do whatever you have to, but resolve this," she hissed. "Stop fighting among yourselves. And don't you dare take your own pain out on Jagged Peak!" With those harsh words, she spun on her paws and stalked away.

Gray Wing could feel the shame radiating off his pelt as he watched her go.

"She's right," Clear Sky mewed. "I didn't come here to watch you two fight. I came for your help. Sparrow Fur is in bad shape, and I'm sure she would rather be home. I think she should come back to your camp. One Eye loathes her, for whatever reason, and until I can—"

"You're not telling me you still welcome One Eye into your camp, after what he did?" Gray Wing asked, astounded.

"No! I told him I never wanted to see his miserable pelt

again. But . . ." Clear Sky's words dried up and he raked the tough moorland grass with his claws. For a few heartbeats he stared at the ground, looking pained, then cleared his throat and continued. "Until I can get my group settled again, I don't think Sparrow Fur should be there."

"You mean her life is in danger?" Gray Wing challenged him. He could feel anger swelling up inside him again. "Because you can't be certain you can protect her from One Eye?"

Clear Sky's only response was a helpless shrug.

For the first time in his life, Gray Wing realized, he felt little respect for his brother. *He's been cowed by a dangerous, violent rogue. Unite or die,* Gray Wing thought, suppressing a sigh. *That's what the spirit-cats told us. But they didn't warn us that there were cats in this forest we should never unite with. And now poor Sparrow Fur has paid the price.*

Gray Wing pushed his brother aside and stormed past him, heading back into the hollow. "I need to go and rescue my kit," he snarled over his shoulder. "I helped raise her from a newborn, and in her mother's memory I won't allow her to be treated like this."

Gray Wing headed straight for Wind Runner's den, where he found Pebble Heart looking after Morning Whisker, still being careful not to touch her sores or breathe her breath. Owl Eyes was looking on, helping to chew up the tansy. Gray Wing beckoned them over with a wave of his tail.

"I have some upsetting news. Sparrow Fur has been hurt," he explained gently to the two kits. "She's in Clear Sky's camp."

Seeing the dismayed glance that the two little toms exchanged, Gray Wing knew he wasn't prepared to tell them that their father was dead. *Maybe we can talk about that in private when we're walking across the moor.* "I need to bring her back home," he went on. "Will you come and help me? I know that seeing you will make her feel better."

Owl Eyes nodded eagerly. "Of course I'll come, Gray Wing. Can we go now?"

Pebble Heart looked anxious, but to Gray Wing's surprise he said nothing.

"Is something wrong?" Gray Wing asked him.

Pebble Heart cast a glance over his shoulder to where Morning Whisker was lying. "Something is telling me to stay here," he confessed at last. "Morning Whisker needs me right now."

"But . . ." Gray Wing could hardly find the words. "Your own sister is injured and alone."

"Yes, injured," Pebble Heart agreed, beginning to sound more confident. "But not alone. Clear Sky's cats will look after her, and you'll bring her back to the hollow. But Morning Whisker . . ." He cast another glance over his shoulder at the sick kit, and lowered his voice. "This is really serious. I feel it in the depths of my belly. It would be wrong for me to leave now."

Gray Wing frowned, but he knew there was no point in arguing. Pebble Heart had made up his mind. "Okay, if you must," he responded. "Come on, Owl Eyes, let's go."

Clear Sky fell into step with Gray Wing as he and Owl

Eyes left the hollow. "I'll run ahead to let my cats know that you're coming," he meowed. "They can start to get Sparrow Fur ready to make the journey back with you."

Gray Wing gave a curt nod, and felt relieved when Clear Sky raced off. He hoped he could forgive his brother someday, but right now, he wasn't sure that he even wanted to look at him again.

"Why was Sparrow Fur so keen to visit Tom?" he asked Owl Eyes as they headed across the moor.

Owl Eyes looked uncomfortable. "We've always been curious about our father," he mewed at last. "It's hard, only knowing about half your kin, especially when your mother is dead and you feel like an orphan."

Gray Wing felt his heart cracking open like a dead tree in the frost. *Doesn't it count for anything that I did my best to be a father to these kits?*

He didn't need to speak. Owl Eyes glanced at him and seemed to realize his mistake at once. "Oh, but of course we love *you*, Gray Wing!" His eyes were wide and guilty as he saw the pain in the older cat's expression. "We will always love you. It's not . . . it's just . . ."

The words fell like stones, giving Gray Wing no reassurance. "I'm not your father, am I?" he asked, unable to keep the bitterness out of his voice.

"We just want to know . . . our other father. The father whose blood we carry. Is that too much to ask?" Owl Eyes pleaded.

Sadly it is. Gray Wing halted, realizing now that he couldn't keep the truth from this sensitive kit. "Owl Eyes, let's stop for a moment. There's something I need to tell you. Your father, Tom, is dead."

Owl Eyes stared up at Gray Wing, his eyes dark with horror. "No! But—but how?" he stammered.

"Sparrow Fur was hurt because One Eye attacked her. Tom saved her, and One Eye killed him." Gray Wing rested his tail across the kit's shoulders. "I'm so sorry."

Owl Eyes's head drooped. "I can't come with you."

Gray Wing felt like he'd been hit in his chest. "I'm sorry I didn't tell you sooner."

The little tom didn't look up, and his voice shook as he went on, "I have to go back to camp. I can't face Clear Sky after he allowed that cat into his group."

When the young cat finally met his gaze, Gray Wing could see the mixture of grief and anger in his expression, and his heart almost broke to think of what these kits had faced in their short lives.

"I understand," he mewed.

Owl Eyes turned away and headed back toward the hollow, his shoulders hunched and his tail trailing along the ground. Gradually he picked up the pace until he was racing along, as if he could outrun the news of his father's death.

With a heavy heart, Gray Wing turned his paw steps toward the forest. As he passed under the outlying trees, hearing the dead leaves crunching under his paws, he braced himself for what he might find in Clear Sky's camp.

Sparrow Fur was so small . . . and One Eye's claws are so cruel. . . .

When Gray Wing finally reached the clearing where Clear Sky and his cats lived, he found Clear Sky waiting for him at the edge of the camp. His brother led him to a sheltered spot underneath an oak tree where Sparrow Fur was sitting up and nibbling on a mouse. There were scratches down her pelt and places where her fur had been torn out. One spot was still covered by a thick poultice of cobwebs. But her eyes were bright and she tried to struggle to her paws when she saw Gray Wing.

"You stay where you are," Petal told her firmly, pressing her back with a gentle paw into a nest of moss and fern. "You need to look after those wounds."

"That's right," Quick Water agreed. She was chewing up some marigold leaves, and began to trickle the juice onto Sparrow Fur's scratches. "Keep still and let this soak in," she told the kit. "Dappled Pelt says it's good to stop infection."

"Thank you for taking such good care of her," Gray Wing told the she-cats as he bent over to touch noses with Sparrow Fur.

Petal ducked her head, looking faintly embarrassed. "I don't know much about healing herbs," she meowed. "But I do know how to survive, after so many seasons living on my own."

The little tom kit, Birch, pattered up with a bundle of dripping moss in his jaws. "There you go," he told Sparrow Fur, dropping it in front of her. "Now you can have a good drink."

Sparrow Fur looked up at him, blinking gratefully. "Thank you."

"You're welcome. Me and Alder like having another young cat in the camp," Birch added to Gray Wing.

Though he was impressed by kindness all these cats were showing Sparrow Fur, Gray Wing still didn't want to spend too long in Clear Sky's camp. He glanced around him, peering among the trees, wondering if he would catch a glimpse of One Eye lurking there. Clear Sky was obviously afraid that the rogue might come sneaking back, or he never would have called Gray Wing here to collect his kit.

"Come on, Sparrow Fur," Clear Sky urged her now. "It's time for you to go home. Owl Eyes and Pebble Heart are waiting for you, and there's good news to share—Jagged Peak is going to be a father."

But Sparrow Fur didn't pay any attention to the news about Jagged Peak. Not moving from her nest, she glanced at Birch. "I'd rather stay here for now," she mewed.

Gray Wing twitched an ear. *What?* But Clear Sky spoke his thoughts before Gray Wing could gather his wits.

"Don't you want to be with your brothers and your own group?" Clear Sky asked, clearly as surprised as Gray Wing.

"It would be nice to see them, but I like it here," Sparrow Fur retorted. "I think I'm just fine where I am."

"In the very place you were attacked!" Gray Wing exclaimed, his pads tingling with alarm.

"She wasn't attacked *here*," Clear Sky pointed out. "And assuming you let her stay, I'll make sure it doesn't happen again."

Gray Wing shot his brother a skeptical glance. *You were the cat who came dashing across the moor to see me, terrified that One Eye would hurt her again!* But as he opened his mouth to protest, he was interrupted by a small mewl of pain as Sparrow Fur shifted on her haunches.

Instantly Birch bent over her, stirring up the moss and fern in her nest to make it more comfortable. Her eyelids were drooping with fatigue and she stretched her jaws wide in a yawn.

She's still weak, Gray Wing realized. As much as he wanted her home, the kit was in no state to be trekking across the moor. "Very well. I can see she needs to stay put for now," he meowed reluctantly. "But I want her home soon."

"Would you like to stay with her?" Clear Sky offered. "You're welcome here."

"Yes, stay," Quick Water urged. "I'll make a nest for you."

For a moment Gray Wing was tempted. But as much as he wanted to watch over the kit, his pelt prickled at the thought of staying in Clear Sky's camp. He didn't belong in the forest. And as much as he doubted his judgment where One Eye was concerned, Gray Wing knew that his brother had only good intentions toward Sparrow Fur, and would make sure she was well cared for. "No, I have to go," he sighed.

"It might be best," Petal murmured gently. "I know your denmates need you. We'll let you know when Sparrow Fur is ready to travel."

Meanwhile Clear Sky had beckoned some of his other cats, including Acorn Fur, who gave a nervous nod to Gray Wing. "Acorn Fur, I'll put you in charge of making sure Sparrow Fur always has enough prey," Clear Sky instructed. "And Quick Water, see if you can find some more marigold leaves to put on her wounds when she wakes up. And all of you, keep your eyes open," he finished. "You know what for."

Gray Wing realized that Sparrow Fur was in good paws. There was no need for him to stay there any longer. He backed up and slipped away through the trees, trying not to feel hurt when no cat called after him.

The sun was setting as Gray Wing reached the edge of the forest. A chill wind had set in, ruffling his fur. The cold seemed to go right through to his bones.

Suddenly Gray Wing drew to a stop. The journey back to the hollow seemed like a huge effort. He felt no joy at the prospect of going home. He would need to see Jagged Peak, and while he knew he should apologize to his brother for his harsh words, he was still finding it hard to forgive him for letting Sparrow Fur go out alone.

Petal was wrong, he thought sadly. *No cat really needs me.*

Instead Gray Wing found his paw steps leading him along the edge of the forest to the place where so many of his friends were buried beneath the spreading branches of the four oaks. By now the ground was covered with dead leaves; there was no sign that there was a grave there at all.

Gray Wing was shivering with cold, but he couldn't bring himself to move away. He gazed up at the sky, not feeling surprised when the spirit-cats failed to appear. But then a voice spoke behind him.

"I thought I told you to stay away from this place." River

Ripple stepped out of the undergrowth and pressed himself against Gray Wing's side. Gray Wing was surprised, but also grateful for the warmth of his thick, silver pelt. "This isn't doing you any good, Gray Wing. Come back to my island with me," he invited.

Gray Wing looked at him, startled. *This independent loner is opening his home to me?*

River Ripple was already padding away, his tail high in the air. "Well? Are you coming, or what?" he asked.

Gray Wing cast a final glance at the grave. "Yes." He stood and followed in River Ripple's paw steps.

CHAPTER 13

❧

Thunder stood at the edge of the hollow, gazing across the moor. The sun was setting, but Gray Wing still hadn't returned from the forest. Three days before, Owl Eyes had come back alone, his head down and a subdued look in his eyes.

"What are you doing here?" Thunder had asked him. "I thought you went with Gray Wing to fetch Sparrow Fur."

"I changed my mind," Owl Eyes replied, as if every word was being dragged out of him.

Thunder wanted to ask him why. It wasn't like Owl Eyes to leave his injured sister to cope without him. But clearly the young cat wasn't going to share, and Thunder knew it wasn't his business. So Thunder had simply seen the kit settled with Jagged Peak and Holly, and hoped that the reason for his behavior would become clear soon.

But Owl Eyes had said nothing more, and day had followed day with no sign of Gray Wing. Thunder had visited Clear Sky, in case Gray Wing had stayed with his brother, but all Clear Sky knew was that he had left the camp after seeing that Sparrow Fur wasn't fit to travel. After that, Tall Shadow had sent out a search party, and Thunder himself had watched for his kin when he was out hunting, but no cat could figure out where Gray Wing had gone. Owl Eyes and Pebble Heart were frantic; it wasn't long since their mother had died, and now the cat who had become their father had disappeared.

This isn't right, Thunder thought. *We have to do something.*

With a last glance over the empty moor, he padded into the hollow and headed for Wind Runner's den. As usual, Morning Whisker lay in her nest, motionless except for the occasional jerk of her legs, as if even in her sleep she was in pain. Her belly was still swollen, and more gashes had opened up in her skin.

Pebble Heart crouched beside her, watching the kit intently. He looked exhausted, and his eyes were despairing. A tail-length away Wind Runner sat with Gorse Fur beside her and her other two kits huddled against her.

"Morning Whisker will be fine," Moth Flight murmured, giving her mother's fur a comforting lick.

"Yes, Cloud Spots and Pebble Heart know what to do," Dust Muzzle added.

Wind Runner only shook her head. Thunder could see that she knew how empty their reassurances were.

She rose to her paws and stretched her neck forward, as if she was about to lick Morning Whiskers's ears.

"No!" Pebble Heart sprang up and blocked Wind Runner from coming any closer. "You know you're not allowed to touch her, not while she has this sickness."

Wind Runner glared at him, then turned away, her head drooping. Gorse Fur pressed himself against her side, but she didn't even look at him.

"Wind Runner, we're doing all—" Thunder began, pain wrenching at his heart to see her grief.

"Leave me alone!" Wind Runner snapped.

Thunder realized there was nothing he could do. He couldn't fathom the pain she was feeling; he couldn't make it better. *This illness is breaking every cat's heart,* he thought as he padded away.

Tall Shadow was still perched on the lookout rock, her gaze scanning the moor. Thunder bounded over and leaped up beside her. "Have you seen any sign of Gray Wing?" he asked.

The black she-cat shook her head. "He should have been back days ago. The last cat who went off by herself died," she added. "Many of us were lost in the battle, we have to face up to the sickness, and now another cat has disappeared." She gave her tail a frustrated lash. "What else can go wrong?"

The setting sun washed the moor in scarlet light, showing nothing but emptiness between the hollow and the dark line of the forest. Thunder let out an anxious sigh.

"I'll keep watch through the night," Tall Shadow assured him.

"But is that enough?" Thunder asked, worry prickling in his pads. "I could go out to look for him again."

Tall Shadow shook her head. "You said it yourself: Our first concern is keeping away from the sickness. We all agreed. In the dark you don't know which animals you'll meet, and you could easily put your paw on dead prey. It's best for you to stay here and be patient."

Though he didn't like it, Thunder knew that she was right. He settled down on top of the rock, willing himself to relax, and finally fell into a doze as the sun vanished and the sky darkened. Drowsing uneasily through the night, he was roused from time to time by the hooting of owls or the bark of a fox. Knowing Gray Wing was far from home made it impossible for him to fully drift off, and all the while he was aware of Tall Shadow watching and waiting beside him, her eyes fixed on the horizon.

The damp chill of dawn brought Thunder back to full wakefulness. Above his head the stars were growing pale, and a milky light was beginning to show on the horizon where the sun would rise.

Thunder rose and stretched his cramped limbs, arching his back and shivering at the dew that misted his pelt. At the foot of the rock he spotted a mouse scuffling among the grass, and bunched his muscles, ready to pounce.

Before he could move, Tall Shadow nudged him. "There's a cat coming!"

Thunder looked up to see a dark shape outlined on the horizon, heading for the camp. "Gray Wing!" he exclaimed thankfully. He leaped down from the rock and raced out across the moor to meet him.

But as he drew nearer to the cat he realized that it wasn't Gray Wing. *Clear Sky! What does my father want now?*

"Have you seen any sign of Gray Wing?" he demanded as soon as Clear Sky was in earshot.

Clear Sky skidded to a halt beside him. "Not since he left my camp," he replied, looking confused. "I already told you that. Hasn't he come home yet?"

Thunder shook his head. "We haven't seen him."

Clear Sky twitched the tip of his tail worriedly. "Well, he certainly—"

"Thunder! Clear Sky!" The distant call that interrupted him came from Tall Shadow, still on her rock. She beckoned them with her tail and leaped down to join them as they padded up.

Clear Sky wrinkled his nose as he entered the camp, and Thunder realized how heavily the taint of sickness hung in the air.

"Morning Whisker is no better, then?" Clear Sky asked.

Thunder shook his head. "I think she's dying," he choked out, his heart breaking as he spoke the words aloud for the first time.

He and Clear Sky followed Tall Shadow as she retreated to the edge of the camp. "Why did you come to see us?" she asked.

Clear Sky looked uncomfortable, his whiskers quivering as he replied. "I'm very worried about this illness. All the trouble with One Eye distracted me, but now that it's quieted down I can see that the biggest danger facing us is exactly that: the sickness that's killing Morning Whisker. I'm afraid other cats were exposed, and I'm keeping my eye out for any signs that any other cat is getting sick. The trouble is," he admitted, "even if one of our cats starts to show symptoms, I have no idea what to do for them." Glancing from Thunder to Tall Shadow and back again, he added, "I want to do all I can to help. After all, we're in this together."

Thunder was impressed. *Only a few moons ago Clear Sky was acting like he owned the forest, attacking cats who dared to set paw over his borders. Now he wants to keep the peace.* "Times *have* changed," he murmured.

Clear Sky's whiskers twitched with irritation. "I haven't changed *that* much!" he protested. "I was always the same cat."

Tall Shadow gave him a long, hard look. "I never doubted it for a moment," she meowed.

Clear Sky blinked, and a rough purr rose from his throat. Thunder could see how much Tall Shadow's words meant to him.

"So, how are we going to stop this sickness?" Clear Sky asked briskly, stepping back.

"Only those tending to them are going close to our sick cats," Tall Shadow explained. "And we're being careful about hunting, so that we don't bring sick prey back into the camp."

"That may not be enough," Clear Sky commented. "I've been thinking . . . that forest fire was probably a good thing. The flames should have cleansed the land, so the area that was burned might be a good place to make a camp if we need to move."

Thunder didn't like the sound of that. "I wouldn't want to move cats as sick as Morning Whisker."

Clear Sky gave him a puzzled look. "Well, we'd leave the sick cats behind," he mewed. "Otherwise we'd bring the sickness with us."

Thunder let out a sigh. *My father still has that ruthless streak!*

He could see that Tall Shadow wasn't keen on Clear Sky's

idea, either. "Why don't we all meet by the four trees and discuss it?" she suggested.

Clear Sky hesitated for a moment, then nodded. "I'll tell my cats. Is sunset okay?"

Once Tall Shadow had assented, Clear Sky bounded off. Thunder watched him go, unable to feel hopeful about the meeting.

Where is Gray Wing?

The rest of the day seemed to stretch out like an entire season. Thunder left the camp, partly to hunt, but mostly to keep his eyes open for his missing kin. Though he hunted well, chasing down a rabbit, he found no trace of Gray Wing.

I wish the day was over, he thought as he returned to the camp with his prey. *Maybe some cat at the meeting will know where Gray Wing is.*

But as Thunder padded down into the hollow, he regretted wishing the moments away. A shriek of grief sounded from Wind Runner's den. Dropping his rabbit, Thunder bounded over there to find Morning Whisker stretched out on the ground. The kit's eyes were rolled back in her head. There were scuff marks on the ground beside her, as though she had raked the earth in some kind of fit. Her tongue lolled out of her mouth, swollen and cracked. As Thunder watched, pity and horror surging through his body, the tiny kit's spine contorted in a final shudder of pain. Then she lay still.

Wind Runner sprang toward her, but Pebble Heart was faster, darting to block her.

"Get out of my way!" Wind Runner snarled.

"I can't let you touch her," Pebble Heart responded. "I'm sorry. But even now, you could catch the sickness."

"She's my kit!" Wind Runner howled, her voice cracking with grief. "I can't lose another one!"

Furiously she lashed out at Pebble Heart, her claws extended. Thunder leaped forward to get between them, taking the blow on his own shoulder.

"Don't," he meowed to Wind Runner. "Pebble Heart is only trying to help."

Wind Runner glared at him for a heartbeat, and Thunder braced himself for an attack. But instead the brown she-cat collapsed to the ground, letting out a thin, heartbroken wail. Gorse Fur crouched beside her, licking her ears, and the rest of the cats gathered around in silent concern.

Tall Shadow was the last to approach; Wind Runner looked up and faced her with hostility in her eyes. "Don't tell me!" she spat. "We'll need to have a burial. You're very good at organizing those, aren't you?"

Thunder rested his tail on Wind Runner's shoulder. "Tall Shadow only wants to help," he told her, trying not to sound harsh. He could see that Wind Runner was out of her mind with grief.

Tall Shadow dipped her head toward Wind Runner, her eyes patient and sorrowful. "What would you like us to do?" she asked.

Wind Runner gazed for a moment at Gorse Fur, then at her dead kit. "I'd like us to send Morning Whisker to live with the spirit-cats," she whispered. "That's what she deserves."

"Yes, I'd like that too," Gorse Fur agreed.

"Then that's what we'll do," Tall Shadow mewed. Turning to the other cats, she continued, "Go and fetch leaves—as many as you can find. Not dried up and crackly, but fresh ones that we can use to wrap Morning Whisker's body."

Grateful for something to do, Thunder bounded out of the hollow with his denmates, heading for the forest. As he reached the outskirts he found plenty of leaves, and collected up a bundle to carry back to camp. The others returned too, piling their leaves in a heap beside the kit's body.

"Pebble Heart," Tall Shadow meowed, "you and Cloud Spots are the only cats who have touched Morning Whisker directly. Will you wrap her in the leaves, please?"

"Of course, Tall Shadow." Pebble Heart dipped his head respectfully.

Leaf by leaf, under the intent gaze of their denmates, Pebble Heart and Cloud Spots wrapped the kit in layer after layer of leaves until her whole body was covered. Then between them, Mouse Ear and Jagged Peak nudged her across the moor, all the weary way to the four trees, with the rest of the group surrounding them in silent escort.

As the sun slid down the sky, casting long shadows over their path, Thunder realized with a start that Morning Whisker would never see another morning in her short life. It wasn't fair—for one so young to be lost, or for Wind Runner to lose another of her kits. His heart started to pound and he didn't know how to go on bearing his sorrow.

At last the cats arrived beside the grave where the cats who had died in the battle were buried.

"Where would you like to put her?" Tall Shadow asked Wind Runner. "We shouldn't disturb the main grave."

Wind Runner's gaze fell on a gorse bush at the foot of the slope that led down into the clearing. "Over there," she meowed. "Morning Whisker always liked hiding in bushes."

She began scraping at the ground underneath the bush. Thunder and the other cats joined in to help her and soon they had dug a hole big enough to bury the kit. Gorse Fur nudged the tiny, leaf-wrapped body into the grave, and helped Wind Runner to paw the soil back over it, patting it down gently. Wind Runner tore a sprig of gorse off the bush and laid it on the grave, her eyes wide with sorrow.

"Good-bye, my little one," she whispered.

Thunder's heart ached as he glanced up at the sky, where clouds had covered the sun. He knew it was still too early for the spirit-cats to appear, but he sent a message up to them.

"Set Wind Runner's kit free of her pain," he murmured. "And let her play among the stars."

When he looked down again, Tall Shadow gave him an approving nod. "Well spoken," she mewed. Glancing around at the other cats, she added, "We may as well stay here. It's not long to sunset, when we have to meet Clear Sky and his cats."

Wind Runner turned away from her kit's grave. "I'm not staying," she told the others with a challenging look. "I can't stand all of this anymore. I should have remained a rogue, alone on the moors. If I'd had my kits alone, maybe Morning

Whisker would still be alive now. Maybe none of this would have happened. I've helped . . ." Her voice shook and she made a massive effort to steady it. "I've helped you hunt and in battle, and all I've had in return is grief and heartbreak."

Thunder's mouth turned dry and it was hard for him to speak. "But where will you go?"

Wind Runner gazed farther out toward the moors. "Back where I came from. I'll take my kits and disappear among the long grasses, and none of you will ever have to care about me again."

"But we want to care about you!" Holly protested. "I was a rogue cat too, and I remember how hard it was, even if you don't. Wind Runner, don't cut yourself off, not when you're having such a tough time."

"She won't be alone," Gorse Fur meowed, stepping forward. "I'll go with her."

They arrived together, Thunder thought. *And now they're leaving together.* "Are you sure?" he asked.

But Wind Runner was already turning away, running through the trees with Moth Flight and Dust Muzzle following her.

Gorse Fur cast a regretful glance at the other cats. "Don't worry," he mewed. "I'll look after them." Breaking into a run, he followed his mate and their kits out of sight.

Will we ever see Wind Runner and Gorse Fur again? Thunder wondered.

CHAPTER 14

Scarlet light slanted through a gap in the clouds as the sun went down. A chilly breeze sprang up, and a few dead leaves whirled down over the waiting cats.

Leaf-bare is almost here, Thunder thought.

Then he noticed movement among the bushes that lined the sides of the hollow, and a heartbeat later Clear Sky padded into the open, the rest of his cats trailing behind him.

"Greetings," he meowed; dipping his head to Tall Shadow and Thunder.

"Greetings," Tall Shadow responded. "Let's all gather around the rock, and—"

She broke off at the sound of more rustling from the bushes. A clump of ferns parted and River Ripple emerged.

"River Ripple!" Thunder exclaimed, pleased to see the silver-gray tom. "How did you know there was going to be a meeting?"

River Ripple paused to give his silky chest fur a couple of licks. "I know everything," he purred. "When are you going to learn that? And I brought a friend with me."

To Thunder's amazement, Gray Wing slipped out of the

ferns behind River Ripple. His whole body was tight with tension, and he didn't meet any cat's gaze.

Thunder felt his whole body sag with relief. *Gray Wing is okay!* He bounded over to the gray tom. "Gray Wing, where have you been?" he demanded, relief and anger mingled in his voice. "How could you go off like that and leave us all to worry about you?"

Gray Wing still didn't look at him. "Sparrow Fur didn't want to come home with me," he explained, "and I couldn't face returning to the hollow alone. I—I just needed to be on my own."

"Yes," River Ripple meowed. "I found him shivering beside the grave. I took him back to my river island with me."

"And that's where I'm staying for now," Gray Wing added with a grateful glance at the silver tom. "I need some time to think."

"To think about what?" Thunder asked. "Where has all this come from? Gray Wing, we need you!"

Gray Wing met his gaze for the first time. "Do you? Or am I just getting in the way? I'm not feeling angry, or anything like that," he went on, overriding Thunder's attempt to protest. "But I do feel like I'm getting in the way. You're a great leader, and so is Tall Shadow. Aren't three cats making decisions too many?"

"No," Thunder responded, hardly able to believe that Gray Wing was thinking this way. "We were all working together! I thought it was going well."

Gray Wing shook his head. "You've grown into your huge

paws, Thunder, and I don't want to keep you from becoming the cat you should be. So I need to think about the next step for me—and I need space to do that."

At last Thunder was shocked into silence. He saw how relieved Gray Wing looked to not have to face any more objections. But before either cat could say more, Tall Shadow stepped forward.

"I see your point, Gray Wing," she rasped. "But did you have to disappear like that? We were all really worried about you—especially Owl Eyes and Pebble Heart."

Gray Wing dipped his head. "I'm sorry," he murmured. "It was shortsighted of me. I'll never do that again."

While they talked the breeze had strengthened, driving the last of the clouds away, and moonlight flooded the clearing, picking out every remaining leaf on the four oak trees.

Clear Sky bounded across to the Great Rock and leaped to the top. "Gather around, all of you!" he called. "Let's begin the meeting."

As the cats found places to sit near the foot of the rock, Thunder noticed another cat slip quietly out of the undergrowth and settle down a few tail-lengths from the others in the shadow of a clump of ferns. With a gasp of amazement he recognized the golden tabby she-cat who had spoken to him after the second meeting with the spirit-cats. Now she turned her intense green eyes toward him and for a moment their gazes locked. Then she glanced away again, looking up at the rock as she waited for Clear Sky to speak.

A shiver ran through Thunder from ears to tail-tip. *Who is she? And what is she doing here?* The thought was quickly followed by another. *If one strange cat can join us, others might do the same.* Suddenly feeling vulnerable and exposed, he took a careful look around the clearing, breathing a sigh of relief when he saw no trace of One Eye.

Tall Shadow leaped up onto the rock and sat beside Clear Sky. "We have had sickness in our camp," she began. "Wind Runner's kit Morning Whisker died earlier today. Her belly was swollen and there were cracks in her skin oozing blood. Has any cat seen this illness anywhere else?"

"We found a mouse that had died the same way," Thunder added.

"And there was that bird," Clear Sky meowed. "The one you argued over with One Eye."

"There was a dead fox near the Thunderpath." Snake sprang to his paws to make his contribution. "It had a swollen belly and froth all over its jaws."

Quick Water nodded. "I saw it too. And a squirrel with half its fur gone, and sores all over its body."

"And I found a dead vole by the river," River Ripple contributed.

"Cloud Spots, you know herbs," Shattered Ice began. "So do you, Dappled Pelt. Have you seen anything like this before?"

"Yes, are there herbs that could help?" Jagged Peak asked.

Cloud Spots rose reluctantly; Thunder saw that he looked bewildered, and knew before he spoke that he wouldn't have any useful answers.

"I advised Pebble Heart to treat Morning Whisker with

tansy," he meowed. "It might have slowed down the progress of her illness, but it didn't cure her. I'm sorry."

"River Ripple, what about you?" Tall Shadow looked down at the silver tom from her place on top of the rock. "Have you come across this before?"

River Ripple dipped his head to her. "I haven't seen this exact sickness before, but I have seen severe illness. There was one greenleaf when many of the rogue cats died. It seemed like it had something to do with the heat."

It's been hot this past greenleaf, too, Thunder thought. *Maybe the same thing is happening again.* "How did you get rid of the illness last time?" he asked.

"Most of the cats split up," River Ripple replied. "I didn't see some of the rogues for a long time. Then after greenleaf we started to mix again, and the sickness seemed to have worked its way out."

"One Eye sounded as if he knew something about it," Clear Sky put in. "He mocked me but wouldn't give me specifics on what he knew, just that some of the cats in my group were as good as dead."

"And now Morning Whisker has died, but no other cats are sick," Acorn Fur added.

"And One Eye isn't here to tell us any more," Clear Sky said, looking down at his paws, embarrassed.

"What happened with that cat isn't your fault," Thunder reassured him.

"I know, but if One Eye were still here, he might be able to advise us," Clear Sky mewed desperately. "He—"

"Yes, but at what cost?" Lightning Tail interrupted angrily. "He's killed one cat and nearly killed another. How many more would have to die, just so that we could listen to his words of wisdom—if he has any wisdom to offer?"

A murmur of agreement rose up from all the cats. *Of course Lightning Tail is right,* Thunder thought. *We'd all be mouse-brained to have any more to do with One Eye.* "Talking about One Eye is distracting us from the real issue," he pointed out.

"But we need to keep our eyes open for him," Clear Sky reminded them in a low voice. "He's dangerous, and he has sworn revenge."

"Everything in its time." Tall Shadow spoke with her usual cool wisdom. "For now we need to figure out how to protect ourselves from the illness."

"We need to separate." Thunder gave a start of surprise as Gray Wing spoke for the first time. "Make sure that our groups don't mix. Set up boundaries and respect them."

Disbelief flashed through Thunder at his kin's words. "But we've spent so long defending unnecessary boundaries," he protested. "And now you of all cats want to set them up again?"

"We're vulnerable now," Gray Wing pointed out. "It's part of what I told you before—we have some good leaders, but too many for only two groups. If we split up, natural leaders can take their rightful places, and all cats will be protected."

"I liked the swampy land beyond the Thunderpath." A quiet voice spoke up, and it took a moment for Thunder to realize it came from Tall Shadow. More briskly she continued, "I think it would make the perfect home. Far enough away from other cats to safeguard whoever goes with me."

Thunder blinked at her in disbelief. "You—you want to leave the hollow and go somewhere else? What are we supposed to do without you? And how many other cats have been hatching big plans behind my back?" he asked, feeling the fur on his shoulders beginning to rise in anger.

Clear Sky looked down at him. "Thunder, this isn't about cats deceiving you or betraying you. Every cat is trying to do the right thing. We just want to save lives."

Huh! Thunder thought. *That's a bit much, coming from you!* But he had the sense to stay silent, and made his bristling fur lie flat again.

"Can we come to a decision?" Holly asked, an edge of irritation in her tone. "For the record, I'm expecting kits, and I'd prefer not to be moving about, trying to set up a new group."

Her question sparked off a discussion, with every cat trying to have their say. There was no clear agreement. Thunder stayed silent, letting the arguments swirl around him, as impatient as Holly to have this settled so they could leave.

"Okay, this is what we'll do," Tall Shadow meowed at last. "I'll stay on the moor with Thunder—for the time being, anyway. Clear Sky will take his group back to his camp, and Gray Wing will go with River Ripple. Agreed?"

"But that's hardly any different from how we're living now," Gray Wing pointed out.

"Because this isn't the time to be making big changes," Tall Shadow retorted. Again her gaze raked the group. "Are we all agreed?"

Thunder didn't object, though he would have preferred for Gray Wing to come home with him. "What about Sparrow Fur?" he asked Clear Sky. "Will she return to the hollow when she's healed?"

"I don't know," Clear Sky replied. "She'll make the decision when the time comes."

Gray Wing winced at these words, but didn't argue. The meeting was clearly over. As the cats began to split up to return to their own camps, Thunder turned away, flicking the tip of his tail in frustration. The spirit-cats hadn't visited, they were no better off in terms of understanding the illness, and he was unsettled by the thought of the cats dividing into more groups. *It hasn't happened yet, but it's clear that's what Gray Wing and Tall Shadow want,* he thought bitterly. *Unite or die—that was the message, wasn't it?* he said to himself. *So much for unity!*

Then he noticed that the strange she-cat had risen to her paws and was weaving among the others until she reached Thunder's side and brushed her pelt against his. Thunder's whole body shivered at her touch, though he tried not to show it.

"My name is Star Flower," she purred, her voice rich and sweet as the scent of honey. "I was named after the white flowers that glow at night with their five petals. If you look closely at my eyes, you'll see the five petal shapes."

She stood in front of Thunder, nose to nose with him, as if she was daring him to gaze at her.

With a huge effort of will, Thunder turned away. A fox-length away he spotted Lightning Tail. The black tom was watching him intently. Thunder felt even more awkward.

"I told you before, I've heard a lot about you," Star Flower continued.

Thunder felt surprised and a bit uneasy. *Which cats have been talking to her about me?*

The golden tabby's glance dropped to his paws and she reached out to give one of them a quick pat. "They're not as big as some cats said," she told him, "but I could train you to fight with them."

With a last, teasing glance, she padded away.

Thoroughly flustered by the encounter, Thunder turned and, seeing most of his own group close by, caught their attention with a wave of his tail. "In the future," he began, "if we meet any strange cats, can we let each other know? It doesn't feel right, letting them slip into our meetings without knowing who they are."

"Oh, Thunder," Tall Shadow meowed. "Stop being so grumpy and hostile."

Thunder's eyes widened, though he didn't respond. *Is that Tall Shadow talking—the cat who wouldn't let any strangers join our group, or even visit for more than a few heartbeats?*

By now full darkness had fallen, and the departing cats melted into the night. Thunder realized that Tall Shadow was padding along by his side. "Did you really like what you saw on the other side of the Thunderpath?" he asked.

Tall Shadow shrugged. "I told you when we were there. I just find it . . . so beautiful."

"But to live there?" Thunder protested. "It's marshland!"

"Some of it, yes," Tall Shadow agreed. "But there are flowers growing there, and trees. I loved the misty air. It felt special, somehow. As if it was a secret place, just inviting me to explore it." She shook her head, looking slightly confused. "I can't explain it. I felt at home."

"But what would I tell the others if you went?" Thunder asked. Though he'd often disagreed with Tall Shadow, there was an ache in his heart at the thought of losing her calm and watchful presence. *I've lost so many who were dear to me . . . and now Tall Shadow too?*

Tall Shadow gave her pelt a shake. "Oh, stop worrying!" she exclaimed. "I'm here, aren't I? I'm going back to the hollow with you."

Thunder didn't feel at all reassured by her words. Things were changing, and not in a good way.

To take his mind off his worries, he thought back to his meeting with the beautiful she-cat, Star Flower. *I can't imagine what she has to teach me,* he thought, *but I'd like to find out.*

CHAPTER 15

Clear Sky headed back to his camp with his cats around him, moving easily among the trees in the starlight. Petal, who had stayed behind to look after the kits, rushed to meet him as soon as he set paw in the clearing.

"Come quick!" she mewed urgently. "It's Alder!"

Fear gripped Clear Sky's heart, remembering the terrible symptoms of the sickness that he had seen on the dead bird. *Are my worst fears starting to come true?* He rushed over to the nest Petal shared with the kits, expecting to see Alder with a bloated belly and sores all over her skin.

But when he reached the nest, all he saw was Alder lying comfortably among the moss. Birch sat beside her, stroking her tail with one paw.

"Hi, Alder, how do you feel?" Clear Sky asked.

Alder blinked up at him sleepily, seeming confused, as if she wasn't sure where she was.

"She's just tired," Clear Sky meowed. "Honestly, Petal, did you have to give me a scare like that?"

The yellow tabby glared at him. "She's *not* just tired!" She waved a paw in front of Alder's face; the gray-and-white kit didn't react. "See how she's not focusing on me?" Petal demanded. "Something's wrong."

"Didn't I tell you?" A sneering voice spoke behind Clear Sky.

Whirling around, Clear Sky saw One Eye standing a couple of fox-lengths away from him, a mocking gleam in his eyes. Nettle, who had been left with Petal to guard the camp, stood behind him, his gaze filled with a mixture of guilt and horror.

Petal shifted suddenly to stand in front of the kits. "Stay in your nest," she warned them.

Clear Sky shot her a glance; the conviction that something terrible was happening swelled up inside him. "What's going on?" he demanded.

Petal couldn't meet his gaze. Her face showed the same guilt as Nettle's, and her ears were flattened to her head.

"What do you know that I don't?" Clear Sky insisted, but Petal still wouldn't answer.

Desperation pulsed through Clear Sky until he felt that every hair on his pelt must be quivering, but he faced up to One Eye boldly, determined not to let the rogue intimidate him.

He humiliated me in front of my own cats, and Thunder and Gray Wing. He killed Tom and injured Sparrow Fur. . . . Sudden realization flooded over Clear Sky, and he glanced wildly around the clearing. *Sparrow Fur! Where is she?*

"What have you done with Sparrow Fur?" he asked One Eye. He was determined not to allow her to be hurt again, not when he had insisted that she should stay in the forest to recover.

One Eye let out a snort of cruel laughter. "You don't need to worry about that stupid little kit," he sneered.

As he spoke a meow of distress sounded from behind Clear Sky. He whirled around to see twigs and branches wedged in a solid barrier, blocking the opening in a hollow tree. He could just make out Sparrow Fur peering out of a small gap. She let out another plaintive mew.

"Clear Sky, help me!" she begged.

Clear Sky turned back to One Eye. Taking a pace forward he let his shoulder fur bristle up and his tail bush out. "Let that kit out," he snarled menacingly. "She still hasn't recovered properly from what *you* did to her. She needs food and rest, not torturing."

One Eye looked not at all threatened by Clear Sky's challenging stance. "You can't tell me what to do," he snapped. "This is my territory now." As Clear Sky stood frozen, stunned by the outrageous claim, One Eye stepped forward in his turn until he confronted Clear Sky nose to nose. "While you were off with your stupid friends sharing tales at the four trees," he went on, "I took *real* action. These cats need protecting from the sickness, and I'm the cat to do it."

Clear Sky glanced around at the cats who had accompanied him to the meeting. They were bunched together, sharing looks of bewilderment and fear, as if they couldn't believe this was happening. *Neither can I,* Clear Sky thought grimly. *But if One Eye thinks he can just stroll in here and take over my territory, he's got another think coming.*

Clear Sky didn't want to tackle One Eye on his own. He

had seen how fiercely the rogue could fight. But with his cats behind him, surely they could drive One Eye out without any trouble.

So why does he look so confident?

Letting his gaze travel over his cats again, Clear Sky wondered how much support he could expect. Petal would stay where she was to protect the kits—and it was right that she should. Quick Water had shown her mistrust of him ever since the battle, even though she was one of the cats who had accompanied him on the journey from the mountains. But he felt he could trust Acorn Fur; she had been hardworking and enthusiastic ever since she left the moor to come and live in his camp. With a hollow feeling inside him, Clear Sky realized that he wasn't sure about the others. Leaf and Thorn, Nettle and Snake had only recently joined his group. Snake in particular was giving him a hostile glare, as if he would join One Eye for a couple of mousetails.

A pang of regret for the friends he had lost in the great battle shook Clear Sky. Now he realized how precarious his position was.

Clear Sky tried not to let One Eye see his doubts. "Get out of here," he meowed firmly. "Or we'll rip your pelt off."

One Eye didn't move. "Don't you remember what I said?" he sneered. "I may only have one eye, but I see everything. I watched these cats carefully when I joined your so-called group, and there's something I noticed. Most of them don't like you very much, Clear Sky."

Mews of protest sounded from Petal and Acorn Fur, but

before either of them could say more One Eye rounded on them furiously. "Shut up!" Turning back to Clear Sky, he added, "And there's something else I noticed. You don't actually know how to keep your cats in line. Oh, yes, you think you're being very clever, guarding territories and hiding in the forest like a coward, but what does that actually achieve?"

"I don't want to keep my cats in line," Clear Sky argued. "I just want to help them survive."

One Eye rolled his single eye. "What a fool!" he exclaimed. "What a deluded fool!"

Without shifting his gaze from Clear Sky, One Eye flicked his tail to beckon Petal forward. She stepped toward him, and for the first time Clear Sky noticed that she was limping. As she approached One Eye lunged toward her, and Petal instinctively jerked away. She fell on her back, paws flailing, and Clear Sky noticed a wound in the pad of her forepaw. It was a raw circle, as if the flesh had been drawn open by a claw.

It looks just like an eye. . . .

"She and Nettle carry my mark now," One Eye stated proudly. "And the rest of them will too, before the night is out."

"But what about the sickness?" Clear Sky asked, hardly able to believe the depths to which this cat's lust for power would lead them. "There's illness in the forest, and you want to open up a wound in every cat? Are you flea-brained?"

"Not flea-brained," One Eye responded, baring his teeth. "Just strict. I like my cats to toe my line." His voice became a low, threatening snarl. "It's time for you to leave—now."

Clear Sky stood his ground. Glancing back at his cats, he made a last, desperate attempt to rally them. "Come on! I need your help. He can't kill all of us!"

He noticed that Acorn Fur and Thorn slid out their claws, but the rest of them didn't move. Petal, who had struggled back onto her paws, shook her head and mewed in a hoarse voice, "No, Clear Sky. You don't understand."

As Clear Sky stared at her in confusion, One Eye raised his head. "Come out now!" he yowled.

At his words the undergrowth rustled and from all around the clearing cats emerged into the open: rogue cats who Clear Sky had never set eyes on before. He took in their scrawny bodies, their sharp teeth and claws, and their cold, malignant eyes. Their fur was clumped and spiky; they had rolled in mud and plant juices to disguise their scent from him and his cats, he realized, so that there would be nothing to warn them as they returned from the meeting. Every hair on Clear Sky's pelt shivered in horror as the strangers stepped forward, surrounding him and his cats.

"Really, Clear Sky," One Eye meowed in mockery. "You didn't think I would move in without a few friends to back me up? Not even you would be that stupid!"

Clear Sky could see that he and his followers were badly outnumbered. If they tried to fight the rogues under One Eye's leadership they would be torn to pieces. His heart began to race as fear throbbed through him, though he continued to face One Eye with a look of defiance.

"I told you to leave, Clear Sky," One Eye meowed. "I'm not

going to kill you. I know that you'll suffer far more knowing that I took the leadership out of your paws because you couldn't hold on to it. So leave, before I have to put my claw marks on you."

Clear Sky cast one final glance at the group of cats. *My cats!* They were bunched together uneasily, thoroughly cowed by the appearance of the strange rogues. Fervently he tried to send them the silent message that he wouldn't abandon them. *Somehow, I'll find a way to come back for you.*

But Snake turned his head away, and Clear Sky felt something die inside him. *Do they really want my help?* he asked himself.

"As for the rest of you," One Eye continued, "you'll stay here and take my mark. You won't be harmed, provided you behave yourselves."

Defeated, Clear Sky turned to go. But as he took the first paw steps, his gaze lighted on the hollow tree, and Sparrow Fur peering out helplessly from between the branches that imprisoned her.

I won't leave her to be tortured by One Eye, Clear Sky resolved.

Letting his head droop and his tail trail along the ground, Clear Sky padded across the clearing in the direction of the hollow tree. The two strange cats nearest to it fell back to let him pass between them.

As soon as he was out of the circle of One Eye's rogues, Clear Sky sprang forward. Darting up to the hollow tree, he tore at the branches with paws given strength from desperation. A gap opened up and Sparrow Fur wriggled through it.

"Run!" Clear Sky yowled.

He thrust the kit in front of him as One Eye let out a screech of rage and the whole gang of rogues turned to pursue him. But Clear Sky knew the forest far better than any newcomer. He showed Sparrow Fur the way between trees, under bushes, through bramble thickets, splashing for several fox-lengths up a narrow stream to break their scent. He was thankful that the young cat's wounds had almost healed, and her strength held out, though her chest heaved with the effort of running and her breath rasped.

At last the furious shrieks and caterwauls died away behind them. Clear Sky burst out of the forest with Sparrow Fur hard on his paws. As she collapsed panting, he turned and looked back at the line of trees, where the last few leaves clung to stark, bare branches.

My home . . . what was my home.

Throwing back his head, Clear Sky sent up a wordless yowling, a desperate cry to any of his cats who could hear him. The sound died away into silence, and there was no response.

Clear Sky glanced down at Sparrow Fur, who met his gaze with wide, troubled eyes.

"What are we going to do, Clear Sky?" she asked.

Clear Sky took a breath to answer, but said nothing. He had nothing to say. He had lost his home and his group of cats. One Eye had defeated him.

CHAPTER 16

Gray Wing crouched under a bush at the edge of River Ripple's island and watched River Ripple and Night, the black she-cat. As the sun glinted on the water the two cats dipped in their paws and scooped fish out onto the bank. The fish writhed there, the rainbow-colored scales reflecting the sunlight.

In the days that Gray Wing had spent with River Ripple, he could not get used to the idea of cats who didn't mind getting their paws wet. He was intrigued by the thought of hunting like that: no scenting the air, no stalking or pouncing, just patience and a swift paw. Gray Wing remembered how Dappled Pelt had sometimes caught fish that way on the journey out of the mountains.

So much has happened since then.

Gray Wing's belly squirmed with guilt at the thought that he was completely reliant on River Ripple and his cats to provide him with food. None of them had complained, seeming to sense that he needed time to think. They had given him a soft nest and all the fish he could eat.

But Gray Wing knew that he couldn't go on like this. *Much more of it, and I'll lose all my hunting skills. I was once a leader of cats, and now I'm being cared for like a kit!*

He was pleased, however, that his breathing was much easier, and he hoped that Thunder was taking his rightful place as a leader.

Night hurled another fish out onto the bank and let out a *mrrow* of exultant laughter. "See that? It's the biggest yet!"

"Nonsense!" River Ripple gave her a friendly nudge. "I've caught one at least a mouse-length bigger than that."

Gray Wing rose to his paws and padded over to them. "I'd like to contribute some prey," he meowed. "I think I'll leave for a while and go hunting on the moor."

"Fine," River Ripple responded. "I'll come with you."

He took the lead as the two cats made their way over the stepping-stones to the riverbank, but once there Gray Wing forged ahead through the long grasses, his ears pricked for the sound of prey. Before he had gone for many paw steps, he came upon Dew, another rogue who had joined River Ripple. Her gaze was fixed on a vole that was crouching under a nearby clump of fern.

Gray Wing halted, not wanting to disturb Dew's hunt. Then as he looked more closely at the vole he saw that its belly was bloated, and that flecks of foam were spotted around its jaws.

"Don't touch that," he mewed. "It's sick."

Dew nodded. "It's like the other one we found. Don't worry. I'm not going near it."

River Ripple peered over Gray Wing's shoulder, then shook his head in frustration. "We're seeing more and more of this. I don't know what we can do to stop it."

Dew let out a disgusted hiss. "It's all well and good for us to separate, but now there's no way of knowing if the others are having the same problem, or how far the illness has spread."

"It has spread at least as far as the hollow," Gray Wing told her somberly.

Dew shrugged, drawing back from the vole. "I'm going back to the island."

River Ripple dipped his head to her. "Night and I caught plenty of fish. Help yourself."

"Thanks." Dew whipped around and vanished into the long grass.

Gray Wing and River Ripple continued, keeping well away from the sick vole.

"If you like, I'll teach you some of my hunting techniques," Gray Wing suggested. "On the moor they seem to think I'm pretty good at working out strategies and sniffing out prey."

River Ripple murmured agreement, though Gray Wing noticed his whiskers twitching as if he was amused.

"Okay," Gray Wing began, "there are obviously voles around here. So what we have to do is track some down. They live in tunnels, right?"

River Ripple nodded.

So hunting them must be much the same as hunting rabbits, Gray Wing decided. *Though even Wind Runner couldn't follow a vole down its hole!*

"This way," he meowed, veering back toward the bank, but farther downstream than the stepping-stones and River

Ripple's island. After a few paw steps he crouched down and pressed his ear to the ground.

"What in the world are you doing?" River Ripple asked, sounding astonished.

"Listening for voles," Gray Wing explained, pleased there was something he knew that the silver tom didn't. "But I don't hear anything."

"Let's try farther on." River Ripple seemed more interested now, and angled his ears toward a spot on the bank with a luxuriant growth of plants. "That's the stuff voles like to eat."

The second time Gray Wing listened he heard faint scratching noises under the ground. "There's at least one vole under there."

He scouted around, opening his jaws to taste the air, until he picked up the scent of vole and tracked it to a small hole in the ground among the roots of a hawthorn bush. "Stay there," he instructed River Ripple.

Listening carefully for the scratching sounds, Gray Wing managed to follow the tunnel all the way to the other end, a hole in the side of the bank. He scrambled down carefully until he stood on the strip of mud and pebbles that separated the side of the bank from the water.

"Okay," he called to River Ripple. "Scratch at that hole and yowl into it, as loud as you can."

From his position he couldn't see River Ripple, but he heard a fearsome screeching coming from the other end of the tunnel. *That should get them moving,* he thought, satisfied.

A moment later there was frantic squeaking and scuffling

coming from inside the tunnel; first two—then three, then four—voles burst out into the open, their eyes wide with terror. Gray Wing felt a rush of exhilaration as he pounced on two of them, one under each paw. Expertly he snapped their necks, but as he turned to pursue the other two, a dark shadow flashed over him and a harsh cry sounded from above. He looked up and saw a hawk plummeting out of the sky, its talons extended. Gray Wing barely had time to leap out of the way, rolling over on the pebbles, while the hawk snatched up one of the other voles as it tried to flee. The fourth vole plopped into the river and vanished.

River Ripple bounded up, peering down at Gray Wing from the top of the bank. "Let's get out of here," he urged. "We don't *need* all this prey. We have more than enough on the island."

Gray Wing rose to his paws, listening to the faint wheezing of his own breath. Ignoring River Ripple, he padded back to where he had left the two dead voles, and checked them all over for signs of illness, giving them a good sniff and parting their fur with careful claws. Satisfied that they were healthy, he picked them up by their tails and scrambled up the bank to drop them at River Ripple's paws.

"I just wanted to contribute," he meowed, his eyes burning with hurt. "To feel useful."

River Ripple's shoulders sagged. "You don't need to prove yourself to me," he murmured. "I've seen everything you've done, the way you've led your cats. But any cat can see that you have been hurting, and I was happy to give you a place to retreat to." Gently he pushed the dead voles back toward Gray Wing. "Maybe you know some other cats who could use some food? Some kits, maybe?"

Gray Wing stared at the silver tom. "How did you know?" he gasped, astonished by his friend's wisdom. "It's true; I haven't been able to stop thinking about Pebble Heart and Owl Eyes . . . and poor Sparrow Fur."

I don't even know if her injuries are better, he thought guiltily. *And how is Pebble Heart coping with being a healer? And Owl Eyes . . . I hope he isn't being overlooked because his brother has grown up so quickly. Does he get the chance to play and enjoy being a kit?*

"I think it's time for me to go home," he told River Ripple.

The silver-furred tom dipped his head in understanding. "I wondered how long it would take for you to realize that," he mewed. "But should you ever need refuge, you know where we are."

Gray Wing felt a pang at the thought of leaving this cat who had become such a good friend. "Would you like to come back to the hollow with me?" he asked. "Maybe you and Night and Dew could—"

He broke off as River Ripple shook his head.

"That's not what we agreed at the four trees, remember? We need to separate and isolate this sickness. Besides, the island is my home. I could not live anywhere else."

Gray Wing sighed regretfully. "I know. But I'll miss you, River Ripple. Thank you for all your help. I'll never forget what you have done for me."

He touched noses with the silver tom, then turned and

headed toward the hollow, picking up the pace as he felt the tough moorland grass under his paws once again. Excitement fluttered in his belly. He would miss River Ripple, but he had missed the kits, too, more than he had realized until now. *Will they be glad to see me again? I hope so. . . .*

On his way to the camp, Gray Wing was crossing the center of the moorland when he heard a faint mewing coming from a scattering of rocks just ahead. To reach them he had to cross a dip in the ground, a sandy hollow that felt itchy against his pads. Halfway across he spotted a cat perched on a flat-topped rock, watching him.

"Wind Runner!" he exclaimed, dropping his prey in his surprise. "What are you doing out here on your own? Are you okay?"

Wind Runner leaped down from the rock and ran across the hollow to touch noses with him. "I'm not on my own," she replied. "Come and say hello to Gorse Fur and the kits."

Retrieving his voles, Gray Wing followed Wind Runner along a winding path through the rocks until they reached a bank where a rabbit burrow had been dug out to make a den like the ones in the moorland camp. Gorse Fur was sitting at the entrance, Moth Flight and Dust Muzzle tussling together on the grass in front of him.

They sprang apart when they saw Gray Wing, and Gorse Fur rose to his paws and came out to meet him. "It's good to see you again," he purred.

Gray Wing couldn't help noticing how scrawny the two kits looked. "Would you like one of these voles?" he asked, setting one down between them.

"Thank you!" the two kits squeaked in chorus, falling on the prey with hungry bites.

Wind Runner cast a grateful glance at Gray Wing, who motioned to her to follow him aside for a few paw steps.

"I was sorry to hear that Morning Whisker had died, when we met at the four trees," he meowed. "I know what it's like to grieve. How are you coping?"

Wind Runner's whole body trembled, but she managed to control her emotion. "Look around you," she responded. "I'm sheltered and dry here. I have my own space, and there's room for my kits to grow and flourish."

Gray Wing bit back a comment that her kits seemed to be doing anything but flourishing. "Life as a rogue is hard," he murmured gently.

"We're not rogues anymore!" Wind Runner snapped at him with some of her old tartness. "Yes, life is hard, but I'm setting up my own group here."

"Really?" Gray Wing asked, surprised.

Wind Runner shrugged. "Okay, maybe now I'm making a home for my family. But I'm doing something that's more than wandering around like a rogue cat, without a real home or friends. I've learned a lot from living with the others, and now I want to put that to use here. The hollow and the forest aren't the only places a group of cats could live."

Gray Wing knew that she was right. River Ripple's home on the island was proof of that.

"Then look after yourself and your family," he mewed. "I'd

better be getting back. Would you like the other vole?"

Wind Runner shook her head. "We'll be fine, but thanks."

Gray Wing was relieved that she had refused. *I want something to take back to Turtle Tail's kits. They're almost grown now, but they'll still enjoy a treat.*

As he turned to leave, he paused, spotting another cat watching him from the shadow of one of the rocks: a she-cat with a thick, dark gray pelt and wide, amber eyes.

"Slate," Wind Runner called, beckoning with her tail. "Come and meet Gray Wing. He's one of the cats from that big group I told you about."

Slate padded forward and dipped her head to Gray Wing, giving him an interested stare. "It's good to meet you," she mewed. "I see we both have colors in our names."

As she spoke her eyes were alight with mischief, and for the first time in moons Gray Wing felt an amused purr bubbling up in his throat. "Great to meet you, too," he responded politely.

"Are you coming to live with us here?" Slate asked.

Gray Wing shook his head. "I have my own home to go to in the hollow," he explained. *Home for now,* he realized. An idea was forming in his mind that he hardly dared put into words; seeing Wind Runner had made that plan seem a little more real.

"I see," Slate murmured. "Can I come with you for part of the way?"

Surprised and pleased, Gray Wing agreed. Saying goodbye to Wind Runner and Gorse Fur, they padded along side by side.

"How is Wind Runner managing?" Gray Wing asked, feeling awkward as he mumbled his question around the vole in his jaws.

Slate dipped her head thoughtfully. "She's surviving, but it's hard. I know what it's like to lose someone I loved. My brother died saving me from a fox attack—look."

She slid to the ground and rolled over so that Gray Wing could see a healed scar on the tender part of her belly. His heart softened in sympathy. *There's something very special about a cat who can show her vulnerable side like this to some cat she's only just met.*

"I'm sorry," he murmured. "Your brother must have been a great cat."

Slate walked with Gray Wing in comfortable silence until the hollow came in sight. Then she halted. "I'll leave you here," she meowed. "Good luck."

"Luck?" Gray Wing was puzzled. "What for?"

The gray she-cat's amber eyes were glinting again: with merriment or wisdom, Gray Wing couldn't tell. "For the challenges ahead," she replied. "I can feel them resting heavy on your shoulders."

She brushed her tail along his side and turned to go.

"Good luck to you, too," Gray Wing called after her, unable to tear his gaze away as she strode confidently across the moor. *She knows more about me from a few moments' talk than some cats I've lived with for seasons. Where in the world did Wind Runner find her?*

As Gray Wing approached the camp, he spotted Tall Shadow standing at the edge of the hollow. Her gaze was fixed on the horizon, toward where the Thunderpath stretched.

Her tail curled up in welcome when she noticed Gray Wing.

"You're back," she meowed in tones of deep satisfaction as she touched noses with him. "Are you glad to be home again?"

"I think so," Gray Wing responded, looking around for the kits and spotting Pebble Heart at the entrance to their den.

"You *think* so?" Tall Shadow called after him as he headed toward the den.

Gray Wing glanced over his shoulder. "It's good for now," he called back.

But for how long . . . ?

CHAPTER 17
❦

Thunder crouched behind a tussock of grass and narrowed his eyes
as he stared at the rabbits feeding outside their burrows. The
sun was slipping down in the sky, and a chilly breeze whispered across the moor. On either side of Thunder, Owl Eyes
and Lightning Tail waited, looking stiff and tense. Owl Eyes's
tail-tip flicked impatiently to and fro.

"Don't you dare move before I tell you to," Thunder warned
him. "This is what we're going to do. You see the rabbit over
there by that rock?" He angled his ears toward the rabbit that
was farthest away from the burrows. It was nibbling the grass,
unaware that the cats were watching it.

Lightning Tail nodded. "I see it."

"Right. Lightning Tail, I want you to run out between the
rabbit and the burrows. Make it run the other way. Owl Eyes,
you stay here and leap out at it if it doubles back this way."
Thunder swiped his tongue around his jaws. "And I'll kill it.
It looks nice and plump."

"I'm ready, Thunder," Owl Eyes mewed, his whiskers quivering with excitement.

"Okay. Lightning Tail, go!"

Pushing off with powerful back legs, Lightning Tail launched himself out of cover. The rabbits closer to the burrows jumped up in alarm and fled, their white tails bobbing as they vanished into safety. The cats' chosen prey tried to follow, but Lightning Tail intercepted it, his teeth bared. For a moment the rabbit seemed not to know which way to run, then dashed off in a panic. As Thunder bore down on it, the prey dodged his pouncing paws and headed straight for Owl Eyes. The kit leaped out of hiding, his tail lashing and his claws tearing at the grass. Letting out a terrified squeal, the rabbit crouched trembling in the grass, not even trying to flee any longer. Thunder brought down one huge paw on its neck—a killing strike.

"Great catch!" Owl Eyes exclaimed, coming up to look at the limp body.

"You both helped," Thunder meowed, with a nod to Lightning Tail as he came padding up. "Owl Eyes, you looked really scary!"

But Thunder's satisfaction with the hunt ebbed away rapidly as he took a closer look at what they had caught. The prey was not succulent and plump—it was actually just bloated and swollen from the sickness. There was froth around its jaws, and a faint, rank smell rising from the body.

"Owl Eyes, keep back," Thunder ordered sharply. "Lightning Tail, we'd better find some leaves to wrap it. If we leave it here some other cat might take it." *No wonder it was easy to cut it out from the rest,* he added silently to himself.

When he and Lightning Tail had found enough leaves to

wrap the rabbit, and shoved it deep into a cleft in a nearby rock, Thunder led the way back to camp.

"It's getting harder and harder to catch enough prey," Owl Eyes complained. "It's like everything is sick."

"I know," Lightning Tail agreed. "We decided separating might help, but we couldn't tell that to the prey. The illness is spreading farther and farther."

His denmates were saying out loud what Thunder was already thinking privately. "That may be true," he meowed, "but as we haven't found a cure yet, all we can do is avoid the sickness as much as we can."

I touched that rabbit, he thought, with a tremor of fear in his belly. *Does that mean that I'm carrying the sickness with me now?*

Halfway back to camp they stopped to collect the prey they had caught earlier, which they had hidden under some stones. "One scrawny rabbit and a couple of mice," Thunder muttered. "It looks like a lean leaf-bare. But Gray Wing would probably say it's still better down here than in the mountains."

Owl Eyes winced at the mention of Gray Wing's name, and Thunder wished he had never spoken of his kin. He knew how much the kit missed Gray Wing, and felt guilty that he had left the hollow.

Owl Eyes thinks it was his fault, because he was angry about Tom's death, and left Gray Wing to fetch Sparrow Fur by himself.

"I'm sure Gray Wing will be back soon," Thunder meowed, rubbing his cheek against the side of Owl Eyes's muzzle.

Owl Eyes looked unconvinced, and did not reply as he picked up one of the mice and started back toward the camp.

Thunder exchanged a glance with Lightning Tail, and padded alongside him in Owl Eyes's paw steps. *I really miss Gray Wing, too,* he thought. He regretted that he had taken his kin too much for granted over the last few moons. *Especially after Turtle Tail died,* he mused. *Gray Wing just seemed to turn in on himself. My support could have helped him.*

More clearly than ever, Thunder realized how important Gray Wing was to their group, and how much he had to offer. *He seems convinced he has to give me room to grow and become leader, but I hope he changes his mind. I want him to come back.*

They were nearing the camp, beginning to hurry as the sun slid closer to the horizon, when Thunder heard the soft, teasing voice of a she-cat calling out from the gorse bush they were passing.

"That's not very much prey for a cat with such big paws!"

Thunder halted and peered into the bush. From the darkness between the branches a pair of brilliant green eyes with starlike pupils stared back at him. His heart began to pound and his mouth felt dry.

Star Flower strolled out of the bush, her tail curling up with amusement. "Quite a comeback," she mewed wryly, padding forward to stand in front of Thunder, whose mouth was still full of the rabbit he carried. Glancing at Lightning Tail, she added, "Is he always this talkative?"

Thunder was surprised to see Lightning Tail narrow his eyes at the rogue she-cat. "Thunder doesn't really like strangers," he said evenly. "Not many cats do these days. Excuse us."

While Thunder watched, bemused, Lightning Tail stalked off toward the camp. He paused a moment later, when he realized that Thunder wasn't following.

Before Thunder could call to his friend, Star Flower had turned back to him. "It's early to be heading home," she meowed, with a quick glance at the sky. "You're going to miss a spectacular sunset. Besides, there's still enough light for me to show you a few killer hunting moves . . . if you're not too proud to learn."

Thunder set down the rabbit he was carrying. "No, I'm not too proud," he said, his voice sounding high and unnatural— even to him. *Why do I always behave like a mouse-brain in front of this she-cat?*

He saw that Lightning Tail was giving him a look of annoyance. "Come on, Thunder," he urged. "We're needed back at camp."

"Actually, we're not," Thunder retorted, forcing more authority into his voice. "You and Owl Eyes can manage the prey. I'll stay behind and catch something to eat by myself."

Lightning Tail gave an irritable shake of his head. "You know we're supposed to be keeping to ourselves because of the sickness," he mewed tersely. "After all, you helped *make* that rule." Lightning Tail stared at him for a moment. When Thunder didn't move, he ran back to Thunder and leaned in close. "I just don't trust her," Lightening Tail meowed quietly. "There's something about her that makes my fur stand on end. She's just . . . not real. I can't explain it but . . ."

Thunder backed away, shaking his head, hoping that Star

Flower hadn't heard. *This she-cat is utterly real. I can't believe it, but she is.*

If Star Flower had heard Lightning Tail's warning, she pretended not to.

Star Flower took a pace toward him with a swish of her plumy golden tail. "Do I look sick to you?" she purred. "Anyway, who's the leader around here?"

"I am." Thunder gave Lightning Tail a hard stare. "Take Owl Eyes back to camp. *Now.*"

Lightning Tail shot Thunder an angry and disappointed look, but he didn't argue anymore. Snatching up Thunder's rabbit, he beckoned with his tail for Owl Eyes to follow, and stalked away. Owl Eyes blinked in bewilderment, then padded after him.

For a few heartbeats Thunder's pelt prickled with dismay at the argument with his friend, but when he turned back to Star Flower and looked into her eyes, it all seemed to melt away.

"Have you seen the secret garden?" she asked him.

Thunder had no idea what she was talking about, but before he could tell her so she turned and sprang away. "Follow me!" she called, glancing back over her shoulder.

Thunder raced after her, exhilaration blowing through him like a gale. Everything looked new and wonderful to him. The sun slanting through the trees seemed to sparkle more brightly than before, and the air was full of delicious scents.

Star Flower led him toward the river, but before they reached it she turned aside through a copse of thick trees where ferns still grew in luxuriant masses. Beyond the ferns they came to the bank of a brook, which bubbled along over stones, then flowed down toward the river in a series of tiny waterfalls. On either side of the water the grass was speckled by innumerable flowers, releasing their scent into the cool air of leaf-fall.

"They'll wilt soon," Star Flower whispered as Thunder caught up with her. "Maybe even before the sun rises again. We're so lucky to see such beauty before it's gone, aren't we?"

Thunder murmured assent. There had been so much stress in his life, so many questions that were difficult to answer, that he had never really been able to relax and enjoy beauty like this secluded spot.

"It is wonderful here," he agreed. A sudden thought struck him, and he continued, "You love flowers so much—do you know one called the Blazing Star?"

Star Flower nodded. "Sure. It grows mostly on the other side of the Thunderpath," she told him. "Why do you want to know?"

"Oh . . . " *Did she hear all the other cats at four trees talking about the spirit-cats? If I bring them up and she didn't, she'll think I have bees in my brain!* "Some cat mentioned it. Do you know what it's used for?"

"It's a healing herb," Star Flower responded.

"Really?" Thunder felt a prickle of excitement in his pads. "That's useful to know." He looked forward to telling his denmates what he had discovered. *And then let Lightning Tail say that I shouldn't talk to Star Flower! If only we'd known that before poor Morning*

Whisker died, he added to himself with a stab of sorrow. *Maybe this herb can help against the sickness.*

Star Flower sat down on a hillock overlooking the water and beckoned Thunder to join her with a flick of her tail. "Tell me about yourself," she meowed as he settled down beside her. "Were you born here on the moor?"

"Not exactly," Thunder replied. Without realizing how it came about, he found himself telling Star Flower about Clear Sky and Storm, how his mother and his littermates had died when the Twoleg den where they lived was destroyed, and how Gray Wing had rescued and raised him.

"But what about Clear Sky?" Star Flower asked. "Don't tell me he didn't want a fantastic cat like you!"

Thunder shrugged. "Clear Sky rejected me—twice, actually. Once when I was a kit, and once when I challenged the way he ran his group."

"That's dreadful." Star Flower's voice was a sympathetic purr. "Clear Sky must be a terrible cat with deep weaknesses. Doesn't he know that family is more important than anything?"

"He's not really weak," Thunder mewed, feeling uncomfortable discussing his father like this. "He made mistakes, but he made them while he was trying to do what he thought was for the best." Hoping to change the subject, he added, "Anyway, what's your story? I'd never seen you before that meeting at the four trees."

"Oh, I was born on the moor," Star Flower told him. "But I mostly kept myself to myself until I heard about cats forming groups. I decided to go to the four trees and find out more, and then I saw you."

"You don't seem like other rogues," Thunder meowed.

Star Flower's green eyes glinted with amusement. "What do you mean?"

"Well," Thunder ducked his head in embarrassment. "You're sort of . . . softer and . . . and more . . ." *Beautiful* was the word he wanted to say, but held his tongue.

"I take very good care of myself," Star Flower murmured with a twitch of her whiskers. "Look at the sunset," she went on, gazing up into the sky, where streaks of scarlet and gold were staining the blue.

Thunder's gaze followed hers, and he let himself relax and enjoy the beauty that was blazing above his head. When Star Flower leaned closer to him and laid her paw over his, he thought that he would burst with happiness. The soft touch of her pelt sent warmth flooding through his fur, and her sweet scent drifted around him.

I've never felt like this before!

Thunder's heart thumped even harder as he wondered how he could ask Star Flower if she might be ready to join a group—*his* group. He was sure that if she would agree to come and live with him, he would be able to smooth over any problems with Lightning Tail or the others.

If they only knew her like I do!

He was desperate to ask her, but he couldn't think of the right words. His tongue felt as dry as a dusty path in greenleaf.

Before he could decide what to say, the light in the sky

began to fade. Star Flower suddenly twitched her ears and sprang up.

"Well," she meowed, "that was magnificent, but it's starting to get dark. We should go home."

"Where is your home?" Thunder asked.

Star Flower brushed her tail along his flank. "I'm not ready to tell you that yet," she replied, "but I'm sure I'll see you again."

Thunder had no time to respond before she whirled around and vanished among the trees. He raced after her, pushing his way through the ferns, but when he burst out into the open there was no sign of the beautiful she-cat.

He had no choice but to make his way back to camp, his heart still pounding. *Did that just happen?* he asked himself. *Was it real? And when will I see her again?*

The sky was clear and the last of the daylight was enough to guide Thunder as he loped across the moor. Once or twice he thought he heard paw steps following him, and once the rustling of a gorse bush after he passed it. His pads tingled with apprehension, but when he spun around to see if some creature was following him, he saw nothing but the empty moor.

I wish it had been Star Flower, he thought longingly.

When Thunder arrived back home, all thoughts of the golden she-cat were driven out of his head. He was amazed to see both Gray Wing and Clear Sky sitting at the edge of the hollow with Tall Shadow.

"Gray Wing!" Thunder yowled excitedly, racing up to them and skidding to a halt in front of his kin. "You're home!"

Purring loudly, he brushed his muzzle against Gray Wing's shoulder.

"Yes, I'm home," Gray Wing responded with a sigh. "It's good to see you again, Thunder."

"And you." Thunder turned toward Clear Sky. "You're becoming a familiar face around here," he added wryly.

As soon as he had spoken, he realized how serious every cat was looking. Clearly this wasn't the right time for humor.

"Where have you been?" his father demanded. "Lightning Tail said you'd gone off with some rogue she-cat. We have a crisis here. One Eye has taken over my camp!"

Thunder gaped at him. "That's not possible!" he gasped. "Why would your cats let him do that?"

"They had no choice," Clear Sky retorted bitterly. "One Eye has brought in a whole bunch of rogues. I don't know where he found them, but they're mean and fierce."

Now Gray Wing looked at Thunder. "And there's even worse news," he said, rising to his paws and leading Thunder down into the hollow, toward the nest that Jagged Peak shared with Holly. Before they reached it, Thunder could hear a familiar moaning. He felt as though all the blood in his veins had turned to ice.

Jagged Peak was crouching outside the nest, and sprang to his paws as Thunder and the others approached. "It's Holly!" he exclaimed. "She has the sickness!"

CHAPTER 18

Clear Sky stood back and let Gray Wing and Thunder go into the hollow ahead of him. It felt strange to be following in the paw steps of his brother and son, but he knew that was the way it had to be now. Not only because of the promises they had made to the spirit-cats, but because of his deep sense of his own humiliation.

How can I lead any cat, when One Eye has so utterly defeated me?

Just before they reached Holly's den, Thunder paused beside a gorse bush where Sparrow Fur was sitting, while Cloud Spots checked over her injuries. Owl Eyes and Pebble Heart crouched a fox-length away, their worried gazes burning into her pelt.

"Sparrow Fur, you're back," Thunder mewed, his voice full of relief. "Are you okay?"

Cloud Spots answered for the kit as he stroked a clump of fur back into place. "Her wounds are healing well. She'll do." Turning to Clear Sky, he dipped his head stiffly and continued, "Thank you for taking care of her while she was in the forest."

Clear Sky returned the nod politely, though he suspected

that the black-and-white tom's thanks were not entirely sincere. He was sure of it a moment later when Cloud Spots muttered, "But it's better that she's back in her rightful home."

Sparrow Fur pulled away from him, her fur fluffing up in indignation. "Clear Sky was good to me," she insisted. "He let me rest, and then he rescued me from a trap."

"Trap?" Thunder's voice was sharp, and he exchanged a glance with Gray Wing. "What trap?"

Sparrow Fur gave her chest fur a couple of licks, clearly reluctant to go into details. "One Eye shoved me into a hollow tree," she admitted, "and then blocked the hole."

Clear Sky felt himself bristle as the other cats all turned identical glares on him.

"How could you let that happen?" Gray Wing asked.

"It wasn't my fault!" he protested, struggling to meet the accusing gazes. "I wasn't even there!" For a long moment he was silent, then let his shoulders slump. "Can we just find a way to sort out this mess? One Eye is out of control—that much is clear—and now the sickness is spreading worse than ever."

"Yes!" Jagged Peak spoke up, drawing closer. "We must do something—anything! I can't bear to see Holly like this."

"I can help!" Thunder announced, excitement pulsing through him again as he remembered what Star Flower had told him. "I just found out that the Blazing Star is a healing herb."

"That's it!" Cloud Spots sprang to his paws. "Remember what the spirit-cats said? 'The claw still blights the forest,' and, 'Only the Blazing Star can blunt the claw!' Suppose that the *sickness* is the claw, and the Blazing Star can heal it. Maybe it can cure Holly. We've tried everything else. . . ."

His last few words were almost drowned out by enthusiastic yowling from Owl Eyes and Jagged Peak.

"We've got to go and fetch some!"

"I'll go!"

Clear Sky waved his tail in a hopeless bid for silence, then raised his voice to ring out over the young cats' clamor. "Okay, okay, but that's enough! What about One Eye? We have to deal with him too."

"That's right," Tall Shadow agreed. "And don't forget that in order to cross the Thunderpath to where the Blazing Star grows, we have to go through the forest. I don't think One Eye will let us do that without a fight. He'll have his rogues guarding the boundaries for sure."

"Let's discuss this as a group," Thunder suggested. "Clear Sky, we need to know exactly what's going on in the forest, and then we might be able to come up with some ideas."

He bounded off to join Tall Shadow, who leaped up onto the lookout rock and called the rest of the group to gather around it. Gray Wing and the others with him padded over, while Dappled Pelt emerged yawning from her den. Lightning Tail and Shattered Ice, who were sharing a rabbit at the other side of the hollow, left their prey and hurried across, tongues swiping over their whiskers. Mud Paws and Mouse Ear followed, breaking off their training session with a final pounce on their imaginary prey.

Pebble Heart was the only cat not to answer the summons.

Clear Sky spotted him slipping into Holly's den, and realized the kit must be taking care of her.

By now the last streaks of sunset had faded from the horizon, and darkness had gathered. The first stars showed frostily in a sky streaked with cloud. Clear Sky looked up at them and wondered if the spirit-cats knew what was happening in the forest. *We can't expect any help from them,* he thought.

"Well, Clear Sky," Tall Shadow began when the group was assembled. "What do you want from us?"

Clear Sky stood at the foot of the rock and faced the other cats. "First, to thank you all for allowing me to come back to the hollow," he meowed. "I feel—"

"Never mind how you *feel*," Jagged Peak interrupted sharply. "We need to know what we're dealing with. Tell us everything you know about One Eye."

Clear Sky had to pause for a moment before answering. Whenever he thought about the vicious rogue he became so full of rage that he found it hard to speak. "He's a bully and a murderer," he spat out at last. "He's a rogue with fierce battle skills, and he's hungry for power. He knows this area very well; he claimed to know about the sickness—"

"Then he won't be easy to defeat," Shattered Ice mewed thoughtfully. "We'll need to come up with a really good plan."

Clear Sky turned to the one cat he knew he could trust with his life: Gray Wing. "What do you think we should do?" he asked.

Gray Wing blinked thoughtfully. While waiting for his reply, Clear Sky noticed that Thunder was watching Gray Wing closely, too.

Please tell us what to do. Clear Sky had never had to beg his brother out loud before. Would this be the first time?

"It's too soon to launch an attack on One Eye," Gray Wing meowed. Then he raised his tail to silence Jagged Peak, who was opening his jaws to interrupt. "No—listen to me. One Eye knows that Clear Sky has fled the forest."

Clear Sky nodded, inwardly wincing to hear his retreat described like that.

"So he'll be able to guess that you've gone for help," Gray Wing continued, gazing around at the assembled cats. "Don't you think he'll be ready for us? With all those rogue cats he has at his command now? We wouldn't stand a chance."

"Just try us," Mud Paws growled.

"Mouse-brain!" Mouse Ear flicked Mud Paws's ear with his tail-tip. "What do you suggest instead?" he asked Gray Wing.

"We need to be patient," Gray Wing replied. "It will take courage to do what I'm about to suggest. Are you in?" He looked each of his denmates in the eye, one by one.

Yowls of enthusiasm rose up from every cat, splitting the peaceful night as if they rose as far as the shivering stars above. Warm admiration flooded over Clear Sky.

Gray Wing really knows how to get cats on his side! If only I could do that. If only I hadn't relied so much on drawing boundaries, maybe we wouldn't be in this position now.

Then Clear Sky gave his pelt a shake, hoping to clear his mind of regret as he cleared his fur of dirt and fluff. It was too late to be thinking about what he could, or should, have done.

"This is what I think we should do." The other cats drew more closely around him as Gray Wing continued. "We should go after the Blazing Star. The samples we brought back before all dried up before we could figure out how to use it. Holly needs it badly, and if we have it we can heal any other cats who fall ill. That means we'll be in a stronger position if—and I mean *if*—we do decide to take on One Eye."

"But the Blazing Star is on the other side of the Thunderpath," Owl Eyes protested, his eyes stretching wide with apprehension.

Gray Wing cast him a pitying glance. "Are you giving up already?"

"No!" Owl Eyes meowed indignantly. "I just think we should be careful. Cats have been killed on the Thunderpath." His voice shook as he added, "I don't want any more cats to die."

Sparrow Fur stretched out a paw and brushed it comfortingly along her littermate's side.

"It's true that cats have died," Gray Wing agreed. "But there are many of us who have crossed Thunderpaths and survived. And some of us have been to where the Blazing Star grows and survived. It's *vital* that we fetch the Blazing Star. If we can't cure this illness, then sooner or later, we will all die. It's as simple as that."

"You're right, Gray Wing." Lightning Tail rose to his paws from where he had been sitting at the back of the group. "It's a risk worth taking, but only if we're sure about the Blazing Star. How do we know it's a healing herb?"

"Star Flower told me," Thunder replied.

"That cat!" Every hair on Lightning Tail's pelt began to bristle. "And you *believe* her?"

"I do!" Thunder sprang to his paws and faced the young black tom. "I believe every word she said."

"Then you're even more mouse-brained than I thought," Lightning Tail retorted.

"You don't even know her!" Thunder meowed angrily. "You don't like her based on what? A random feeling that you can't explain?"

Clear Sky listened in surprise to the young toms' hostile words. *I thought those two were friends.* Now tension was thrilling between them, and more cats were turning to one another, muttering in low voices, as if they were as reluctant as Lightning Tail to trust Star Flower.

I don't know this cat, Clear Sky thought. *But she certainly rouses some strong feelings!*

"That's enough!" Gray Wing's voice was full of authority. "Lightning Tail, you're right that we have no reason to trust Star Flower—but we have no reason to *distrust* her, either. And if we don't do something soon, Holly will die."

His words silenced all protests. Lightning Tail gave an uneasy shrug and sat down again.

"I'll lead the expedition," Thunder stated, taking a pace forward to stand beside Gray Wing. He blinked in surprise as Gray Wing shook his head.

"We need cats to guard the hollow," Gray Wing explained. "We still have no idea what One Eye may have planned."

Reluctantly, Thunder nodded.

"Jagged Peak," Gray Wing began, turning to the gray tabby tom, "will you lead the party across the Thunderpath?"

Jagged Peak gaped. "Me?"

Clear Sky's belly cramped with a mixture of compassion and guilt as he gazed at his young brother. *I thought he would be no good to any cat after his fall from the tree. And now he believes it himself.*

"I'm sure you'll manage just fine," Gray Wing assured Jagged Peak. "Will you do it?"

"I—I want to, Gray Wing," Jagged Peak stammered. "But I can't leave Holly."

"Mouse droppings!" a hoarse voice called out from the other side of the camp.

Clear Sky turned his head to see that Holly had dragged herself to the entrance to her den, and was listening to the discussion.

"Of course you can do it, Jagged Peak," she went on. "It's about time you took your proper place as a leader of cats."

"But what if . . ." Jagged Peak began to protest, but his voice trailed off; he couldn't put words to his worst fear.

Holly snorted. "I'm not going anywhere. Now get across that Thunderpath and fetch me some Blazing Star!"

"So . . . are you willing to go?" Gray Wing asked.

Jagged Peak turned back to him, his eyes brimming with emotion. "I will," he choked out.

Gray Wing wasted no more time. "We have to act tonight," he mewed. "Jagged Peak, you and the cats you take with you had better rest for a while before you set off. You should reach the Thunderpath as the sun starts rising. Once it has, you'll be able to see what you're doing."

Jagged Peak nodded. "Who is going with me, Gray Wing?"

"You'd better have Lightning Tail," Gray Wing replied after a moment's thought.

Lightning Tail looked surprised, and Clear Sky could understand why. *Choosing the one cat who* really *doesn't trust Star Flower?* But then he realized how clever Gray Wing was being. Of all cats, Lightning Tail would be expecting trouble, which meant that he would be alert for the first signs of it.

Now the young black tom gave a curt nod. "Okay."

Gray Wing hesitated, as if he was thinking of choosing a third cat. Before he spoke, Clear Sky slid up to his side. "I want to go," he meowed. "I've been there before, so I know where to find the Blazing Star."

Gray Wing faced him, looking deep into his eyes. "Okay," he responded at last, though there was a trace of reluctance in his tone. Lowering his voice, he continued, "Just make sure you don't try to take over. This is a mission I've given our younger brother, and I want him to have the chance to prove himself. Can you accept that?"

Clear Sky swallowed hard before he replied. "Sure I can." *But only if everything goes smoothly,* he added silently to himself.

Glancing around, he saw Thunder moving among the other cats, setting guards on the camp, while the cats chosen for the expedition headed for their dens for a brief rest.

It's good that we're pulling together, Clear Sky thought. Then the doubts crept in, as he wondered if the cats were walking to their deaths.

Will One Eye be lying in wait for us?

CHAPTER 19

❧

Gray Wing shared his den with Clear Sky for what remained of the night, but Clear Sky slept uneasily. When Gray Wing prodded him in the side and mewed, "It's time," he was instantly alert.

A chilly breeze flowed into the den; beyond the entrance the darkness was beginning to lift. When Clear Sky emerged into the open, he could just make out Tall Shadow on the lookout rock, while Thunder stood guard at the top of the slope. Mud Paws, Shattered Ice, and Dappled Pelt were there, too, spaced at intervals around the hollow.

Lightning Tail was already waiting, standing at the foot of the rock. At first Clear Sky couldn't see Jagged Peak; then he spotted his brother as he appeared just outside the den he'd shared with Holly until she fell ill.

The sick she-cat was just behind him, standing unsteadily on her paws. "Take care, Jagged Peak," she rasped. "You'll be brilliant; I know it."

"I'm doing it for you," Jagged Peak replied. "I'll bring back the Blazing Star to make you well again."

As the two cats looked deeply into each other's eyes, Clear

Sky turned away, embarrassed. He bounded across the hollow toward Lightning Tail. A couple of heartbeats later, Jagged Peak had joined them, meowing briskly, "Right. Let's go." He led the way to the top of the hollow and the other cats followed, crowding around to see them on their way.

"Good luck!" Dappled Pelt called. "Bring back lots of the herb!"

"And watch out for One Eye!" Shattered Ice added.

Jagged Peak raised his head proudly. "He'd better not mess with us!"

Clear Sky couldn't help thinking that his younger brother had no idea how much danger they would be in if One Eye learned that they were venturing through the forest, but he said nothing.

"Clear Sky, you'll take the lead as soon as we get to the Thunderpath," Jagged Peak instructed his cats as they trekked across the moor toward the forest. "Then you and Lightning Tail gather as much of the herb as you can carry—huge bunches of it. I'll keep watch while you do that. Then I'll lead on the way back. Lightning Tail, you bring up the rear and warn us if there's trouble." His gaze flicked across each of the cats in turn. "Is that clear to every cat?"

"That's fine," Lightning Tail responded, while Clear Sky nodded.

Clear Sky found it hard to hide his amusement. He wasn't sure they needed to be told all this in such detail, but at the same time it was good to see Jagged Peak relishing his role. *Maybe there's a leader in him yet.*

Suiting his pace to his brother's limping gait, Clear Sky padded alongside Jagged Peak. "How do you feel about becoming a father?" he asked.

He expected Jagged Peak to be excited, and pathetically grateful to Holly for carrying their kits, but his brother's response was quite different.

"I've been helping Holly prepare our nest," he mewed. "And I've been hunting extra-hard to bring her more prey. She needs to keep her strength up. And I've had practice, of course . . . helping out with Turtle Tail's litter when they were younger."

Clear Sky was surprised at how practical he sounded. "But how do you *feel*?" he asked again.

Jagged Peak hesitated, casting a glance over his shoulder to see that Lightning Tail had dropped a couple of fox-lengths behind. "Am I allowed to admit . . . terrified?" he asked. "I mean, I've never done *this* before!"

Clear Sky let out a snort of laughter, and a heartbeat later Jagged Peak joined him.

"You know," Clear Sky meowed when he had managed to control himself again, "there was a time when you wouldn't have been able to admit to feeling terrified. You'd have gotten angry and picked a fight with me, and then you'd have tried to prove yourself by doing something foolish. You—" He broke off, wondering if he had gone too far.

"That's true," Jagged Peak responded in a neutral tone. "I had a lot to get my head around after I was injured."

Clear Sky nodded. "I'm sure I didn't help matters," he

admitted. "I should never have made you leave my group. You deserved better from me."

Jagged Peak halted, staring his brother full in the face. "Thank you," he mewed. "That means a lot to me. There was a time when you would never have been able to apologize."

Before Clear Sky could say more, Lightning Tail caught up with them, glancing from Clear Sky to Jagged Peak and back again. "It's good to see you getting along so well," he commented wryly.

"What about you and Thunder?" Jagged Peak asked. "You didn't seem glad to see him when he got back to camp last night."

"Well, you know what *that's* about, don't you?" Lightning Tail replied.

"Um . . . no," Jagged Peak replied, with a shake of his head, though Clear Sky felt he had a good idea.

Lightning Tail let out a small yowl of frustration. "That she-cat Star Flower's got Thunder in a trance, and he's too stupid to see what she's doing."

"What *is* she doing?" Clear Sky asked.

"I don't know exactly," he meowed slowly, obviously trying to keep calm. "But something about her is not quite right. It's clear to me she's up to *something*. And if Thunder weren't so taken with her, he would see it too!" Lightning Tail declared, the fur on his shoulders rising.

"Let's not leap to judge other cats," Jagged Peak meowed. "It was Star Flower who told us that the Blazing Star can heal, remember."

"Right, and I *still* don't believe it." With that, Lightning Tail gave a shrug and stalked into the lead.

By this time they had reached the outskirts of the forest. The leafless trees stood in front of them in a dark and threatening line, barely visible in the first faint light of dawn.

"Quiet from now on," Jagged Peak ordered. "We have to get through here without alerting One Eye. Clear Sky, can you take us the quickest route to the Thunderpath?"

Clear Sky nodded. "We need to come out near the dead ash tree. It's not too far from there to where the Blazing Star grows."

He took the lead as the three cats slipped silently between the trees. Clear Sky kept his ears pricked, his jaws parting to taste the air. The reek of One Eye and his rogues had soaked into the forest like a shower of thundery rain, yet all the scents were stale; no cat had been this way since the day before. Even so, Clear Sky was relieved when they finally emerged from the forest at the edge of the Thunderpath near the place where the ash tree stretched bleached boughs across the strip of grass.

"Mouse Ear says he can tell if a monster is coming through vibrations in the ground," Jagged Peak meowed.

"That's right." Clear Sky stretched out a paw and laid it on the hard black surface of the Thunderpath. His pads couldn't pick up the faintest hint of movement. "I think it's fine now," he reported.

Jagged Peak waved his tail to beckon the other cats, and limped across the first half of the Thunderpath to the stretch of grass that ran down the middle. Clear Sky checked for vibrations again; then they completed the crossing. Not a single monster had appeared from either direction.

"It's very early," Clear Sky murmured. "Maybe the monsters are all still asleep."

"Whatever the reason," Jagged Peak agreed, "I'm glad it was so easy."

Clear Sky's pelt prickled at his brother's words. *I don't trust easy. It makes me feel like something is bound to go wrong soon.*

He took the lead again, heading into the marshes along the same route they had taken before. The stench of One Eye and his rogues faded behind them. Clear Sky began to pick up scents of mud and stagnant water and rotting vegetation.

"Tall Shadow loves it here," he remarked to Lightning Tail, wrinkling his nose against the smells. "I can't imagine why."

By now dawn light was strengthening in the sky. Clear Sky could make out pools of water reflecting the pale light, surrounded by reeds and long grasses. Somewhere unseen a single bird sent up a thin, piping call. The ground underpaw was damp, with moisture welling through his pads every time he took a step.

"If I lived here, I'd turn into a frog," he muttered.

At last Clear Sky drew to a halt. He became aware of a sharp, clean scent all around him. The outlines of spiky branches were visible against the sky, bearing yellow, five-petaled flowers. "This is the place," he mewed.

He and Lightning Tail set to work biting off stems, while Jagged Peak climbed to the top of a hillock and kept watch. By the time they had amassed a huge mound of the herb, the sun was up, shedding cold, clear light over the marshes. Bird-song was all around them, and a breeze rattled the tops of the rushes.

All right. Now I can almost understand what Tall Shadow sees in this place, Clear Sky thought.

"I just wish I could believe Star Flower was telling the truth," Lightning Tail meowed, contemplating the heap of flowers. "It would be so wonderful if this stuff really could help Holly."

"Let's hope it will," Clear Sky responded.

He thought of Petal and the kits and other cats, cut off from him now in One Eye's camp. One Eye had said other cats would get sick and were as good as dead. Had any of them gotten the sickness?

I wish I could take them some of the Blazing Star just in case, he thought anxiously. *But what if One Eye takes advantage of the situation?* Then he gave his pelt a shake. *You stupid furball! Of course One Eye will take advantage!*

"Come on!" he called to the others. "It's time we were getting back."

He and Lightning Tail divided the herbs between them, gripping them tightly in their jaws, while Jagged Peak took the lead, glancing warily around as they headed back to the Thunderpath.

While they were in the marshes, it seemed, the monsters had woken up and were roaring angrily. Their acrid tang rolled over the cats as they approached the Thunderpath and watched the glittering creatures speed past in front of their noses. The wind of their passing buffeted the cats' fur and they choked in the reek they left behind.

"We could be here all day," Jagged Peak grumbled as moments slid by without any break in the lines of monsters.

At last the noise died away and the air cleared slightly. The first section of the Thunderpath was clear as far as the strip of grass down the center. Clear Sky checked for vibrations and nodded.

"Now!" Jagged Peak yowled.

Tightly bunched together, the three cats darted across the black surface of the Thunderpath. Clear Sky hated the way it felt under his paws. Still keeping close to one another, they waited on the central grassy stretch until it was safe to cross the second half.

Jagged Peak watched Clear Sky as he set his paw on the surface again to feel the vibrations of oncoming monsters. Clear Sky thought at first that there was hardly any point, since he could see the monsters sweeping past a tail-length from his nose. But eventually a gap opened up, and he could only feel the faintest quivering beneath his pads.

"Okay," he mumbled around his mouthful of stems.

Jagged Peak waved his tail, and the three cats set out across the Thunderpath. When they were barely halfway across, a monster appeared as if from nowhere. It let out an earsplitting shriek as it bore down on them with blazing eyes.

"Faster!" Clear Sky screeched, dropping most of his bundle of herbs.

He got behind Jagged Peak and gave him a strong shove,

propelling him to the safety of the grass, where they both tumbled, a tangle of flailing paws. Lightning Tail landed beside them and rolled over as the monster swept past and growled away into the distance.

"What have we here?" A voice spoke somewhere above their heads.

Clear Sky stiffened. Looking up, he saw One Eye gazing down at him, a mocking twist to his mouth.

"Flea-pelt!" Clear Sky spat.

One Eye made no response, only circling them with the same mockery on his face as all three cats scrambled to their paws and shook debris off their pelts.

"And what's this?" he went on, padding up to Lightning Tail. He gave the young cat a hard blow on the side of the head, making him drop his bunch of herbs. "Oh dear," he went on. "I really don't think I can allow you to take that."

"It's got nothing to do with you!" Jagged Peak protested, bravely facing up to One Eye. "We don't need your permission."

One Eye tilted his head to one side, as if he was pretending to think. "I guess not," he meowed. "Yes, yes, you're right. I shouldn't have been so presumptuous."

Clear Sky watched the rogue cat warily. He knew this had to be a trick.

A moment later, One Eye's glance grew icy, and his voice was clipped and cold. "Rogue cats, attack!" he commanded, stepping aside.

Clear Sky stared as One Eye's rogues streamed out of the

undergrowth. Their pelts were matted; their rheumy eyes were filled with spite. There seemed to be even more of them than when One Eye drove him out of the camp.

The leading rogue leaped at Clear Sky, who rolled out of the way just in time.

"Coward!" One Eye sneered. "You'd never win a fight with me, one-on-one."

With a snarl of rage, Clear Sky hurled himself at One Eye, but the weight of several rogues landing on top of him bore him to the ground. Twisting his head to one side he saw that Lightning Tail and Jagged Peak were lashing out at the mass of rogue cats who were attacking them. In spite of their scrawny bodies, One Eye's followers were vicious fighters.

We're hopelessly outnumbered, Clear Sky thought, as two rogues bundled him to the ground.

With a pang of pure horror he saw that two more rogues were forcing Lightning Tail back onto the Thunderpath, almost under the crushing, black paws of the passing monsters. Clear Sky heaved at the rogues who were pinning him down, but their weight was too much for him to throw off.

There's nothing I can do!

Then a loud yowling sounded from the other side of the bramble thicket. Acorn Fur burst out into the open. Throwing herself at the rogues who were attacking her brother, she sank her claws into the nearest shoulder.

The rogue let out a screech of pain. Arching his back, he let go of Lightning Tail to take a swipe at Acorn Fur. While he was distracted, Lightning Tail squirmed free from the other rogue and flung himself back onto the grass just as a huge monster growled past.

At the sight of Acorn Fur, One Eye let out a furious screech. The rogues turned toward him, briefly breaking off the fight.

"Now! Run!" Clear Sky yowled.

He scrambled to his paws, thrusting Lightning Tail and Jagged Peak in front of him as he headed for the depths of the forest.

"I can't leave Acorn Fur!" Lightning Tail protested.

"There's nothing you can do!" Clear Sky gave him another shove. "Now, *run!*"

Lightning Tail growled in frustration, but he ran. The three cats pelted into the depths of the forest, blindly blundering through brambles and clumps of bracken in their desperate urge to escape.

Clear Sky took a last glance over his shoulder. He caught a glimpse of One Eye buffeting Acorn Fur around the head. The claw of regret tore at his heart. He didn't want to leave her there, but there was nothing he could do to rescue her now.

One Eye will destroy the forest, Clear Sky thought as he raced after Jagged Peak and Lightning Tail. *Somehow we have to drive him out.*

CHAPTER 20

♣

Clear Sky and his companions slowed their pace when they realized that One Eye and his rogues weren't pursuing them. Their route back to the moorland hollow had never seemed so long. Lightning Tail was bleeding from a scratch on his shoulder, and limping almost as badly as Jagged Peak. Clear Sky's tail stung as if a rogue had bitten it, and every muscle in his body seemed to ache.

Jagged Peak was trudging along with his head down. He had no obvious injuries, but his tail drooped and he looked as if every step took great effort.

Clear Sky watched him sympathetically, but didn't say anything. His younger brother's first mission as leader had ended disastrously, even though it wasn't his fault. There was no way any cat could fight against One Eye and his rogues, and escape with a whole pelt.

When they reached the camp, the rest of the cats eagerly crowded around and began questioning them.

"What happened?"

"Why are you hurt?"

"Where's the Blazing Star?"

At first no cat replied. Clear Sky felt exhausted, his chest still heaving from the aftermath of the fight and the desperate race to escape. Lightning Tail and Jagged Peak were struggling for breath too. The press of bodies around them made Clear Sky feel he was going to suffocate.

Then Pebble Heart wriggled his way to the front of the crowd. "Back off!" he told the other cats. "Give them some air."

As the other cats obeyed, Clear Sky gradually felt the tension in his chest ease, and looked around for Gray Wing. His brother was standing to one side, a couple of tail-lengths away, waiting for the excitement to die down.

Jagged Peak was the first to speak. He padded up to Gray Wing and stood in front of him with his head hanging. "I failed," he choked out. "I'm sorry."

"What happened?" Gray Wing asked.

"I don't have the Blazing Star."

Clear Sky slipped up to his side and rested his tail across his young brother's shoulders. "One Eye attacked us on the way back," he explained to Gray Wing. "We had to fight him and his rogues, and we lost the Blazing Star. Jagged Peak was not to blame."

To his surprise, though his face was grave, there was a gleam of approval in Gray Wing's eyes. "It's bad news about the Blazing Star," he meowed, "but good news about One Eye. I'm sorry you were attacked, but in a way I was hoping something like that would happen."

"What?" Clear Sky's tail curled up in astonishment. "You

wanted One Eye to rip our pelts off?"

"Not that, of course," Gray Wing replied. "But it's good that you ran away. Now that he thinks we're all a bunch of cowardly cats, he won't be expecting any more trouble from us. And that means we can go on to the next stage of our plan."

"And what's that?" Clear Sky asked, his interest stirring. He refused to show his annoyance that his brother had almost accused him of cowardice.

"I'm working out the last details now," Gray Wing told him. "Let's all meet at sunset, and I'll explain it to you then."

Clear Sky's pads itched with impatience. He opened his jaws to protest, but Gray Wing forestalled him.

"You all need to let Cloud Spots check you out," he meowed. "And then you can rest, and eat. Tall Shadow led a hunting patrol out, so there's plenty of prey."

Clear Sky's shoulders sagged. All he wanted was to find a way of defeating One Eye, but he knew that his brother was talking sense. "Okay," he muttered.

"And I'll go and talk to Holly," Jagged Peak added, still looking dejected. "I promise I won't get too close, but I need to tell her face-to-face. I just hope she understands why I failed to bring back the Blazing Star."

"I'm sure she will," Gray Wing assured him. "And Jagged Peak," he added as his young brother turned away, "you *didn't* fail. You put us exactly where we need to be for my plan against One Eye to have a chance of working. Thanks to you, we have a real chance of winning this battle."

* * *

"Let all cats gather together at the foot of the rock!"

The sun was going down, streaking the sky with scarlet, when Tall Shadow's yowl echoed around the camp. Clear Sky watched from the tunnel he was sharing with Gray Wing as Cloud Spots and Jagged Peak emerged from Holly's den. Lightning Tail, Mud Paws, and Dappled Pelt, who were sharing prey beneath a gorse bush, hastily swallowed the last mouthfuls and found places to sit near the rock. Mouse Ear broke off the game he was playing with Sparrow Fur and Owl Eyes, and led the way to join their denmates. Shattered Ice and Thunder padded down the slope from where they had been keeping watch at the top of the hollow.

When the rest of the cats were assembled, Gray Wing and Clear Sky padded over from the den they were sharing, and thrust their way into the center of the crowd. Tall Shadow remained on her rock, her ears angled to listen while her eyes scanned the moor for intruders.

"So what is this plan, then?" Clear Sky demanded. He felt better after resting and eating, and from the burdock root Cloud Spots had put on his bitten tail, but his impatience was like ants crawling through his pelt.

Gray Wing signaled with his tail for the other cats to draw back, leaving him alone in the center of a ragged circle. Then he began to draw lines in the earth with his claws.

"Look," he explained as Clear Sky peered closer. "Here's the forest, and here's the hollow where we are. There's the Thunderpath, and there's the river. This is the rocky outcrop where Wind Runner is living, and this is the clearing with the four oak trees. And here . . ." Gray Wing smacked a paw down in the middle of his drawing, then looked around inquiringly to see if any cat had gotten his point.

Clear Sky frowned in confusion. "But there . . . there's nothing."

"Exactly!" Gray Wing gave his brother a satisfied nod. "An empty space a good way away from anywhere cats live. Free, open space where a single cat on his own would be terribly vulnerable."

Owl Eyes had crept forward and was studying the markings. His eyes stretched wide until they were as big as the eyes of the bird he was named for. "You mean . . . attack One Eye there?" he breathed out.

"That's exactly what I mean," Gray Wing confirmed.

Clear Sky was aware of the cats sharing worried glances, until Thunder spoke up. "I'm not sure," he meowed.

Gasps of astonishment came from the cats around him, and Clear Sky himself was shocked. "Is that my son talking?" he asked. "The brave warrior Thunder, with his great leaps and huge paws? He's really backing away from action?"

Thunder took a pace forward, glancing around the assembled cats. "We've seen so much death and destruction," he explained. "The spirit-cats told us to unite or die. Maybe One Eye will be happy now that he has the forest, so we should give it to him."

Clear Sky stared at his son, feeling that he scarcely recognized him. "You'd be happy with that, would you? Think how well you hunt in among the trees. You'd be happy never to go back there?"

Doubt clouded Thunder's face. "I don't know," he confessed, scraping at the ground with one massive paw. "I'm just trying to do the right thing."

"We all are," Clear Sky retorted. "But the right thing isn't nothing."

"And what about Acorn Fur?" Lightning Tail asked. "I'm not going to abandon my sister to stay in the forest with One Eye."

"Okay," Thunder conceded, though he still didn't look happy. "But we drive One Eye out. We don't kill him. That would make us just as bad as he is."

Good luck with that, Clear Sky thought, knowing how vicious the rogue was. Aloud, he said, "That's fine with me . . . provided we *can* make him leave."

As Thunder and Clear Sky faced each other, a she-cat's voice rang out from the top of the hollow. "Can I help at all?"

Lightning Tail turned around, his pelt bristling with irritation. But he said nothing.

"Who is this?" Clear Sky asked his son as the she-cat began padding gracefully down the slope. *She's certainly a beautiful cat,* he thought, admiring her golden tabby fur and her green eyes that shone brilliantly in the fading daylight.

No cat replied until the newcomer reached the bottom of the hollow. "My name is Star Flower," she purred, giving Clear Sky a polite nod. "I'm a rogue cat looking for a home. And if there's any fighting to be done, I'm a great cat to have on your side. Just ask Thunder. . . ."

Every cat turned to look at Thunder. Clear Sky saw his son shifting about on his paws, looking utterly embarrassed. *So that's Star Flower!* Clear Sky was unable to stifle his amusement in spite of the serious problems they were facing. *Who would have thought it? Thunder is padding after this pretty she-cat!*

But the other cats clearly didn't share his amusement.

"Your help isn't needed," Lightning Tail meowed, still stiff and bristling. Quickly he drew a paw through the markings Gray Wing had made in the earth, though Clear Sky noticed that Star Flower had already managed to take a quick glance at them.

Star Flower met Lightning Tail's glare. "That's fine," she mewed smoothly. "I won't stay where I'm not wanted." She began to move off.

Clear Sky opened his jaws to say something, but Thunder got there first. "Star Flower, come back!" he exclaimed.

The other cats didn't bother to hide their murmurs of surprise.

"What's wrong?" Thunder demanded, rounding on them. "Don't you think we need help right now? Didn't you hear her name? Star Flower! She is the one who told me that the Blazing Star can save us from the sickness. She might know where more is growing, and you want to turn her away?"

Star Flower halted, dipping her head modestly. "I do know a lot about the plants around here," she purred. "But I think I should leave now. I sense that I'm not entirely welcome."

"No, don't go!" Thunder begged.

Clear Sky watched as Thunder and Star Flower gazed into each other's eyes. "I'll come back tomorrow," the rogue she-cat promised. "Maybe by then, things will have had a chance to calm down." She turned and padded away.

As he faced the group of cats again, Thunder's eyes blazed with fury, and he flexed his claws angrily. "Thank you for your 'support,'" he choked out, his voice thick with sarcasm.

"Thunder," Clear Sky began diplomatically, "these are confusing times. It's hard to know which cat to trust."

"You trusted One Eye, didn't you?" Thunder spat at him.

"Yes, and look where that got me!" Clear Sky retorted.

Thunder shook his head in disgust, and Clear Sky expected him to race off in pursuit of Star Flower. He was surprised when the young cat showed enough maturity to stay with the group.

"So, what is our plan?" Thunder asked in a grudging tone. "We lure One Eye into the empty space on the moors and . . . what then?"

Gray Wing retraced his markings in the earth and then continued. "I think we should attack from all sides," he meowed, pointing with his paw as he named each place. "From here, from Wind Runner's home . . . maybe we should see if any of the forest cats will help us."

"I'll never believe Acorn Fur would willingly support One Eye," Lightning Tail put in.

"Or Quick Water, either," Tall Shadow meowed from her place on top of the rock.

"And I'm sure Petal will be on my side," Clear Sky added.

Gray Wing nodded agreement. "I'll ask River Ripple for his help, too."

"That could work," Tall Shadow pronounced from where

she still sat on the rock. "But how do we get One Eye onto the moor in the first place?"

"And without his rogues," Jagged Peak pointed out. "We can't attack One Eye if he hides behind that mangy lot."

Clear Sky felt a heavy weight in his belly, as if he had swallowed a rock. He knew that this was his moment to make it up to his friends for all the mistakes he had made. "Which cat does One Eye despise more than any other cat?" he asked. They all stared at him, but no cat dared utter a word, so he answered for them. "Me. One Eye taunted me when we met by the Thunderpath, saying I could never beat him. If he thinks I've challenged him to a one-on-one fight, he's sure to come.

"I'll go out there on my own," he continued, "but you all need to make it count. If you don't spring out in time, I'm a dead cat."

"Clear Sky, you can't," Gray Wing protested. "It's too dangerous."

But Clear Sky had made up his mind. "I brought One Eye here, and I'll be the one to see him thrown out again. I don't want to die, but I won't stand back and see other cats die, either. Let's drive out One Eye, and then we can tackle this sickness."

Seeing his friends' nods of assent, and hearing a few murmurs of admiration, Clear Sky allowed a flicker of hope to awaken in his chest. *We're uniting against the rogue,* he thought. *Maybe this is what the spirit-cats meant.*

CHAPTER 21

When the discussion was over, Gray Wing did not retire to his den. Instead he padded up the slope to the edge of the hollow and sat for a while, gazing at the sky as night fell and the moon appeared, swollen, almost full. Not a cloud could be seen, and the silver shape shed its frosty radiance over the moor, lighting up every rock and blade of grass.

Good, Gray Wing thought. *I need all the help I can get tonight.*

Glancing over his shoulder to make sure no cat was following him, he headed onto the moor, making his way toward the empty area in the center where he had suggested that Clear Sky should confront One Eye. He intended to use the night to survey the terrain, pick out a good spot for Clear Sky to wait, and make sure there were no nasty surprises lurking.

It's all very well, scratching out battle plans in the earth, but if anything goes wrong it will be my fault. I meant to give the leadership to Thunder, he added wryly to himself. *And here I am, back in the middle of the trouble.*

When the hollow was a good way behind him, Gray Wing began searching for the best place for the fight. He needed an open space that was near to some cover. Outcrops of rock, dips in the ground, thorn bushes . . . all places where Clear Sky's allies could hide. It would be no good if the cats who were ready to help Clear Sky had no chance of reaching him in time.

Gray Wing was padding around a gorse thicket, working out how many cats could be concealed inside it, when the hot stink of fox hit him in the throat.

Ugh, what a reek! he thought, stiffening.

There was a tang of blood on the air, too; the creature had killed, and would be on its way back to its den. *And good riddance.*

Leaving the gorse thicket, Gray Wing padded off to investigate a tumble of boulders that gleamed eerily white in the moonlight, except where patches of lichen stained the surface.

They cast a deep shadow over the moor, and as Gray Wing stepped into it his paws gave way beneath him. The ground was loose and sandy; he slid down helplessly, paws scrabbling for a grip. From the bottom of the pit something darker than the shadows reared up, and a terrible snarling filled the air.

The fox!

Panic gave Gray Wing extra strength. Digging his claws into the loose earth he forced himself upward. The top of the dip was a tail-length away.

Yeowch!

A sharp pain pierced Gray Wing's hind leg as the fox's teeth met in it, and he was dragged down to the bottom again.

No! With a yowl of agony and terror Gray Wing struggled to pull away, but the fox's teeth only sank deeper. He had never felt such excruciating pain, not even in the forest fire. Fierce, hungry eyes gleamed from the darkness as Gray Wing twisted his body and lashed out with his forepaws, trying to sink his claws into his attacker. But the fox didn't let go.

In the midst of the struggle Gray Wing spotted a couple of bats flitting across the face of the moon. Their shadows swept over him. He closed his eyes and thought of the kits he had raised with Turtle Tail. *Will that be the last thing I ever see?*

The fox was flinging him to and fro by his hind leg; as Gray Wing thumped against the ground, the breath was driven out of him and he felt the familiar tightness in his chest. His strength was ebbing; there was nothing he could do to save himself.

Then he heard a loud and angry hissing coming from somewhere up above. The fox must have heard it too, and paused for a moment, letting Gray Wing dangle from its jaws. In the brief respite Gray Wing looked up and saw Slate, Wind Runner's friend, peering around the nearest boulder.

"Run!" Gray Wing choked out.

Instead Slate stepped out of cover and circled the top of the dip, her hissing changing to a deep, threatening growl. She didn't seem at all afraid of the fox.

"You think you can fight, flea-pelt?" she taunted it. "Come and try!"

Though the fox couldn't understand her words, the mockery was clear enough. With a snarl of rage it dropped Gray Wing to the floor of the dip. Winded and shaking, Gray

Wing looked up to see the fox leaping up the slope and flinging itself at Slate.

But Slate was faster. Spinning around, she darted away. Gray Wing lost sight of her until he managed to scramble out of the dip. Then he saw her racing for the nearest thorn tree, her tail streaming out behind her.

The fox pursued her more slowly; Gray Wing saw that it was limping, and briefly glimpsed the gleam of exposed bone on its shoulder.

Ah, it's been injured, he thought. *That must be why it was lurking down there.*

Slate reached the thorn tree and leaped into the branches, climbing nimbly to the very top. The moonlight turned her thick, gray pelt to silver and her eyes shone like two tiny moons. The branch swayed beneath her and she balanced there without a trace of fear.

"Oh, aren't you clever!" she teased the fox. "You've trapped me in this tree. I'm *so* scared!"

Even though he was injured and exhausted, Gray Wing could feel laughter bubbling up inside him. The fox looked so frustrated, snarling and scraping at the tree trunk. It couldn't get at Slate, and it must have realized that she could jump down and outpace him anytime she liked.

Creeping cautiously, hampered by the pain in his leg, Gray Wing slid between two of the boulders into a narrow gap where the fox couldn't follow. Turning in the tight space, he settled down to rest and watch what would happen next.

He had to admit, he admired Slate's bravery. *She was attacked by a fox, and her brother died saving her. But she still risked being attacked again to help me.*

For a long time neither Slate nor the fox moved. All Gray Wing could hear was the flutter and squeaking of the bats. Then from farther across the moor he heard the bark of another fox.

Oh, no! he thought, tensing with fear. *How are we going to cope with two of them?*

But to his relief the injured fox staggered to its paws, and when the distant barking was repeated it limped off in the direction of the sound. Slate waited for a few moments after it vanished into the darkness, then jumped down from the tree and headed back toward the boulders.

Gathering his strength, Gray Wing crawled out of his hiding place to meet her. "Thank you!" he exclaimed. "You were great!"

Slate padded past him without a pause and Gray Wing gazed after her. Bemused, she cast a glance over her shoulder. "Follow me!" she called.

Gray Wing did as she told him, trying to get his breathing back under control. *I don't want her to think I'm* totally *pathetic!*

Slate led him across the moor until they came to a small, hidden pool surrounded by rushes that bent and swayed in the night breeze with a peaceful rustling sound. The gray she-cat padded out into the water until it covered her paws, breaking up the smooth surface into a silver dazzle.

"Come on," she meowed to Gray Wing, beckoning him with a flick of her ears.

As Gray Wing waded out to join her, he was surprised to feel that the water was almost warm, even though it was the middle of the night.

"Why—" he began.

"The water is very shallow here," Slate explained, guessing what he was about to say. "It sits on top of black rocks that soak up the sun's heat. Even at night the pool keeps some of the warmth. It feels good, doesn't it?"

"It feels wonderful!" Gray Wing agreed, relaxing into the gentle lapping. *Who would have thought wet paws could be so pleasant?*

"The rocks around here are called slate," the she-cat told him. "I was named after them. We can use the water to clean your pelt from that fox attack."

Gray Wing stood still and allowed Slate to scoop water over his hind leg until the pain had almost faded away. "That feels much better," he mewed.

"You're very lucky," Slate told him, giving the wound a sniff. "The teethmarks haven't gone too deep." Looking up into Gray Wing's face, she continued, "How do you like my secret hideaway? You should feel very lucky I've shared it with you. Only *special* cats are invited here."

Gray Wing felt his pelt prickle with embarrassment. "I'm not used to any cat making such a fuss over me," he muttered.

Slate's amber eyes stretched wide with surprise. "You don't know how respected you are?" she asked.

Now it was Gray Wing's turn to be surprised. "How do *you* know what any other cats think of me?" he asked curiously.

"You live with Wind Runner, far away from any other cats on the moor."

"But I believe everything Wind Runner has to say," Slate responded. "And she has a lot to say about you—all of it good."

Gray Wing was so stunned by the she-cat's words that he didn't know what to say. Wading out of the shallow pond, he gave each paw in turn a shake. "I . . . uh . . . must get back to the hollow," he mumbled. "They need me there."

"Really?" Slate jumped gracefully out of the water and stood on the bank by his side. "When we met the other day, you gave me the impression that you had mixed feelings about your home in the hollow."

Gray Wing looked at her, confused. "What do you mean?"

"You just didn't seem very settled," Slate replied with a shrug. "I mean, what were you doing wandering around on the moor by yourself at night, anyway?"

Her questions disconcerted Gray Wing. "If you must know," he meowed defensively, "I was surveying the land."

Slate let out a surprised *mrrow* of laughter. "You were what?"

"To find a good spot for a battle," Gray Wing explained. A moment later, not knowing quite how it happened, he found the whole story pouring out: how One Eye had driven Clear Sky out of the forest, and how Gray Wing and his friends had planned to lure him out onto the moor and confront him. "It was my plan, and I had to make sure it was going to work," he finished. "I just hadn't counted on meeting angry foxes in pain. . . ."

As she listened, Slate dried her fur on some of the long

grasses that grew beside the pool. "It sounds like a great plan," she mewed as she weaved in and out among the stems. "I'd like to help."

"No!" Gray Wing protested immediately. "This isn't your problem. We can't involve you in the fighting."

"Who said anything about fighting?" Slate asked. "But you'll need help from Wind Runner and Gorse Fur, and they surely won't want to leave their kits alone. If they're willing to fight One Eye, then I'll look after the kits. You *had* thought about their kits' safety, hadn't you?"

"Yes, I had!" Gray Wing spluttered, realizing that he had not. "I'd be so grateful if you'd take care of them while we fight," he went on, his head hanging in shame. "Will I ever have any reason to stop thanking you for your help? I don't seem very capable without you. . . ."

"Of course you are!" Slate reassured him. She made her way over to him and touched his shoulder with her tail-tip. "Which cat came up with the whole plan to defeat One Eye? You! Come on," she continued. "I'll walk with you back to your hollow—you know, that place you love so much."

Gray Wing felt curiously peaceful as he and Slate padded side by side back toward the camp. Their paw steps matched so well, and he felt as though he'd known her for seasons.

I may as well tell her everything, he thought.

"If all goes well in the battle," he began, "I may have the chance to explore other ideas. To try living somewhere else, even if it does mean being on my own for a while."

Slate did not pause in her steady pacing across the moor,

but she drew closer to him so that their pelts brushed. "You don't have to be alone," she murmured, her eyes glimmering in the moonlight.

Gray Wing felt his belly lurch. *Does she mean what I think she means?* But he couldn't reply, because no words seemed big enough to express what he was feeling.

How did I come to rely so heavily on a cat I've only just met?

CHAPTER 22

Thunder woke to the first faint light of dawn creeping through the entrance of his den. He stumbled to his paws and ventured into the hollow, pausing to arch his back in a good, long stretch. The air was clear and cold; every leaf and blade of grass was edged with frost.

Leaf-bare is almost here, he thought.

When he had given his pelt a quick grooming, Thunder was ready to head out to visit Wind Runner and River Ripple, to ask for their help in the fight against One Eye. *I don't have much hope that Wind Runner will join us,* he thought doubtfully. *She made it clear that she wants to be left alone. And I'll leave the forest cats for now,* he decided, remembering how any cat who crossed the border had been attacked when Clear Sky first took over. One Eye was likely to be even more aggressive in guarding his territory. *Maybe I can work out how to speak to some of them when our plans are in place.*

As he padded toward the edge of the hollow, Thunder was surprised to see Gray Wing perched on Tall Shadow's rock. He veered over to talk to him.

"Can you see anything?" Thunder called from the foot of the rock.

Gray Wing shook his head. "Everything's quiet."

For a moment the two cats fell silent, but Thunder felt too disturbed not to say what was in his heart. "Why did you leave, Gray Wing?" he blurted out. "I need you!"

Gray Wing narrowed his eyes as he gazed down at Thunder. "You don't need me," he responded. "If you keep believing that you do, it will hold you back."

I wonder if that's true, Thunder thought uncomfortably, not wanting to accept his kin's words. "But you'll stay now, won't you?" he asked.

Gray Wing twitched one ear, gazing far out across the moor. There was something in his eyes that Thunder couldn't read. Before he could respond, Lightning Tail popped out of his den and bounded over to Thunder's side. "I'm coming with you," he announced roughly.

Thunder suppressed a hiss of irritation. *Why does Lightning Tail think I'll want him with me, after the way he treated Star Flower?* But then Thunder reminded himself how often Lightning Tail had been there for him. *Our bond is too important for us to fight now. Lightning Tail will come around. When he gets to know Star Flower better, he'll realize his suspicions are unfounded.* "Okay," he mewed.

Gray Wing looked down again from his perch. "You'd better get going. The sooner we know who will help us with this, the better."

Thunder's thoughts were still with Gray Wing as he headed across the moor with Lightning Tail by his side. He didn't feel like talking, and it was Lightning Tail who broke the silence in a disbelieving tone. "You're not even going to apologize?"

Surprised, Thunder halted and stared at him. "Apologize? For what?"

"You know very well," Lightning Tail retorted with a lash of his tail. "You left the group vulnerable when you went off . . . cavorting with that *rogue*."

Anger began to swell up inside Thunder. "Don't call her that!" he hissed.

"Why? That's what she is," Lightning Tail asserted. "And you'd better remember that. She's not one of us."

Now Thunder had to make a massive effort to hold on to his anger and not lash out at his denmate. "What do you mean by 'one of us'?" he asked. "Being one of the original cats from the mountains, or being born in the hollow?"

Lightning Tail sputtered for a moment, as if he hadn't expected that question. "Well . . . yes, that's a pretty good definition," he managed to say at last.

"Then I'm not 'one of us,' either," Thunder spat. "I was born in the Twolegplace! My mother was a rogue, and I would have been one, too, if Gray Wing hadn't taken me in."

"But that's different—" Lightning Tail protested.

"Maybe that's why Star Flower and I have such a deep connection," Thunder went on, dismissing his friend's words with a flick of his tail. "In our hearts, we both know that we're outsiders."

"That's ridiculous!" Lightning Tail exclaimed. "You only just met her. And you're not an outsider."

"I don't want to talk about this anymore," Thunder meowed, sinking his claws into the ground to stop himself from catching Lightning Tail with a blow over the ear. "I'm leader of the group, and I'm certainly capable of deciding who to spend my time with."

There was a hurt expression in Lightning Tail's eyes. "So that's how it is, then? Other cats' opinions don't count for anything?"

Thunder didn't respond, but merely turned his back and stalked on across the moor. He realized that Lightning Tail hadn't followed him, and for a moment he was afraid that his denmate would go home. Then he heard a patter of paw steps as Lightning Tail ran to catch up and padded along just behind him.

Gray Wing had told Thunder where to find the rocky outcrop in which Wind Runner had made her den. But before he reached it, he spotted Wind Runner herself beside a small pool, slinking out from a patch of reeds with a mouse in her jaws. She stopped and waited for Thunder and Lightning Tail to approach her, but there was no welcome in her eyes.

"What do you want?" she asked, setting down her prey.

"We're sorry to bother you," Thunder meowed, dipping his head politely. "How are your kits doing?"

"Better," Wind Runner replied tersely. "But we're seeing more and more sick prey."

"That's partly why I'm here," Thunder told her. "You remember the Blazing Star plant the spirit-cats told us about? We think it might be a cure for the sickness."

Wind Runner's eyes stretched wide. "You think you've found a cure? Well, who's gone to look for the flower?"

"Some of our cats tried yesterday, but One Eye attacked them," Thunder began. "And we haven't tried again yet."

"Why not?" Wind Runner snapped.

"Because we have another problem," Thunder told her. "We've come to ask for your help."

Wind Runner was instantly suspicious. "What for?"

"That evil rogue cat, One Eye, has driven Clear Sky out of his group," Thunder explained. "We have a plan to defeat him, but we'll need all the help we can get."

Wind Runner's eyes seemed to glaze over. "You want my help in battle to aid . . . Clear Sky? Are you mouse-brained?" Thunder opened his jaws to start giving her reasons, but the brown she-cat cut him off with a snarl. "No."

"But remember what the spirit-cats said," Thunder urged her. "Unite or die! We need to help each other."

"No," Wind Runner repeated, her tone implacable. "I left your group to protect my family, and that's what I'm doing. We have a perfectly nice life here."

Thunder narrowed his eyes with a glance at the small mouse that was her only piece of prey. "Is your life really all that nice?" he asked. "We've been struggling to find prey that isn't sick, and there are far more cats with us than with you."

"Then you have more mouths to feed," Wind Runner retorted.

"Maybe. But are your kits actually getting enough to eat?"

Wind Runner twitched her ears. "I've given you my answer," she rasped. "You can go now. But you can come back with news of the flower."

Lightning Tail took a pace forward. "So you're willing to take the group's wisdom, but do nothing for us in return?"

The she-cat gave him a cold look from baleful, yellow eyes. "I lost two kits when I was with your group," she reminded him. "Surely you owe me a few scraggly flowers?" Picking up her prey, she stalked away.

Thunder let out a sigh as he watched her go. *That went well.*

With a dissatisfied shrug, he headed toward the river, hoping he would have better luck with River Ripple. "You might want to be a bit more tactful this time," he told Lightning Tail after a few moments. "We really need River Ripple's help in the battle, and a more friendly approach might work better."

Lightning Tail didn't respond.

"Really?" Thunder's exasperation burst out of him. "We're not speaking now?"

His denmate was quiet for a couple of heartbeats longer. "My loyalty is to the group now," he mewed at last. "Not to you."

I can't believe it! Thunder stared at him. "Are you really abandoning me over a she-cat?" he demanded. "What? Are you jealous?"

Rage flared in Lightning Tail's eyes. Without warning, he swiped at Thunder's face and followed up the blow by leaping on him, tackling him to the ground. The two toms wrestled together among the dried leaves and the cold, frostbitten grass.

"I don't need your approval," Thunder snarled through gritted teeth as he thrust his hind paws into Lightning Tail's belly. "I've led the group well so far, haven't I?"

For an answer Lightning Tail rolled Thunder over and landed on his back, wrapping his forelegs around his neck. "You're falling right into that rogue's trap!" he growled. "And you're the only one who can't see it!"

"Well, if it's a trap, what does she want from me?" Thunder asked, straining to throw Lightning Tail off.

"I don't know," Lightning Tail admitted. "But ever since I first saw her, I've known she was up to something. And whatever it is, it's not good." Abruptly he gave up the fight, springing to his paws and giving his pelt a shake before he stalked off toward the river. "This is stupid," he meowed as he went. "We should be concentrating on finding cats to help us in the battle."

Thunder jumped up and followed him. "Does that mean you'll stop nagging me about Star Flower?" he asked.

Lightning Tail didn't look at him. "Just come on," he hissed.

The sun had risen by the time the river came into sight, dazzling on the water. Thunder headed for the stepping-stones, but as he jumped out onto the first one he realized that Lightning Tail had halted at the water's edge with a bewildered expression.

"We have to cross the water?" he asked. "I didn't know that."

"Yes," Thunder replied. "River Ripple lives on that island. He's a bit weird. . . . He doesn't mind the water."

Lightning Tail nodded grimly. Water was washing over the stepping-stones, and as he followed Thunder he winced at the touch of it on his pads. Thunder didn't like getting his feet wet, either, but he didn't say anything. *I'm not going to let Lightning Tail hear me complain.*

Reeds grew around River Ripple's island, and the interior was screened by bushes that grew close to the water's edge. The reeds made a soft sound as they brushed together, and with the rushing of the river in his ears Thunder had a flash of understanding why River Ripple loved this spot. But the understanding vanished when he had to push his way through the tough stalks of the reeds and get his paws muddy to climb out onto a narrow strip of grass that edged the river. Lightning Tail followed with an annoyed hiss, shaking each of his paws in turn.

"Not very subtle, are you?"

Thunder jumped at the voice and looked up to see that River Ripple had emerged from the bushes and was watching the two cats with amusement glinting in his eyes. His long-furred pelt shone silver in the sunlight.

"You're as bad as a pack of dogs," he went on. "I saw you coming ages ago. Well, what can I do for you?"

Thunder dipped his head respectfully before he settled down and explained to River Ripple about the Blazing Star. Meanwhile Lightning Tail sat silently and washed his paws.

River Ripple nodded understandingly when Thunder had finished. "And what else?" he asked.

How does he know there's something else? Thunder wondered. "One Eye has driven Clear Sky out of the forest, and taken over his group," he meowed. "Gray Wing has a plan to defeat him, but we need help. Will you join us to drive One Eye away?"

River Ripple paused thoughtfully before replying. "I will," he agreed at last. "But I have to warn you—I've had problems with One Eye in the past, and believe me, he won't back down. It's not a question of driving him out; you'll have to kill him."

"We're prepared for that," Thunder told him, doing his best to hide his dismay. "That's what Gray Wing's plan will do."

River Ripple nodded, a grim look in his eyes. "If Gray Wing is behind it, I'll be a part of it, and I'll see that my cats help, too."

"We were thinking of reaching out to some of the cats in the forest," Thunder went on, pleased to have such a formidable cat as River Ripple on their side. "They can't all want One Eye to be their leader. But I can't think of a good way to get to them without running into One Eye and his rogues. Do you have any ideas about that?"

River Ripple shook his head. "Don't even think about it," he advised. "If One Eye found out that any of the forest cats spoke to you, he'd make them suffer. And he'd enjoy doing it," he finished.

Thunder had to accept that the older cat was probably right. He thanked River Ripple, and was saying good-bye when the silver tom's gaze turned serious.

"Be careful, young one," River Ripple mewed solemnly.

"What do you mean?" Thunder asked, puzzled.

"I think you know," River Ripple responded. "I've told Gray Wing many times: I know everything."

Bemused, Thunder thanked him again, then padded away,

shaking his head as he crossed the stepping-stones. *If I thought I understood anything this morning, clearly I was wrong. . . .*

The two cats traveled back to their camp in silence. Thunder remembered that Acorn Fur was still in One Eye's camp, and tried not to worry too much about her. She was strong; Thunder hoped she was taking care of herself. *Maybe that's why Lightning Tail is so touchy; he's upset about his sister.*

But still, seeing Lightning Tail stalking ahead, Thunder couldn't help feeling hurt. He couldn't understand why his friend didn't trust him enough to make his own decisions. *I always felt I could count on him. Why is this turning him away, of all things?*

Thunder was feeling like things couldn't get any worse, until he arrived back at the camp and spotted Star Flower at the bottom of the hollow, talking to Tall Shadow. At the sight of her, Lightning Tail let out a disgusted snort and ran off.

Thunder's heart started to race again as Star Flower bounded up the slope to his side.

"I'm so glad to see you," she purred, brushing against his side. "I was disappointed when Tall Shadow said you weren't here."

"Well, I'm here now," Thunder meowed, then winced, feeling annoyed with himself for sounding so stupid.

"I've got good news for you!" Star Flower announced, her green eyes shining. "I found a small patch of Blazing Star growing near the river. Not many flowers, but enough to treat the sick. And no need to cross the Thunderpath!" After a pause when Thunder didn't respond, she asked,

"Why don't you look more excited?"

Thunder swallowed hard. *Why* aren't *I more excited?* Star Flower had just given him an amazing piece of news, yet he found himself reacting with suspicion, just like Lightning Tail might. *Could Star Flower really be up to something? Or has Lightning Tail ruined this for me by putting his own doubts into my head?*

"It's great news," he told Star Flower hastily, hoping she wouldn't be upset with him. "Can you take me there?"

"I thought you'd never ask," Star Flower meowed with a whisk of her tail. "Come on."

As Thunder followed her out of the camp, he glanced over his shoulder to see Lightning Tail staring after him with a look of disapproval. It gave him an odd feeling of satisfaction to be showing his trust in Star Flower.

"I spent some time with Gray Wing's kits," Star Flower told him as they padded side by side across the moor toward the river. "Owl Eyes and Pebble Heart, and the injured one, Sparrow Fur. They're very cute."

"Yes, they're great kits," Thunder agreed. "I can't believe One Eye would hurt her like that! You know One Eye?"

Star Flower nodded. "We've met."

"Then you know what he's like. He's even driven Clear Sky out of his own camp! But we're not going to stand for that," Thunder went on confidingly. "We're making a plan to corner him on the open moor. If you want, you could really help. . . ."

CHAPTER 23

❧

Clear Sky stretched his jaws in a massive yawn and blinked in the strengthening dawn light. The sky above the hollow was the clear blue of a robin's egg, and on the horizon a rosy flush showed where the sun would rise.

He was sitting at the mouth of Gray Wing's den. Around him other cats were emerging, getting ready for the new day. For a couple of moments Clear Sky watched Turtle Tail's three kits, grooming themselves just a few paw steps away. Pebble Heart was taking particular care with Sparrow Fur's injuries, and Clear Sky's heart warmed toward the wise little cat.

Nearer the center of the hollow, Lightning Tail was crouched over a mouse, devouring it in hungry bites, while his gaze remained fixed on Thunder and Star Flower, their heads close together near the foot of Tall Shadow's rock. Dislike and distrust were rising from him, as clear as the scent of warm prey.

Clear Sky wasn't sure if it had been wise for the moorland cats to allow Star Flower to stay overnight in the hollow. She had taken Thunder to find the herb that would heal the sickness, but to every cat's disappointment the flowers she had found weren't actually Blazing Star, only another plant that looked vaguely like it. Star Flower herself had seemed as upset as any cat, but Clear Sky couldn't be certain that her feelings were genuine.

But Thunder still trusts her, he thought. *That cat is smitten!*

Thunder and Star Flower had stayed talking together far into the night, until Tall Shadow had emerged from her den, tired and irritable, and told them to shut up and let other cats get some sleep.

Clear Sky's feelings of amusement faded as he realized that none of the waking cats were coming to speak to him, or even acknowledging his presence. Not even the cats he had known all his life, had traveled down from the mountains with. *I feel like an outsider . . . because it's what I am.*

Finally Gray Wing padded over to him. "How are you feeling?" he asked. "Are you ready to challenge One Eye to a fight on the moor?"

Clear Sky didn't need to be reminded. *Do I have to tell my brother that I feel sick to the bottom of my stomach?* The knowledge that he was putting his life at risk meant that he hadn't eaten since the previous sunrise.

Thunder and Lightning Tail had told him that River Ripple would support them, but they weren't sure about Wind Runner. And they hadn't even tried to talk to the forest cats. Clear Sky's heart ached at the thought that he couldn't rely on the help of the very cats he was trying so hard to protect.

They can't want One Eye as their leader. Are they all such cowards? Then he remembered One Eye's rogues, and admitted to himself that perhaps his own cats didn't have much choice. They could very well be prisoners in the forest. A moment later, a less comforting thought crept into his mind. *But surely they could escape if they tried hard enough.*

"Has it all been worth it?" he asked Gray Wing despondently.

His brother's eyes widened with shock. "I can't believe you're asking that!" he meowed. "Hasn't it always been worth it?"

Clear Sky had no answer to that question, and he silently rose to his paws and padded beside his brother to the edge of the hollow. Tall Shadow leaped down from her rock to join them, and the other cats gathered around. Clear Sky realized that the only cats missing were Holly, still lying sick in her den, Cloud Spots, and Jagged Peak, who, despite warnings about the sickness, hardly ever left Holly's side.

"Good-bye," Tall Shadow mewed, dipping her head to Clear Sky. "And good luck."

The other cats joined in, repeating her words and calling out their good wishes.

"You can do it, Clear Sky!"

"Rip that crazy cat's pelt off!"

"Good luck!"

"We'll be with you!"

Their enthusiasm warmed Clear Sky and put strength into his muscles. But as he took the first paw step out of the camp, he realized there was one more thing he had to do. He wanted to see Holly, to remind himself why he was doing this.

Turning back, he pushed his way gently through the crowd of cats and bounded across the hollow to her den. Holly lay on her side in her mossy nest, her belly bulging with her growing kits. Jagged Peak crouched beside her; his tail lashed with concern and his eyes were dark with trouble.

Cloud Spots was there, too, encouraging Holly to eat some tansy. "Holly, you have to hold on," he meowed. "This should help until we can get the Blazing Star. The sooner we can get rid of One Eye, the sooner we can get safely across the Thunderpath to fetch some."

"It won't be long now," Jagged Peak promised. "You'll be fine, Holly, and so will our kits."

Clear Sky couldn't tell whether his younger brother actually believed what he was saying.

Holly had a faraway look in her eyes, and didn't seem to hear what Cloud Spots or Jagged Peak said. As Clear Sky gazed at her—knowing he couldn't come closer than the entrance to the den—he noticed the sores on her body and the way her chest heaved with short, panting breaths.

This can't go on, he thought.

Turning away with his resolve renewed, he halted as a cracked, broken voice called out, "Good luck, Clear Sky."

Glancing back over his shoulder, Clear Sky saw Holly's gaze trained on him. Then slowly her eyes closed as she winced in a fresh onset of pain.

Clear Sky felt his motivation surge. He could save Holly. He could save all the sick cats. *Let's do this!*

Clear Sky left the den to rejoin Gray Wing, Thunder, and

Tall Shadow. The rest of the cats drew back respectfully.

"I'll go to the edge of the forest and call out to One Eye," Clear Sky began. "I'll lure him to the spot on the moor that you drew in the earth, Gray Wing." With a glance at the sky, he went on, "Let's say that I'll be there at sunhigh. Can you be waiting, hidden?"

Gray Wing nodded. "We'll be there."

"And we'll send the same message to Wind Runner and River Ripple," Tall Shadow added. "We can only hope that Wind Runner has had a change of heart."

"If we can't summon enough cats," Thunder asked worriedly, "how will we get a message to you to abandon the plan?"

"You don't need to," Clear Sky replied, summoning all his determination. "I'm not abandoning this plan. Whatever it takes, this is the last day that One Eye draws breath." *Or maybe it's my last day. . . .* He gave his pelt a vigorous shake, refusing to think about that. "We're doing this!" he asserted. "The only failure is not to try, and I've never stopped trying."

Gray Wing gave him an approving purr and touched noses with him. "We won't abandon you," he promised.

Clear Sky drew himself up and headed for the forest with a final flick of his tail. *What if this is the end?* he asked himself. *What if this is the last time I see these cats? Would I be satisfied if my life ended today?* He drew a deep breath. *At least Gray Wing and I are reconciled.*

It took an effort not to glance back at the hollow, but he forced himself to keep looking ahead, facing his fate.

* * *

Crouching behind a rock, Clear Sky peered cautiously at the edge of the forest, only a few fox-lengths in front of him. Although the lush growth of greenleaf had died back, leaving the trees gray and bare, there were very few traces of the burned patches from the fire.

But Clear Sky's satisfaction at seeing the end of the devastation was short-lived. It didn't take him long to spot deep claw scratches on several trees, forming the round shape that he had already seen on Petal's pads.

Is One Eye leaving his mark everywhere now? he asked himself, ashamed to remember that although he'd never etched anything into the trees, he'd left his own mark all around the borders of his territory not long ago. Now he gagged at the wave of One Eye's stench that rolled toward him out of the trees, and stiffened at the thought that One Eye could be hiding somewhere in the undergrowth, already aware of Clear Sky's presence.

Stop that! Clear Sky told himself, giving his pelt a shake. *If you imagine One Eye squatting under every bush, you'll never dare do anything.* He let out a sigh, wondering when this vile invasion would end.

Today, he reminded himself.

Tucking his paws underneath him, Clear Sky waited. Sooner or later, he knew, one of his own cats would appear on a patrol. *I just hope they're alone, and not with One Eye's rogues,* he thought gloomily.

"Clear Sky! Clear Sky, is that you?"

A tremor of anticipation ran through Clear Sky at the sound of Acorn Fur's voice. Taking a breath, he distinguished her scent, but it took a moment to spot her crouching underneath a thick clump of bracken at the very edge of the trees.

"Clear Sky?" she called out again, her voice low and urgent.

For a heartbeat Clear Sky hesitated. *Is she luring me out so that One Eye and his rogues can finish me off?* Then he took a calming breath. He would never believe that the brave chestnut brown she-cat could be such a traitor. *I trust her completely, even though she had only just joined my group when One Eye took over.*

Pressing himself to the ground and using the long grass for cover, Clear Sky crawled forward until he could join Acorn Fur beneath the bracken.

"Oh, Clear Sky, I was so relieved when I picked up your scent!" the young cat mewed, trembling as she pressed herself against his side. "It's terrible here with One Eye. Every heartbeat I'm scared he's going to claw me."

"Then why stay?" Clear Sky found it hard to feel sympathetic. "Escape; go back to the hollow on the moor. You could have come with us when One Eye attacked us by the Thunderpath."

Acorn Fur's eyes widened and her trembling was replaced by the stiffness of fury. "You don't imagine I *want* to be here?" she demanded. "I'm only staying to see if I can find some way to help you. I've been volunteering for border patrols so that I might see you or some cat to take a message to you."

"I'm sorry." Clear Sky gave her ear a quick lick. "And have you found out anything?" he added hopefully.

Pacified by his apology, Acorn Fur shook her head. "No, but I'll keep trying." Nervously she angled her ears back toward the forest. "I'm with a patrol now," she murmured. "They must be somewhere around. We don't have much time. Tell me what I can do."

"There is something." Clear Sky couldn't believe his luck, finding a faithful cat like Acorn Fur in the middle of his enemies. "I'm going to fight One Eye," he explained in a rapid undertone. "I need you to take my challenge to him. Claws out—a fight to the death. Just him and me, one-on-one. Tell him I'll be waiting for him on the moor at sunhigh."

"Are you mouse-brained? You can't fight One Eye alone!" Acorn Fur protested, horror in her eyes. "He'll claw you to pieces. I'm not taking a message like that."

"I won't be alone," Clear Sky reassured her. "The other moorland cats are going to help, and River Ripple, and maybe Wind Runner and Gorse Fur. You'll have to lie to One Eye," he added. "Do you think you can convince him?"

Acorn Fur took a deep breath, bracing herself. "I'll do anything to get rid of that mange-ridden excuse for a cat," she promised.

"Acorn Fur!" A harsh voice, unknown to Clear Sky, rang out from deeper within the forest. "Where are you? Get your flea-bitten tail over here before I have to teach you a lesson."

Acorn Fur shuddered. "I've got to go. You can trust me, Clear Sky. I'll do my best."

Before Clear Sky could respond, she had vanished into the undergrowth.

"What have you been up to?" the same voice growled. "I can scent that flea-pelt Clear Sky. I hope you haven't been talking to him."

"Yes, I have." Acorn Fur's voice reached Clear Sky's ears, steady and undaunted. "And you can put your claws away. He gave me an important message to take to One Eye."

"What message?"

"I'll tell that to One Eye," Acorn Fur retorted. "And if you're not careful, I'll tell him you were nosing around in his *private* business."

No response followed, only the sound of retreating paw steps and the rustle of cats brushing through long grass. Clear Sky breathed a sigh of relief.

It's done. Now there's no going back.

CHAPTER 24

Sunhigh had almost come. In the cold, clear light of approaching leaf-bare, Thunder peered out at the expanse of the moor from behind an outcrop of rock. Lightning Tail crouched beside him on one side, but the space on the other side felt terribly empty.

Where is Star Flower? he wondered.

The golden tabby had promised to help him in the battle, but Thunder hadn't seen her since she left the hollow, telling him she was going to find some rogue recruits. Thunder shifted uneasily, hoping she hadn't run into trouble.

"Missing your precious Star Flower?" Lightning Tail asked, an edge to his voice.

"Don't start." Thunder let out a sigh. "Today is too important."

Lightning Tail was silent, a look of shame creeping over his face. "You're right. It's just . . . I don't want to see you get hurt."

Thunder turned to him, thankful that his best friend's hostility was fading. "Star Flower would never do anything to hurt me," he assured Lightning Tail, briefly resting his tail-tip on the younger cat's shoulder. "We understand each other!"

The twitch of Lightning Tail's whiskers told Thunder that his friend wasn't convinced, but to Thunder's relief he said nothing.

A soft paw step behind Thunder announced the arrival of Gray Wing. "Tall Shadow, Cloud Spots, and Shattered Ice are hiding in the hollow over there," he muttered, angling his ears toward a dip in the moor partly screened by gorse bushes. "Mud Paws and Mouse Ear are with them. And see that thorn tree over there?" he added with a purr. "Owl Eyes and Sparrow Fur are hiding in the branches—"

"What?" Thunder protested, stiffening. "They're only kits! They shouldn't be part of this!"

Gray Wing gave him a long look. "Have you tried controlling kits who are just about to be grown cats? I remember another kit with big paws who was keen to get involved in everything."

Thunder nodded, admitting that Gray Wing was right. *If I were their age, I'd want to help, too. At least Pebble Heart has stayed behind to care for Holly.*

"Jagged Peak and Dappled Pelt took the messages to River Ripple and Wind Runner," Gray Wing went on. "River Ripple said he'd keep watch on the riverbank, and Wind Runner . . . well, she didn't say no this time. We can only hope that she and Gorse Fur will come and do what they can to help."

Thunder glanced across the moor in the direction of the sandy dip and the rocks where Wind Runner lived, but he couldn't see any sign at all of approaching cats.

A gasp from Lightning Tail drew Thunder's attention and

he squinted into the bright sunlight. Clear Sky was padding into the center of the moor.

He's clever! Thunder thought admiringly as he watched his father's stride, self-assured yet wary. *No cat would ever know that he feels his friends all around him.*

Clear Sky reached the top of a small hillock, turned to face the forest, and sat down. Motionless, he waited.

Thunder realized that he was holding his breath as he gazed into the distance for the approach of One Eye. The sun beat down on his pelt. Beside him, Lightning Tail flicked his tail impatiently. "Where is he?" he muttered.

Movement flashed in the corner of Thunder's eye. Whirling around, he spotted One Eye. But the rogue hadn't come from the forest. Instead he exploded out of a nearby rabbit hole.

"The tunnels!" Gray Wing hissed in frustration. "Why didn't we think of those?"

"We should have known One Eye would do something sneaky," Thunder responded, all the hair on his pelt beginning to bristle.

Clear Sky spun around, but a heartbeat too late. One Eye's paw was already raking through the air, his claws tearing at Clear Sky's ear. Blood poured down Clear Sky's face, and he let out a screech of mingled pain and anger. Thunder saw him shake his head, trying to clear the blood from his eyes.

This is the worst possible start! Thunder thought.

He flexed his claws, digging them into the ground. All his instincts were shrieking at him to spring out from hiding and help his father, but Clear Sky had insisted that he wanted to fight One Eye alone for a few moments. "I want him to feel overconfident," he had explained.

Clear Sky lashed out at One Eye, striking a hard blow to the rogue's shoulder. One Eye countered by aiming for Clear Sky's throat, but Clear Sky leaped backward in time to avoid his slashing claws.

Then to Thunder's amazement One Eye drew back, padding around Clear Sky about a tail-length away from him. His words reached Thunder on the still air.

"You said you'd fight me, Clear Sky. Are you ready to die?"

Clear Sky's answer rang out. "There's only one cat who'll die today, and that's you."

One Eye let out a furious snarl and launched himself again at Clear Sky. For a few moments they tussled together on the grass. At first it was hard for Thunder to see which cat was winning, until a heartbeat later Clear Sky was lying on his back with his belly exposed. One Eye raised his paw to slice down through the soft flesh.

Now!

Thunder leaped out of his hiding place, raising his voice in a great yowl of defiance. That was the signal for the other cats to launch themselves at One Eye.

As he bounded over the springy moorland grass, Thunder saw Clear Sky scramble back onto his paws. He faced One Eye, hissing to distract him, but One Eye had heard Thunder's cry and spun around, gazing at the cats who were converging on him.

Yes, One Eye, we're coming! Thunder's paws skimmed the ground and he could sense Lightning Tail racing along at his shoulder and Gray Wing close behind. Cloud Spots was leading the other cats who had hidden behind the gorse bushes.

Beyond One Eye, Thunder spotted River Ripple, Dew, and Night charging across the moor from the river, and . . . *Yes, there's Wind Runner!* Gorse Fur was by her side, and as they closed in on One Eye, Clear Sky leaped aside to join them.

They must have left their kits with Slate. The thought flashed through Thunder's mind as he remembered what Gray Wing had told him about his nighttime encounter. *She sounds like a cat worth knowing.*

That fleeting thought distracted Thunder, and he caught his paw in a rabbit hole, hitting the ground hard and rolling over in a tangle of paws and tail.

Lightning Tail's voice rang out. "Thunder, look!"

Struggling to his paws, Thunder saw a line of cats rushing across the moor from the direction of the forest. He half expected to see some of Clear Sky's cats among them, but all of them were strangers to him. *One Eye's rogues! There are so many!*

The group of rogues divided as they drew closer. One section barreled between One Eye and River Ripple, while another darted into Wind Runner's path. Three cats raced toward Thunder and Lightning Tail, who were leading the moorland cats, and snarled at them with claws extended. Thunder had to veer to one side, confusing the cats who were pelting up behind him. They all stumbled to a halt, panting, as the rogue cats hissed in their faces.

"Get out of here!" Thunder responded to the hissing with a hostile growl. "This isn't your fight!"

The rogues didn't move. Thunder's glance darted over to One Eye, who had leaped up onto a rock and was watching with sardonic satisfaction in his single eye. Thunder and his cats were being held back by the rogues. Thunder couldn't imagine how their plan had gone so wrong.

Did One Eye know that we would be in hiding to help Clear Sky?

One Eye let out a *mrrow* of harsh laughter. "Did you really think you could get the better of me?" he asked, his voice filled with mockery. "Oh, daughter dear, won't you show yourself?"

A golden tabby cat broke away from the back of the crowd of rogues. *No . . . it can't be! Star Flower . . .* Thunder stared in horror as the beautiful rogue leaped up beside her father.

Her father? I don't believe it! Thunder felt his mouth go dry and his heart begin to beat faster with shock. He couldn't even look at Lightning Tail. Guilt crashed over him; his head spun, and for a heartbeat the sky darkened.

"Thunder." Gray Wing's voice spoke from somewhere by his side, heavy with sorrow. "You've been betrayed."

CHAPTER 25

Gray Wing could hardly believe that his plans had been so utterly torn apart. *How could I have let my cats down so badly?* He felt even greater pain at the shattered look on Thunder's face.

But there was no time to think about that now. The rogue cats were clustering around him and his denmates, hissing and showing their claws. In the lead was a raw-boned tabby tom with one shredded ear. His jaws gaped, showing snaggly teeth, and his claws worked eagerly as he pressed forward. *They're trying to scare us—and they're succeeding! We're way outnumbered.*

Then a screech came from the branches of the thorn tree, and in a blur of movement Owl Eyes and Sparrow Fur hurled themselves at the crowd of rogues.

No! Panic gripped Gray Wing's limbs. *This is too dangerous for kits!*

Then he saw that their brave leap had worked. Startled, the rogues staggered back; the distraction was just enough for Gray Wing and the others to dart away.

"Follow me!" River Ripple yowled with a wave of his tail.

Streaking across the moor, he led the cats toward the river. Gray Wing glanced over his shoulder and saw that the rogues weren't bothering to follow.

Why should they? he asked himself, tasting the bitterness of defeat. *They've chased us off.*

River Ripple leaped down from the riverbank onto the narrow strip of pebbles where, not long ago, Gray Wing had lain in wait for a vole. Now he shuddered at making his escape so close to the water.

Once all the cats had jumped down, River Ripple halted, giving them a moment to catch their breath. His chest heaving, Gray Wing glanced around to make sure all his cats had made it. The two kits were there, he noticed with relief, and all the others except for Wind Runner and Gorse Fur. *And Clear Sky himself,* Gray Wing realized, remembering his last glimpse of his brother surrounded by snarling rogues. *Oh, please let him be alive.*

The cats huddled together on the pebbles, gazing at one another with wide eyes. "What are we going to do?" Jagged Peak asked. "Clear Sky is still out there. We can't leave him!"

River Ripple shouldered his way through the cluster of cats and headed upstream. "Come on! This way!" he called.

Gray Wing followed, the pebbles feeling cold and wet beneath his paws. The current sucked at the edge, and sometimes the strip of solid ground was only wide enough for the cats to pass in single file. *This had better be worth it,* he thought as he struggled to keep his balance on the slick stones.

Finally River Ripple paused at the mouth of a tunnel in the bank. "This will take us back onto the moor," he meowed.

Tall Shadow balked at the entrance, gazing down into

the gaping darkness. "There could be anything living down there," she objected.

"It was a badger set, but the badgers are long gone," River Ripple responded. "You'll have to trust me. Do you want to save Clear Sky or not?"

Without waiting for a reply, he headed into the tunnel. Tall Shadow shrugged and followed, with the rest of the cats hard on her paws.

In the first few tail-lengths, Gray Wing could see white tree roots interlacing above his head, holding up the roof of the tunnel, but soon the light from the entrance faded and he padded along in darkness. He could feel damp soil beneath his paws, and smell earth all around him, and the scent of Tall Shadow just ahead of him.

In the lead, River Ripple was moving swiftly, passing a side tunnel with no hesitation. Gray Wing began to feel the familiar ache in his chest as he forced himself to keep up. He began to feel like he had been loping along forever in the darkness. *Surely Clear Sky will be dead before we can get to him!*

Then he realized that a faint light was filtering into the tunnel from somewhere ahead, and he could make out Tall Shadow and River Ripple in front of him. The light grew until it became a wide circle of daylight. *We're almost there!* Gray Wing thought thankfully.

At the tunnel entrance, River Ripple halted. "We need to be careful," he mewed softly. "Wait here while I see what's outside." He pressed himself flat to the ground and crept into the open.

Gray Wing could see him looking around; then he glanced back and beckoned with his tail. "You can come out," he told the others.

The rest of the cats followed him cautiously. Gray Wing saw that they had emerged in the middle of a gorse thicket. Peering through the branches, he looked around for Clear Sky, then drew in a gasp of horror at what he saw.

One Eye and the rogues had backed Clear Sky against a rock and were surrounding him, caterwauling insults and threats of what they would do to him.

"Mange-pelt! Fox dung–eater!"

"We'll spread your guts all over the moor!"

Each rogue in turn was padding up to him and aiming fierce kicks at his ribs with their hind legs.

Clear Sky was still on his paws, but just barely so, and Gray Wing feared that each kick might knock him over. Blood from his torn ear matted his pelt, but his eyes still blazed with defiance.

"We have to stop this, before they kill him," Gray Wing meowed.

A rustle among the branches announced the arrival of Wind Runner and Gorse Fur. "We waited for you," Wind Runner explained rapidly. "We knew you would come back. One Eye has been too busy torturing Clear Sky to worry about where you went. What should we do now?"

Gray Wing realized that the eyes of every cat had turned toward him. *I'd better come up with a really good plan,* he thought. The cold sun of leaf-bare was still high in the cloudless sky, shedding its brilliant light down on the moor. The beginnings of an idea stirred in Gray Wing's mind.

"We can use the sun to help us," he murmured, thinking aloud. "We need to get high up—maybe in the thorn tree where Sparrow Fur and Owl Eyes were hiding." More confidently as his plan took shape, he went on, "We'll climb into the tree and call out to One Eye. He'll come to investigate, peering up with the sun in his eyes. He won't be able to see that the tree is full of cats. And then we pounce!"

"Great plan!" Shattered Ice meowed warmly.

One by one the cats slid out of the gorse thicket and crept toward the tree, their bellies pressed to the ground as if they were stalking prey. When they reached it they climbed into the branches on the opposite side from One Eye and the rogues. As he clambered up, Gray Wing felt terribly exposed, and wished there were more leaves remaining to conceal the cats. But One Eye and his rogues were having too much fun tormenting Clear Sky to pay much attention to what was going on around them.

From his vantage point in the tree Gray Wing had a good view of Star Flower standing just outside the circle, watching as her father and the rogues attacked Clear Sky. He hoped that Thunder, crouching on the next branch, hadn't spotted her, but when he glanced at him, the shocked look on his young kin's face told him that he had seen everything.

"I'm sorry," Gray Wing murmured.

"It's fine." Thunder's voice was cold. "This just makes me more determined to defeat One Eye."

"Who's going to call out?" Wind Runner whispered, when all the cats had made it into the tree. "It needs to be a cat who One Eye hates almost as much as Clear Sky."

"That would be me," Sparrow Fur meowed.

"But you're only a kit," Dappled Pelt objected. "It's too dangerous."

"One Eye killed my father!" Sparrow Fur bared her teeth. "I'm doing this for Tom. *I'll* lure One Eye over here."

No cat argued any more. Gray Wing watched admiringly as Sparrow Fur bravely scrambled around the trunk of the tree and walked carefully out onto a branch. It trembled under her weight and she had trouble keeping her balance, but she never paused until she was in full view at the outer edge of the tree.

"Hey, One Eye!" she yowled. "Aren't you going to come and finish what you started? You were so stupid, letting me escape with Clear Sky! You'd like another fight with me, wouldn't you?" Gray Wing saw One Eye stiffen and slowly turn away from Clear Sky, who by now had slumped to the ground, his body writhing in agony. Yet he still kept trying to get to his paws and face his attackers. Gray Wing felt like his heart would crack in two at the sight of his brother in such pain.

He's so badly hurt. Even if we win the fight, will he survive?

"You and you!" One Eye snapped, pointing with his tail at a couple of the rogues. "Guard this piece of mangefur. The rest of you, follow me, and surround that tree!"

The rogues obeyed him, racing fluidly over the moor toward the thorn tree. When they were in position, One Eye followed more slowly. "Is that you, Sparrow Fur?" he snarled. "If you want a fight, I'll give you one you won't forget—because you'll be dead."

"Flea-pelt!" Sparrow Fur spat. Nimbly she leaped up to a higher branch, then one higher still, always moving into the sun.

His hunger for the fight blazing from his baleful eye, One Eye padded closer and closer to the tree, craning his neck upward to spot where Sparrow Fur had gone. He narrowed his eye against the bright rays of the sun.

"Now!" Gray Wing whispered.

On his word of command, the cats in the tree leaped down, pouncing on One Eye and the rogues nearest him. Yowls of shock and alarm rose into the air. Gray Wing saw most of the rogues streaking off across the moor, leaving only one or two to grapple with his cats.

"Cowards!" he snarled, though he was relieved to see so many of their enemies fleeing.

One of the rogues who had stayed was Star Flower. Confronting Thunder, she flashed out an angry paw, though as Thunder jerked backward her claws only riffled through his fur. Thunder raised his paw, claws extended, then froze for a heartbeat before dealing a raking blow down her side. Both cats snarled furiously and leaped at each other to tussle on the ground in a writhing bundle of fur.

Gray Wing couldn't go on watching; he had other things to worry about. With Lightning Tail and Cloud Spots on either side of him, he launched himself at One Eye. The rogue went limp and fell to the ground, but as soon as Gray Wing landed on top of him he exploded into movement, battering Gray Wing's belly with his hind paws.

Cloud Spots tried to get a grip on One Eye's throat, but the rogue twisted his head aside and fastened his teeth in Cloud Spots's shoulder. When Lightning Tail tried to grab the rogue from the other side, One Eye raked his claws over the young cat's ear.

It's like fighting three different cats! Gray Wing thought. He could feel his chest tightening with the effort as he struggled to get a grip on One Eye's wildly flailing body. He had never known a cat so hard to defeat.

At last Cloud Spots and Lightning Tail darted in from either side and managed to pin One Eye down. Gray Wing stood over him, panting, while One Eye glared up at him with his malevolent yellow eye.

Gray Wing raised a paw to slash One Eye's throat open and finish the fight. But before he could strike, he heard Thunder's voice raised in a furious yowl.

"He's mine!"

Thunder rushed over to One Eye, motioning Cloud Spots and Lightning Tail aside with a fierce gesture of his paw. He even waited for the rogue to regain his paws before launching himself at him. Screeching and snarling, the two cats rolled together on the ground in a flurry of teeth and claws.

A flash of movement alerted Gray Wing and he turned in time to block Star Flower as she threw herself toward the fight. "Get back!" he spat, following up the words with a hard kick to Star Flower's chest. She cringed back, whimpering.

That was for Thunder, Gray Wing thought with satisfaction.

Certain that Star Flower was no longer a threat, he turned back to the battle. Everything was suddenly quiet. Thunder, Lightning Tail, and Cloud Spots were standing over One Eye's unmoving body. His head lay at an awkward angle, his neck clearly broken.

"He's dead," Thunder meowed.

Star Flower let out a moan of grief and dragged herself across the ground to touch her nose to her father's. Watching her, Gray Wing's heart was almost touched. *Almost.*

"Get her away from there," Thunder ordered, his voice cold. "She doesn't deserve to grieve. Drive her out!"

CHAPTER 26

Thunder watched in silence as Star Flower padded over to him, her brilliant green gaze pleading. "Thunder, he's my father," she mewed. "Please let me say good-bye."

Thunder felt as if everything in him was frozen, like the icy peaks Gray Wing had told him about. "How interesting that you never mentioned that when we were together." He let out a snort of disgusted laughter. "But then, we were never 'together,' were we? It was all a lie."

Hurt flashed into Star Flower's eyes. *But it's for her father, not for me,* Thunder told himself. *I feel so stupid,* he thought, embarrassment flooding through him at the memory. And worst of all, he still felt something when he looked at her. It was a struggle to pretend that he no longer cared, though knowing how she had used him made it easier.

"Please listen to me, Thunder," Star Flower went on, taking another pace toward him, so that her sweet scent wreathed around him. "I *did* like you, truly. Meeting you by the four trees, and calling out to you on the moor. Taking you to the secret garden . . . that was all my idea."

"Like I'd believe that!" Thunder scoffed.

"It *was*. It was only after my father found out that I'd been spending time with you that he suggested I should use our closeness to find out what the other cats were doing." She looked down and studied her paws. "When I left you at the secret garden, One Eye was waiting for me. He'd been listening to us, and he sent me to follow you. I hid outside your camp and listened to what you were planning."

Thunder winced. *I even heard paw steps; I thought some cat was following me!* "So that's how One Eye came to be waiting for us beside the Thunderpath," he meowed. "And then you showed me a plant that was nothing like the Blazing Star. It was a trick to pump me for information."

Star Flower hung her head. "That's true. But I told you the truth when I said that the Blazing Star is a healing herb. You have to believe that."

"I believed every word you said," Thunder told her. "I was . . . I was . . ."

"What?" Star Flower asked encouragingly, looking up at him again.

"Tricked," Thunder replied, letting all the bitterness he felt seep into the one word. "And I won't let it happen again."

He turned his back on Star Flower, ignoring her as he saw Tall Shadow stepping forward with a commanding whisk of her tail. "Why are we standing here doing nothing?" she asked. "Now that One Eye has been defeated, we need to get the Blazing Star."

"You're right," Thunder agreed. *I do believe Star Flower when she says the Blazing Star heals. She has nothing to gain by lying now.*

"I'll lead an expedition to go across the Thunderpath to

fetch it," Tall Shadow announced briskly.

By now River Ripple and Wind Runner had padded over to where Clear Sky still lay bleeding on the grass. Cloud Spots and Dappled Pelt were bending over him, while Sparrow Fur and Owl Eyes dashed up with pawfuls of cobwebs and bunches of herbs in their jaws.

Gray Wing nodded at them, and then turned back to Tall Shadow. "And I'll come with you," Gray Wing added, padding up to her side.

"What about One Eye's rogues?" Shattered Ice asked. "They could still be lurking in the forest."

Tall Shadow swiveled her head, her gaze raking the moorland. None of the strangers One Eye had brought with him were in sight. "I doubt it," she meowed in reply to Shattered Ice. "They ran away pretty quickly when we ambushed their leader. It's my guess that we won't see so much as a tail-tip. And if I'm wrong . . ." She slid out her claws. "We'll deal with them."

"We'll come with you," Mouse Ear meowed, beckoning with his tail to Mud Paws. "Just in case. It'll feel good to do something for Holly."

Tall Shadow dipped her head to the big tabby tom. "Thank you," she responded, before setting off across the moor at the head of the patrol.

As she and Gray Wing headed toward the forest, Thunder felt a sudden panic at being left in charge. *What am I supposed to do now?* Desperately he ran after them. "Gray Wing, I need to know—" he began.

Gray Wing halted and turned toward him. "Do as your

heart tells you, Thunder," he mewed calmly. He stretched out his neck to touch noses with Thunder, his eyes warm and affectionate. "I trust you," he added, before hurrying after Tall Shadow.

Thunder watched the older cat—almost his father—walk away. He felt a twinge of sadness at the realization that Gray Wing didn't want to advise him anymore. But at the same time Gray Wing's faith in him had sent new energy flowing through his body.

Thunder turned back toward Clear Sky as Sparrow Fur and Owl Eyes ran over to him with even more cobwebs. Reassured that his injured father was receiving the best care possible, Thunder took a deep breath and turned back to where Star Flower was crouching over One Eye's body. A soft keening sound came from her. *How did something so beautiful come from something so ugly?* he asked himself, looking at the grotesquely sprawled limbs of the dead rogue. *One Eye was ugly inside and out. But Star Flower . . .*

Thunder paced slowly up to the golden tabby she-cat and stood beside her. "It's time for you to leave," he meowed quietly. "You're not welcome among any of our groups, and if you won't leave by yourself we'll have to make you."

Star Flower looked up at him, and seeing the despair in her eyes made Thunder feel as though a giant claw was piercing his heart. "Please," she whispered, "can't we at least bury him? Then I'll leave you alone and never bother you again."

Thunder hesitated, then gave her a curt nod. Leaping up onto a nearby rock, he cleared his throat and called the cats around him. "It's time to bury the dead," he announced when they had all gathered.

Sparrow Fur's eyes stretched wide with amazement. "Why would we give him the respect he would never have given any of us?" she demanded.

Thunder glanced over at River Ripple, Wind Runner, and Clear Sky, who had managed to sit up, looking shaky but determined. "It's because we're different from One Eye," he responded, "and we always have been."

The other leaders nodded their agreement.

"One Eye believed every cat was out for themselves," Clear Sky meowed. "But we believe that life is better for every cat when each of us acts for the greater good."

A murmur of approval rose from the crowd at Clear Sky's words. Thunder glanced around and picked out cats who seemed to have suffered least from their enemies' claws: Shattered Ice, Lightning Tail, and Night. "Come and help me dig the grave," he instructed, leaping down among them.

"I want to help, too," Star Flower mewed as Thunder led the way to the foot of the thorn tree where One Eye was lying.

With so many paws working together, it didn't take long to dig a hole deep enough to bury One Eye. Then Star Flower nudged his body into the hole and watched as the others covered him with earth and leaves.

When the task was finished, the cats who had gathered looked at one another uncertainly, murmuring together as if they weren't sure what to do now. *Should one of us say something?* Thunder wondered.

Then Star Flower stepped forward, raising her face to the sunshine. "To my father, a true ray of light," she mewed.

Thunder narrowly stopped himself from gaping, and heard scornful snorts of disbelief from one or two of the others. But no cat said anything.

River Ripple came to stand beside her, and dipped his head toward the grave. "One Eye was a survivor," he pronounced. "A cat like no other who will be missed by those who loved him."

Perfectly true, Thunder thought, admiring River Ripple's cleverness. *But it leaves an awful lot out!*

Star Flower stretched out a paw and laid it gently on her father's grave. For several heartbeats she remained motionless, her eyes closed. Then at last she opened her eyes again and slowly padded up to Thunder.

"Thank you," she whispered. "I won't trouble you anymore." She slipped past him and headed toward the forest.

Thunder stood with his back to her. A massive urge to turn and call her back crashed over him like a storm, and he had to fight with all his strength not to yield to it. When he finally couldn't fight anymore, he spun around to see that Star Flower had disappeared over the swell of the moor.

Meanwhile, River Ripple was rounding up his cats, while Wind Runner joined Gorse Fur. Cloud Spots helped Clear Sky to his paws and let him lean on his shoulder.

"I'll come with you back to the forest," Cloud Spots meowed. "No—don't argue. I don't want you collapsing halfway there."

"I'll come too," Shattered Ice offered. "Just in case there's trouble."

"And me!" Sparrow Fur bounced up enthusiastically.

As they set out, Clear Sky paused and looked back, his gaze traveling over the cats who had fought for him. "Thank you," he mewed. "Thank you, every cat. I'll never forget this."

Watching them go, Thunder realized that River Ripple had sidled up to him and was angling his ears toward the place where Star Flower had disappeared. His eyes were alight with a mixture of sympathy and amusement.

"Don't worry," he murmured. "There will be others."

Thunder felt his heart pounding hard in his chest. "Right," he meowed with a casual flick of his ears.

But while River Ripple padded away, Thunder couldn't tear his gaze away from the spot where he had last seen Star Flower.

I'm not so sure there will be others. . . .

CHAPTER 27

Clear Sky forged ahead, ignoring the pain of his wounds and the ache of exhaustion in his chest. His eagerness to return to the forest was growing with every paw step. Though he had only been away for a few days, it felt like a lifetime. He drank in the familiar forest scent and feasted his eyes on every tree and bush as he drew closer.

I haven't lived here very long, he thought, his spirits lifting. *But the forest has truly become my home.*

"Hey!" Cloud Spots, who was falling behind, called out to him. "Take it a bit slower! You're still hurt, and the forest isn't going anywhere."

But Clear Sky yearned to feel leaf-mold beneath his paws again, and to listen to the creak and rustle of branches above his head. And he was desperate to return to his camp, to find out what One Eye had done to his cats.

Shattered Ice quickened his pace to lope alongside him, with Sparrow Fur scampering behind. "So what now, Clear Sky?" he asked. "Don't you think you'll find life . . . uneventful without One Eye?"

Clear Sky glared at him. "Don't be such a mouse-brain!"

"I can just imagine you, curled up in your nest," Shattered Ice went on, a teasing look in his eyes. "Bored with hunting and training, and wishing you had One Eye back to liven things up a bit."

Clear Sky halted, feeling his shoulder fur beginning to rise. "Are you trying to be annoying?" he demanded. "Do you think I went through all this, nearly got my pelt ripped off, put you and your denmates in danger, just so that I could wish for that mangy excuse for a cat to come back again?"

Unbothered by his sharp tone, Shattered Ice let out a *mrrow* of laughter. "Sorry, Clear Sky. But at least I got you to slow down!"

Clear Sky heaved a deep sigh, unable to hide his amusement. "Thank you, Shattered Ice." The words welled up from deep within his heart. "Thank you for helping me to get my territory back. I know I haven't always been . . ." His voice trailed off as he failed to find the right words.

"It's okay," Shattered Ice meowed understandingly, as the two cats walked on more slowly toward the outskirts of the forest. "I've known you since you were a kit. Perhaps you haven't always made the right decisions, but I know who you truly are, deep inside. Maybe this fresh start will help you to remember that, too."

His words gave Clear Sky a lot to think about, but before he could respond, Shattered Ice halted again, beneath the boughs of the outlying trees. "Who's there?" he called sharply. "Come out and show yourself!"

Acorn Fur poked her head out cautiously from behind a tree,

relief flooding into her gaze as she saw who was approaching. "It's you!" she exclaimed, bounding out into the open. "You've come to save us!"

She ran up to Shattered Ice and touched noses with him, then with Cloud Spots. Clear Sky felt a prickle of annoyance in his pads that she had greeted the moorland cats and ignored him. *What am I, invisible or something?*

"Yes," he meowed. "One Eye is dead, and I've come to take back leadership of the forest cats."

Acorn Fur turned to him at last. "You'd better come quickly, then," she responded.

She whirled around and took off into the forest at a fast trot, not waiting to see whether the other cats were following her. Apprehension trickled down Clear Sky's spine like melting snow, and he exchanged a worried glance with Shattered Ice before heading after Acorn Fur.

The young she-cat was making for the clearing where Clear Sky had made camp, but before she reached it she veered off into the trees. A low moaning came from up ahead, making every hair on Clear Sky's pelt rise with horror.

Skirting a bramble thicket in Acorn Fur's paw steps, Clear Sky emerged into a small clearing. In front of him he saw Petal and the two kits, Birch and Alder, lying in a makeshift nest at the foot of an elder bush. All three of them had the bloated bellies, the sores on their skin, and the foam around their jaws that were the signs of the sickness. The moans were coming from Petal as she made pitiful efforts to lick and comfort the kits.

"What are they doing here?" Clear Sky asked, stunned.

"One Eye made them come," Acorn Fur mewed, her voice shaking with a mixture of pity and outrage. "He wouldn't let us help them. He posted a guard and said we should leave them here to die, because they weren't doing us any good." She almost broke down, beginning to tremble, then forced herself to continue. "I couldn't get here until today, when One Eye and his rogues left for the battle. Quick Water and I brought them water and food, but I'm afraid it's too late!"

"Maybe not." Cloud Spots shouldered his way past Clear Sky and rushed over to the sick cats. "Tall Shadow and Gray Wing have gone to fetch the Blazing Star from the other side of the Thunderpath. We must find tansy, quickly, to use until they return."

There was a rustle in the undergrowth as Shattered Ice, Acorn Fur, and Sparrow Fur darted off immediately to find the herb.

Clear Sky's legs felt shaky as he padded forward and stood looking down at Petal. As if his scent or the sound of movement had alerted her, she stirred, and her clouded eyes focused on him. "Clear Sky!" she whispered through cracked lips. "You came!"

Crouching beside the nest, Clear Sky lowered his head close to Petal's. "Of course I came," he murmured. "I couldn't let that rogue—"

"I knew you would come!" Petal interrupted, her voice suddenly sounding stronger. "Of course you would! I've always been able to count on you, Clear Sky, ever since . . ." Her voice faded, the brief flash of strength ebbing away. Her eyes clouded again.

"Petal!" Clear Sky mewed urgently.

He could see the huge effort Petal was making to focus on him again. "I have to get better. . . ." she croaked. "I want to help you, Clear Sky . . . to repay all you've done for me!"

As she spoke the last words her eyes seemed to fix on something in the distance. Her body gave a massive shudder, and went limp.

"Petal!" Clear Sky called out, sickness rising in his belly.

There was no response.

Cloud Spots padded up with Acorn Fur just behind him, a bunch of tansy in her jaws. He gave Petal a brief sniff and shook his head. "I'm sorry, Clear Sky. She's gone." As Clear Sky dug his claws into the ground, rigid with grief, the older tom continued, "She went untreated for too long. The kits are younger, more able to fight it. There's hope for them still."

"When we brought Petal the food she wouldn't eat it," Acorn Fur mewed, setting her herbs down beside the nest. "She took one bite and gave the rest to the kits."

"They weren't even hers." Clear Sky's voice was bleak. "But she was dedicated to them, right up to the end." He was still struggling to accept that he had lost Petal, the cat who had given him unfailing support from the first time they met. *I didn't deserve her.*

"We should bury her . . . *quickly*," Cloud Spots meowed. They covered Petal's body with leaves so that the sickness would not spread. Then with the help of Shattered Ice, who had also returned with tansy, Acorn Fur gently lifted Petal's body out of the nest, trying not to disturb the kits. Finally they began to dig a grave at the side of the clearing.

Meanwhile Cloud Spots chewed up some of the tansy and began trickling the juices into the kits' mouths. They were barely conscious, but their tongues lapped eagerly at the moisture as if they were tormented by thirst.

Clear Sky dipped his head until he could nuzzle the kits affectionately, not caring about the risk of infection. "Hello, my little ones," he murmured. "You'll feel better soon, I promise."

Birch blinked up at him. "Where's Petal?" he asked.

Clear Sky's heart ached. "She's gone back to camp," he lied, fixing Cloud Spots with a gaze that forbade the other tom to contradict him. *They're too weak to bear the truth now. I'll tell them when they're stronger.* He wondered what had happened to the expedition led by Gray Wing and Tall Shadow. *They can't get back with that plant soon enough.*

Birch sighed and snuggled down in the nest again, pressing himself close to his sister.

"Should we move them back to camp?" Clear Sky asked.

Cloud Spots shook his head. "They're better than Petal, but they're still not doing well. They need the Blazing Star. Besides, it's best to keep the kits away from the cats who are still healthy."

Clear Sky nodded. "When we've buried Petal, Shattered Ice can go find Gray Wing and ask him to let us have some of the flowers."

Leaving Cloud Spots with the kits, Clear Sky limped across the clearing to where Shattered Ice and Acorn Fur were digging the grave. His injuries made it hard for him to help, but in any case they had almost finished, and he contented himself with tidying up the scattered earth and removing the bigger stones.

"That'll do," Shattered Ice meowed after a few moments, standing back with a nod of satisfaction.

Clear Sky gently nudged Petal's leaf-wrapped body into the hole and raised his head to the sky, his eyes closed, as the other two cats covered her with earth.

Please take care of Petal, determined and loyal to the last, he prayed silently to the spirit-cats. *Let her join your ranks and give us guidance. I will miss her.*

Opening his eyes again, he wondered if the spirit-cats had heard him. Oddly the prayer had made him feel better.

Shattered Ice and Acorn Fur stood silently beside the grave for a few heartbeats, until Acorn Fur gave her pelt a shake. "Clear Sky, we ought to go back to camp," she mewed.

Clear Sky nodded. "Right. Shattered Ice," he added, "will you go to the hollow, and when Gray Wing comes back with the Blazing Star, tell him we need some here?"

"I'm on my way," Shattered Ice replied briskly, loping toward the edge of the clearing.

"I'll stay with the kits until the herb comes," Cloud Spots offered. "I need to make sure it will help them."

"Thank you." Clear Sky dipped his head. "Will you be okay on your own here?"

"I think One Eye's rogues are long gone," Cloud Spots responded. "But on your way to camp, will you keep an eye out for Sparrow Fur? She went to collect tansy, and she hasn't come back."

Uneasiness tingled through Clear Sky from ears to tail-tip. Sparrow Fur was one of the bravest cats he had ever known, but she was still only a half-grown kit. *And we don't know there aren't still rogues lurking about.*

"I'll do that," he promised Cloud Spots. "And if she hasn't turned up when I've spoken to my cats, I'll send a patrol out to look for her." Turning back to Acorn Fur, he flicked his tail in the direction of the camp. "Lead the way."

All of Clear Sky's senses were alert as he followed Acorn Fur, but he didn't see or scent any sign of Sparrow Fur. *I'll get my cats to follow her scent trail from the clearing,* he decided. *Thorn is good at tracking. We'll find her.*

When he and Acorn Fur emerged from the undergrowth and entered the camp, Clear Sky saw the rest of his cats huddled around the pool in the center. They spun around, their shoulder fur rising apprehensively as he padded toward them.

Then Quick Water jumped to her paws. "Clear Sky!" she exclaimed, sounding both surprised and relieved. "You're alive! Are you okay?"

"Apart from having half my pelt ripped off, I'm fine," Clear Sky replied, his glance raking across the others. "It's good to see you all again."

Thorn, Leaf, and Nettle looked glad to see him, too, but Snake was glaring at him with clear hostility in his eyes. As

Clear Sky was speaking he leaped up and padded forward to face him.

"Good to see us?" he snarled. "Like I'd believe that! You let this happen! We're all scarred by One Eye's mark now."

"I know." Clear Sky bowed his head. "I'm more sorry than I can say. It was my poor judgment that allowed One Eye into our group in the first place. But I intend to spend the rest of my life making up for that mistake." When Snake didn't respond, he continued, his voice choking with the strength of his emotion. "This forest is my home and you're all my family. I would do anything for you, and I risked my life to get rid of One Eye and come back to you. Can't you see that?" he appealed to Snake.

Snake stared at him for a moment. Then without warning he leaped at Clear Sky, striking at his face with claws extended. Shaky from his injuries and the stress of Petal's death and burial, Clear Sky was knocked to the ground, letting out a yowl. Summoning all the strength he could, he battered at Snake with his hind paws and managed to throw him off.

The two cats crouched on the ground, facing each other. Clear Sky could see the burning hatred in Snake's eyes; he tried to stare him down, but he could see that Snake intended to attack again.

What am I going to do? Clear Sky flattened his ears. His chest was heaving from their brief tussle, and he knew that in his injured state he couldn't win a fight. *What will the other cats do when they see their leader beaten?*

But before either of them could make a move, a wild screech

sounded from the undergrowth at the edge of the clearing. A blur of tortoiseshell fur shot into the open and barreled into Snake.

Sparrow Fur! Clear Sky stared in astonishment as the little she-cat tackled the tom—who was twice her size—her paws flailing wildly. Snake could have flattened her with a couple of blows, but for a heartbeat he was too confused to defend himself.

In that moment, Nettle threw himself into the battle, raking his claws across Snake's ears. "Come on!" he yowled to the other cats. "We can't let some kit fight for our leader!"

"Yes!" From the other side, Quick Water hurled herself at Snake. "Come on!"

At her words, Acorn Fur, Thorn, and Leaf leaped into the fray. Snake went down underneath a mound of spitting, clawing cats.

"Stop!" Clear Sky exclaimed, stepping forward to haul Acorn Fur off. "That's enough. I don't want him dead."

He had to grab Leaf, too, and shove him away. Finally, his order sank in and the enraged cats backed off. They stood in a circle around Snake, who struggled to his paws, spitting out dirt and debris. Blood was trickling from a scratch on his forehead and he had lost several clumps of fur.

Clear Sky paced forward to face him. "You can accept me as leader," he meowed, "or leave the forest."

"Then I'll leave," Snake snapped.

With a grim nod, Clear Sky motioned for the other cats to move back, to leave Snake an open passage out of the clearing.

Snake turned and stalked off into the undergrowth.

As the sound of his departure died away, the rest of the cats encircled Clear Sky, each touching noses with him in turn. Gratitude shone in their eyes.

"It's good to have you back," Acorn Fur murmured.

"Thank you." Clear Sky blinked happily at his cats, and gave Sparrow Fur a swift lick around the ears. "You are without doubt the most flea-brained kit I've ever come across," he meowed. "And the bravest. Thank you, too."

Before Sparrow Fur could reply, Clear Sky heard the sound of a cat pushing its way through the bracken toward the clearing. He whirled around, half expecting to see Snake returning for another attack. Instead it was Tall Shadow who emerged into the open. Relief flooded through Clear Sky as he saw the bundle of yellow flowers and spiky leaves that she carried in her mouth.

"You brought the Blazing Star!" he exclaimed. "Where's Gray Wing?"

"Back in the hollow," Tall Shadow replied, dropping the herbs at Clear Sky's paws. "Shattered Ice said you needed this."

Clear Sky nodded. "Petal died of the sickness," he told her, "and the kits are very ill. Cloud Spots is with them."

"Where?" Tall Shadow asked, glancing around the camp. "I must see him."

"I'll show you." Clear Sky picked up the stems of Blazing Star and limped off in the direction of the small clearing where the kits were lying.

"You'll need to go faster than that," Tall Shadow meowed.

"Sorry, but I'm doing the best I can," Clear Sky mumbled around his mouthful of herbs. "The kits are that way," he added, pointing with his tail. "A few extra seconds won't make a difference, will they?"

"We just left the hollow," Tall Shadow replied, "and Holly is responding well to the Blazing Star. But that's not all—her kits are coming early!"

❧

CHAPTER 28

The sun was going down, casting long shadows across the hollow. A raw, damp breeze ruffled the tough moorland grass and stirred the branches of the gorse bushes. Thunder yawned and arched his back in a long stretch, trying to ease the aches in his muscles. The demands of the day had exhausted him. *And it's not over yet.*

He settled down again on the grass at the foot of the look-out rock and cast a glance at Tall Shadow, who was sitting beside him. She had finished grooming her black pelt; now she looked neat and composed, her tail wrapped over her fore-paws. Her gaze was fixed intently on the nest where Holly was giving birth to her kits.

This was the first time Thunder had been able to draw breath since he had led the attack on One Eye and his rogues. At least the malignant cat wouldn't trouble them any further, and nor would his deceitful, treacherous daughter, Star Flower.

Best not to think about her. . . .

Once River Ripple had set off back to the river with his cats, and Wind Runner and Gorse Fur returned to their kits,

Thunder had raced across the moor after Gray Wing and the other cats who had set out to gather the Blazing Star, and caught up with them at the edge of the Thunderpath.

"What are you doing here?" Tall Shadow asked, adding anxiously, "Is there trouble back at camp?"

Thunder shook his head. "No, everything's fine. I just felt restless," he confessed. "And I wanted to make sure you were okay, and that One Eye's rogues weren't around."

"Huh!" Mouse Ear kneaded the grass with his claws. "We've smelled plenty of their reek, but we haven't seen a hair of their miserable pelts."

They had crossed the Thunderpath without any trouble, but as they searched the marshes for the Blazing Star Thunder had noticed how Tall Shadow gazed across the reed-filled pools with longing in her eyes, and turned back with reluctant paw steps once they had collected as much of the plant as they could carry.

Now as he examined her calm profile, Thunder had to ask himself how far the black she-cat's fascination with the marshes would carry her.

"Would you have come back?" he asked her, with a flutter of anxiety in his belly as he dared to put words to his uncertainty. "If we hadn't needed you to help carry the Blazing Star, would you have stayed over there in the marshes?"

Tall Shadow didn't shift her gaze from Holly's den, where they could just make out the group of cats a tail-length back from the entrance. Pebble Heart was tending to Holly, smoothing her fur with one paw and licking her ears. Cloud

Spots stood beside him, supervising; he had only just returned from treating Petal's kits in the forest. Jagged Peak was crouching beside Holly, too, murmuring words of encouragement into her ear. Though she was responding to the Blazing Star, Thunder knew it was still very dangerous for her to be giving birth so soon.

For several heartbeats Tall Shadow did not speak, and when she did, it was not in reply to Thunder. "Who would have thought Jagged Peak would have ended up being such a wonderful mate and father?" she mewed.

"You didn't answer my question," Thunder retorted.

Before Tall Shadow could respond, a high-pitched wailing came from Holly, a sound that made every hair on Thunder's pelt prickle with anticipation.

Tall Shadow leaped to her paws. "The kits are coming!"

All Thunder's instincts told him to race across to Holly's nest and see what was happening. But he knew that too many cats crowding around would be bad for Holly and her kits. Tall Shadow seemed to feel the same, and she paced impatiently in tight circles.

The next moments were the longest of Thunder's life, but at last Cloud Spots broke away from the cluster of cats in the mouth of the den, and bounded over to them.

"Holly's kits are here!" he announced triumphantly. "Three of them—all well, and Holly is fine too! This is as good as we could possibly have hoped for."

Thunder felt a loud purr rising in his throat, but Tall Shadow twitched her tail anxiously. "But how is Holly really?"

she asked. "I've seen illness before, and it doesn't just vanish in a couple of heartbeats. Will she make it through the night?"

"We've given her another dose of the Blazing Star," Cloud Spots replied, his elation fading. "Now all we can do is watch and wait."

By now the last of the sunlight had vanished and twilight covered the moor. Thunder stifled another massive yawn and said good night to Tall Shadow and Cloud Spots before withdrawing to his den.

Sleep? I've almost forgotten what it's like to rest my bones!

Some cat had renewed the moss and bracken in his nest, and Thunder sank into the soft bedding with a weary sigh. He began grooming his pelt, running his tongue over the scratches he had received in the battle with One Eye. But his tongue moved more and more slowly, and his eyelids were growing heavy.

I'll just sleep for a bit. . . .

Thunder felt a paw on his shoulder, gently shaking him. He opened his eyes and made out the figure of Gray Wing, his gray pelt turned to silver by the moonlight that shone through the entrance to the den.

"It's time," Gray Wing mewed.

Thunder stifled a yawn, feeling utterly confused. "Time for what?" he mumbled.

"To go to the four trees," Gray Wing replied. "Can't you feel it?"

Struggling back to full wakefulness, Thunder turned his

attention inward. Waves of energy were surging through his body, growing stronger with every heartbeat. He could hear faint voices calling in the distance, and he realized that he recognized them.

Rainswept Flower . . . and Turtle Tail!

Thunder locked his gaze with Gray Wing's and spotted a flutter of grief in his kin's face at the sound of his dead mate's voice. He rose to his paws. "You're right. Let's go."

Taking the lead out of the camp, Thunder almost tripped over Mouse Ear, who was sleeping in the open, curled up in the shadow of a rock. But the tabby tom didn't stir. Thunder drew a breath of relief. *We don't want any cat asking us where we're going.*

Thunder and Gray Wing were silent as they headed for the clearing with the four great oaks. The air was mild, not at all like a night on the edge of leaf-bare. Thunder could hardly feel the long grasses brushing against his pelt, and the speed of his own movement surprised him. It was almost as though they were floating, not walking at all.

When they arrived in the clearing Thunder saw that more cats were already assembled there, sitting in a ragged half circle in front of the rock: Tall Shadow, River Ripple, Wind Runner, and Clear Sky. They acknowledged the newcomers by dipping their heads, but no cat spoke.

Thunder looked around for Turtle Tail and Rainswept Flower, and spotted them on top of the rock. Their pelts glimmered with starlight and frosty sparkles shone from their eyes. They too dipped their heads in greeting.

"You heard us call to you," Rainswept Flower meowed. "You came."

At the sight of the two beautiful she-cats, Thunder felt himself choking with emotion, his throat so tight that he could scarcely breathe. *Why were they taken from us? Why did we have to be parted in the first place?*

"Because now we can see everything you see, and more." Turtle Tail responded as if she was reading his thoughts. "Because we can help you. Are we really parted, when we can send you messages in your dreams?"

Thunder's eyes stretched wide in shock. *This is a dream! Now I understand! That's why I never disturbed Mouse Ear, and why we seemed to float over here, and why I don't feel the night cold.*

Glancing at Gray Wing, he saw that the older cat shared his astonishment. "We're sharing the same dream!" he whispered. His breathing sounded easy, without the problems that had plagued him ever since the forest fire.

"And so are we," River Ripple added. His eyes were full of wonder, so different from his usual amused detachment. "All the leaders."

"Don't get too excited," Turtle Tail warned them. "Now—think. Can you remember what we told you when we last spoke with you?"

Thunder nodded. "You said we had to unite or die, and you were right. We united against One Eye and defeated him. And we shared the Blazing Star to fight off the sickness." He paused, and when neither of the spirit-cats spoke, he continued. "What now?" For the first time he realized that he didn't know what the future held. "Why did you summon us in our sleep?"

Rainswept Flower's blue eyes shone with star-fire as she gazed down at him. "What else did we tell you?" she asked.

Almost overwhelmed by the strangeness of what was happening to him, Thunder struggled to remember. It was Gray Wing who spoke up. "That to survive we must grow and spread like the Blazing Star."

Rainswept Flower gave him a nod of approval. "That's right. You cannot forget those words. They will help you in the coming seasons."

Thunder exchanged a bewildered glance with Gray Wing, then shrugged. *Why can't these star cats ever tell us something so we can understand it?*

"Can you give us any more of a clue as to what that means?" Tall Shadow asked.

"Yes." Wind Runner flicked her tail, sounding irritated. "Why bring us here and then speak to us in riddles?"

Turtle Tail held up her paw, the pads facing the living cats, and extended her claws. "The Blazing Star has five petals, just as a cat's paw has five claws."

It's like she's teaching kits, Thunder thought, frustrated. "Yes, but so what?"

"Grow and spread . . . grow and spread . . ." Turtle Tail and Rainswept Flower spoke in chorus, repeating the same phrase over and over.

As Thunder gazed up at them, still bewildered, the starry forms of the spirit-cats began to fade. Their voices grew fainter, too, as if they were calling out from an immense distance.

"No!" Thunder yowled. "Don't leave us! Stay and explain!"

But it was too late. Turtle Tail and Rainswept Flower seemed to dissolve until they were no more than wisps of mist above the rock; then they were gone.

Thunder threw back his head and let out another long caterwaul to the stars that blazed down from an empty sky. Then before his eyes the stars seemed to shift, blotted out as darkness swirled in front of his eyes. He lashed out with one paw and felt the soft touch of moss against his pads. His eyes flew open and he realized that he was back in his own den.

Thunder's heart was racing, and shivers ran through him as if he had just struggled out of icy water. He lay still in his nest for several heartbeats, going over in his mind what the spirit-cats had said.

After a few moments the moonlight that washed into his den was suddenly cut off as another cat slipped through the entrance. Gray Wing's scent wreathed around him.

"Well done," Gray Wing muttered, sounding unusually irritable. "You called the dream to a halt."

"They were leaving anyway," Thunder retorted, sitting up and shaking scraps of moss from his pelt.

Gray Wing padded farther into the den, letting the light flow back, and sat down beside Thunder. "We have to work out what the message means," he meowed.

Thunder rolled his eyes. "Good luck with that." He was still frustrated by the spirit-cats' riddling talk, and by the way they had vanished instead of explaining themselves.

"I have an idea," Gray Wing continued, sounding more like his calm self. "But we need to discuss it with the others."

Thankful to have something he could do, Thunder leaped to his paws. "Do you want me to fetch Clear Sky, River Ripple, and Wind Runner?"

"Wait." Gray Wing stretched out a paw to stop Thunder from leaving the den. "Let's talk to Tall Shadow first just to see whether she had the dream too."

Thunder nodded. "Good plan!"

Gray Wing rose to his paws and padded out of the den. When Thunder followed him into the open he saw that the moon had already set. The stars were fading and pink streaks stretched across the sky where the sun would rise. The air was damp and misty, with dew clinging to every rock and blade of grass.

The rest of the cats were beginning to stir. Tiny squeaks came from the den where Holly and Jagged Peak were caring for their kits, and as Thunder watched, Pebble Heart emerged from his own den and slipped in to join them. The sound of their cheerful greetings told Thunder that Holly was doing well.

Shattered Ice slid out of the tunnel where he slept and sat down to scratch one ear vigorously with his hind paw, while Dappled Pelt sat at the mouth of her den, giving herself a thorough grooming.

His glance sweeping across the camp, Thunder spotted the small, dark shape of Tall Shadow sitting at the foot of the lookout rock. As soon as she saw Gray Wing and Thunder she leaped up and bounded across the hollow toward them.

"Did you have a dream?" she demanded when she reached them.

Gray Wing dipped his head. "So you had it too?"

"Yes," Tall Shadow confirmed. "What are we going to do about it?"

"We need to discuss it with the other leaders," Thunder meowed. "I'll go fetch them."

"Wait." Once again Gray Wing stretched out a paw. "I can feel a kind of tingling in my pads. It reminds me of what the spirit-cats said. . . . I think we should go back to the four trees."

Tall Shadow twitched her ears in surprise. "If that's what you want."

With Gray Wing in the lead, the three cats left the hollow and set out across the moor. Mist still wreathed around them, but above their heads the sky was clear. Thunder enjoyed the cool touch of the dewy grass on his paws, reviving him from his interrupted sleep and sending new energy through his limbs.

By the time they crossed into the forest the sun was peering over the horizon; every drop of moisture glittered in its rays, though ragged scraps of mist still remained under the shadow of the trees.

When they reached the top of the slope that led down into the clearing, Thunder spotted Clear Sky, Wind Runner, and River Ripple perched among the bare branches of one of the great oaks.

"There you are!" River Ripple called out to them, leaping down to join them as they bounded rapidly down the slope. "I wondered how long it would take the three of you to turn up."

"You were expecting us?" Gray Wing asked, as Clear Sky and Wind Runner also jumped down and padded up to them.

For answer, River Ripple simply dipped his head.

"Did you see the same thing, then?" Clear Sky asked, tearing at the ground in agitation. "The meeting with the spirit-cats? What did you make of their message?"

"We all saw it," Wind Runner responded. "And my encounters with death have colored everything for me. 'Unite or die,' they told us. All I can take from that is that we have to face more death and grief."

"But I think their message tonight was more hopeful than that," River Ripple told her quietly, brushing his plumy tail sympathetically against Wind Runner's shoulder. "Besides, shouldn't we all feel grateful? How lucky we are, to be . . ." He paused, struggling to find the right word.

"The chosen ones?" Thunder asked.

River Ripple tilted his head, looking both surprised and impressed. "Yes, maybe that's what we are. We're lucky that the spirit-cats want to speak with all of us and allow us to meet with them in our dreams." His habitual amusement glimmered in his eyes. "Think how terrifying it would be if you received these messages and you were the only one."

"We've been told to grow and spread. But are we still being told to unite or die?" Thunder asked, remembering what he had said in the dream. "I think we would all have died if we hadn't united against One Eye. So is that part of the message over and done with now?"

"You want to go back to fighting among ourselves?" Tall Shadow asked. "Having another battle, maybe?"

"No, of course not—" Thunder began to protest.

"Then I think both messages are important. We just have to figure out what the second message means. Grow and spread . . ."

"I hope the spirits aren't blaming me for leaving the hollow," Wind Runner interrupted waspishly.

"Well, it can't mean that we all have to live together," Gray Wing meowed. "That never worked, right from the beginning."

"Only because some cats argued about where to live," Tall Shadow pointed out.

Clear Sky's neck fur began to bristle. "Are you saying we have no right to make that decision?"

Thunder could see that the meeting was going to break down in squabbling if he didn't do something. Bunching his muscles, he leaped up onto the top of the Great Rock.

"Stop!" he yowled. When silence fell, with all the others gazing up at him, he went on, "We mustn't fight among ourselves. We need to work together to find the exact meaning of their most recent message."

Murmurs of agreement came from the other cats, except for Clear Sky, who barely seemed to be listening. Instead he seemed to be carefully scanning the area.

Choosing new boundaries? Thunder wondered, feeling his belly tense at the thought of more confrontation with his father. *I hope not. I've had enough of boundaries to last me a lifetime.*

The other four leaders jumped up to join Thunder on top of the rock, and after a pause, much to Thunder's relief, Clear Sky followed them.

By now the morning sun was rising high in the sky, casting its slanting rays between the branches of the oaks and burning off the last of the dawn mist. The creak and rustle of the trees was all around them. Thunder felt peace like dew soaking through his pelt, and as the others relaxed he realized that they felt it too.

Clear Sky's gaze was fixed on the horizon. "We need to work together," he murmured. "We can do that, even if we don't live as one group."

Even greater relief flooded through Thunder, and he drew closer to his father. "Of course we can," he responded.

"I'm not sure that I can take direction from other cats on my own territory," Wind Runner mewed stiffly. "But I'll think about it."

Gray Wing and Tall Shadow exchanged a glance. "I'll do whatever the rest of you ask of me," Gray Wing stated firmly.

"So will I," Tall Shadow added.

River Ripple was the only cat who hadn't spoken. As Thunder turned to the loner who had already helped them so much, the silver-furred tom dipped his head in answer to the unspoken question. "I'll unite with you," he meowed. "Haven't you noticed? I've been doing that ever since the day you first arrived here from the mountains."

"The only difference," Thunder told him, "is that now our survival depends on your help."

Every cat fell silent, as if they were thinking of the enormous commitment they had just made to one another. But Thunder couldn't feel satisfied.

"But what about when they said we had to grow and spread like the Blazing Star?" Thunder asked. "What does that mean?"

For a moment the six cats exchanged baffled glances. Then Gray Wing mewed, "I think I understand."

DAWN OF THE CLANS

WARRIORS

THE BLAZING STAR

BONUS SCENE!

Read on to see what was happening in the mountains
while sickness spread in the forest. . . .

CHAPTER ONE

Sun Shadow slipped out from beneath a scrubby bush rooted in the shallow soil between two boulders. As he halted to sniff the cold mountain air he saw that the sun was already going down, flooding the gray rock walls with scarlet light.

Maybe I should head home, he thought. The rest of the Tribe would already be gathering to share the day's prey in the cave behind the waterfall. *Sharp Hail will claw my fur off if I'm late!*

Curiosity had led Sun Shadow's paws farther down the mountain than he had ever ventured before. But he knew that his mother's new mate, Sharp Hail, would never understand his urge to explore.

My real father wouldn't be so strict, he told himself sadly as he hurried along a winding path between sharp, jutting stones. *I wish I could have known him.*

The path curved around a massive outcrop; following it, Sun Shadow found himself facing an almost sheer cliff. Squinting through the fading light of sunset, he spotted a narrow crevasse gaping open in the rock face ahead.

Instantly Sun Shadow forgot the need for haste. His ears twitched curiously and his pads itched with the compulsion to find out what lay beyond the dark gap. It felt like the crevasse was tugging at him.

It might lead into a cave, like the one where we live. And it won't take long to check it out....

Sun Shadow's pelt prickled with excitement as he padded cautiously forward. Ever since he was a kit, he had loved to explore. He'd always yearned to know what lay beyond the mountain peaks that surrounded his home.

Not that I get much chance to find out, with Sharp Hail always looking over my shoulder. Sun Shadow's mother's new mate was always finding chores to keep Sun Shadow close to the cave. *But all I want to do is get out and see the world,* he thought resentfully.

Envy bit into him like thorns when he thought of how his real father, Moon Shadow, had left before Sun Shadow was even born to follow the Sun Trail and find a new home. Several cats had left with him, and without so many mouths to feed, the Tribe was doing better—or so Sun Shadow's mother, Dewy Leaf, said. Hunting had improved, and no cat was in danger of starving anymore.

So why is Sharp Hail so obsessed with keeping every cat safe? Sun Shadow asked himself. *If I'd been born when my father left, I'd have gone with him.*

Reaching the rock face, Sun Shadow stretched one paw out into the cleft and tentatively patted the ground. It felt solid, though when he tried to peer down the narrow passage he could see nothing beyond the first tail-length. When he tasted the air he picked up a strange scent, musty like earth, but it seemed a long way away.

Sun Shadow stepped into the opening, feeling his pelt brush against the walls on either side, and glanced over his shoulder at the dimming sunlight.

Just a quick look . . . It won't hurt any cat.

As he slowly padded forward, Sun Shadow's own body blocked out the last of the light, leaving him with only his whiskers and his sense of smell to guide him. He sensed that he was heading along a tall, narrow tunnel that sloped gently downward. From somewhere farther ahead he could hear the sound of dripping water, each drop waking a flurry of sharp echoes.

Maybe the tunnel opens into a larger cave, Sun Shadow thought. His heart thudded with excitement; he couldn't wait to find out what lay ahead of him.

Then a sound from farther down the tunnel brought Sun Shadow to an abrupt halt. *What is that?* he wondered. He had never heard the high-pitched chittering before, or the oddly loud flapping, like many wings rustling together. It sounded like it was moving. . . .

Panic froze Sun Shadow, fixing his paws to the ground. *It's coming right toward me!* he thought. *Could it be an eagle?*

The sounds grew louder. Whatever was making them was just a short distance away now. Sun Shadow crouched low, his shoulder fur bristling in terror, and let out a yowl as a whole flock of hideous creatures swept over his head, screeching and beating their wings. He choked as a musty smell filled the air.

In the darkness Sun Shadow couldn't tell what the creatures were, and he didn't care; he only knew he had to get away from them. Terrified, he tried to run back the way he'd come, only to crash face-first into a craggy rock wall.

"Ow!" Sun Shadow staggered back, letting out a yowl of pain. The scent and harsh taste of blood flowed over him.

The horrible creatures were still passing above his head. Sun Shadow stumbled forward, desperate to get out of the tunnel. He panted hard with relief as he burst into the open and saw twilight glimmering in the sky.

Sun Shadow's whole face ached, and when he raised a paw, hesitantly touching his nose, it came back covered in blood. *Oh, haredung . . . that hurts!*

Looking up, he saw a blur of brown, mouselike creatures disappearing into the sky, darting here and there on tough, featherless wings. *Bats!* Sun Shadow had seen a dead bat before, but never a whole group of them in flight.

And I don't care if I never see them again.

Sun Shadow stood watching the ugly creatures for a few moments more, until his racing heart gradually slowed and his shoulder fur lay flat again. *I'm glad no other cat saw me,* he thought, beginning to feel stupid. *Those things are disgusting, but they couldn't hurt me.*

"Sun Shadow! Sun Shadow!"

The young cat's heart lurched again as he recognized the distant voice calling his name. "Sharp Hail!" he muttered. "Now I'll have to put up with one of his lectures." His head and tail drooped as he set off toward the cave. "But what choice do I have?"

* * *

Sun Shadow's paws tingled with apprehension as he followed Sharp Hail back into the cave. By now darkness had fallen and moonlight glimmered on the waterfall, sending silver light dancing around the cavern walls.

Once inside, Sharp Hail swung around and thrust out his muzzle toward Sun Shadow. "Why did I have to go looking for you among the rocks *again*?" he demanded, narrowing his ice-blue eyes. "When will you learn to come back to the cave by sunset? And what in the world has happened to your *face*?"

Sun Shadow extended his tongue and licked toward his nose, tasting blood again. His pelt grew hot with embarrassment at the thought of confessing how he had fled from the bats. "I . . . uh . . . I ran into a hawk," he mumbled.

Sharp Hail lashed his tail in frustration. "You expect me to believe that?" he snarled. "A scrawny thing like you would never stand a chance against a hawk. Besides, that injury is a bump, not a scratch—like you crashed into something."

He waited, flexing his claws impatiently, but Sun Shadow had nothing more to say. He blinked miserably as he stared at the cave floor.

"We just want you to be *safe*." Dewy Leaf spoke gently behind him. "Don't you understand? After all that's happened to us, here in the mountains . . ."

"Nothing has happened to us!" Sun Shadow blurted out, whipping around to face Dewy Leaf. "Not in my lifetime. I wish something *would* happen! Then living here might not be so boring."

A look of horror flashed into Dewy Leaf's eyes. At the same

moment, Sun Shadow felt a stinging blow across his ears, and turned to see Sharp Hail glaring at him with one paw raised.

"That's enough!" Sharp Hail yowled. "I've had it up to here with you whining about being safe and having enough to eat. You're just like your father! Moon Shadow was always too restless to appreciate what he had."

Sun Shadow had heard that accusation before, if not exactly in those words, and the truth of it stabbed him like a thorn in his pad. *I am restless! And if I were with my father, at least I'd be around someone who understands me!*

He had been too young to remember how his sister, Crow Muzzle, had died during her birth, and he had only a vague memory of his brother, Dancing Leaf, falling sick and dying a moon later. He had grown up alone. There had never been any cat who would listen to his dreams of life beyond the mountain.

"You need to be taught a lesson," Sharp Hail went on, his voice cold. "To make up for worrying your mother tonight, you'll spend the next half moon caring for Stoneteller."

Sun Shadow nodded, feeling slightly bewildered. He liked Stoneteller, and admired how her wisdom guided the Tribe and how she cared for each of them as if they were her own kits. Ordinarily caring for her would have been an honor, not a punishment. But in the last few days Stoneteller had fallen ill with some kind of vomiting sickness. Sun Shadow had overheard the older cats reassuring one another that she would get better soon. They all believed she had many more seasons in her, and couldn't imagine life without her.

I hope they're right, Sun Shadow thought. *But meanwhile, cleaning up after her will be pretty yucky.*

"Well?" Sharp Hail's voice broke into Sun Shadow's thoughts. "Are you going to stand there all night? Get on with it!"

His belly still churning with resentment, Sun Shadow padded toward the back of the cave and the tunnel that led to Stoneteller's den. He had never been allowed there before, and at the end of the passage he halted, his eyes wide with wonder.

The tunnel opened into a smaller cave, lit by starlight from a jagged hole in the roof. Reflections glinted from pools on the cave floor. Most astonishing of all, stone pinnacles rose from the cave floor, rising to meet spikes of stone that hung from the roof. Some of them were joined in the middle, so that Sun Shadow felt that he was gazing into a forest made of stone.

Hardly daring to breathe, Sun Shadow padded forward. "Stoneteller?" he called softly.

There was no reply. But a moment later Sun Shadow spotted the old white she-cat curled up beside one of the pools, her tail wrapped over her nose. Her body rose and fell gently with the rhythm of her breathing. She looked perfectly fine; there was no scent of vomit around her.

Sun Shadow retreated quietly and returned to the main cave. He crouched at the end of Stoneteller's tunnel, trying to ignore the rumbling of his belly.

All the prey had been shared by the time I got back. And I'm not going to ask Sharp Hail if there's any left!

A few tail-lengths away, Sun Shadow spotted Quiet Rain sitting beside her sleeping hollow and nibbling daintily on a mouse. As he watched her, his jaws watering, Quiet Rain glanced his way, then picked up her prey and padded over to him.

"You look like you could use some kindness," she murmured, blinking sympathetically at his injured face. "Here." She tore the mouse in two and pushed half of it toward him.

"Thank you!" Sun Shadow meowed, tearing hungrily into the prey.

"You look so much like your father," Quiet Rain went on. "The same slender build and black pelt. It's a pity he never saw you."

Sun Shadow looked up, gulping down the last mouthful. "My father is a hero," he declared. "He left the mountains and risked the dangerous journey down the Sun Trail to find new hunting grounds and save all the cats who stayed in the mountains."

To his surprise, Quiet Rain seemed not to share his admiration. "That's true, but to do that, he left your mother on her own, even though she was expecting kits," she pointed out.

A pulse of anger shot through Sun Shadow. "It was a sacrifice he had to make!" But his anger died as he met Quiet Rain's steady gaze, and he remembered that she too had been left behind. "Your kits—Clear Sky, Gray Wing, and Jagged Peak—were heroes too," he went on. "Do you ever wonder about them?"

Quiet Rain did not reply, though her eyes misted over, as if she was gazing into the far distance. Sun Shadow found himself questioning whether the she-cat was lonely. *She never took another mate, or had another litter. All her kits are gone.*

"Do you ever think about what life is like at the end of the Sun Trail?" Sun Shadow asked her. "Beyond this mountain?"

Quiet Rain remained silent for a few heartbeats, and Sun Shadow hoped he hadn't upset her. But when she met his gaze again, her expression was resolute.

"I often wonder how my kits are faring," she replied. "I would like to see them once more before I die. But my place is here, on this mountain, with these cats." She paused, running the tip of her tail along Sun Shadow's back. "Perhaps every cat wonders about life beyond the mountain," she mewed. "But you must find your place in the group *here*, where you belong."

Without waiting for a reply, she padded back to her sleeping hollow and curled up inside it.

Sun Shadow watched her, impressed by her wisdom. But before he could think more about what she had said, he heard the sound of Stoneteller's voice coming from her den at the end of the tunnel. It was too far away for him to make out the words, but there was an urgency in her tone that made him spring to his paws and race down the tunnel toward her.

Maybe she's ill! I have to help her!

But when Sun Shadow erupted into Stoneteller's cave, he saw her standing erect on her paws, her head raised and her gaze fixed on the jagged gap in the roof. Her green eyes shone brilliantly, as if what she saw there filled her with mingled joy and sorrow. Sun Shadow didn't dare speak; he could only watch and listen in wonder.

"Fluttering Bird . . . Shaded Moss . . . Bright Stream . . . Turtle Tail . . ." She breathed out. "Oh, my dear friends! I thought I would never see you again. How is it that you're here now, with me?"

Stoneteller paused, as if she was listening to an answer, though Sun Shadow couldn't hear or see anything.

Then Stoneteller bowed her head. "Now I understand," she murmured. "I am not ready yet, but if that is what you wish . . ."

Fear gripped Sun Shadow, piercing his body like claws of ice as he realized what the old she-cat meant. *Fluttering Bird was Quiet Rain's kit who died of hunger. If Stoneteller's talking about joining her, she must be talking about dying. . . . But she can't!* His heart thumped and his chest felt tight with panic. *What will we do without our leader?*

CHAPTER TWO

Stoneteller's vision seemed to fade, and at last she turned with slow paw steps toward her nest at the far end of the cave. Sun Shadow followed her, ready to offer help if she seemed to need it, but she curled up among the moss and fell asleep almost at once.

Sun Shadow crouched in the shelter of one of the stone trees, reluctant to leave his leader yet knowing there was nothing he could do for her. Though his body ached with exhaustion, his horror at what he had overheard kept him awake.

We need Stoneteller! Every cat said she had many seasons left. What are we going to do when she's gone?

Eventually Sun Shadow rose to his paws, stretched cramped limbs, and slipped back through the tunnel into the main cave. The sky beyond the screen of falling water at the entrance was dim gray, telling Sun Shadow that a new day was dawning.

Wearily Sun Shadow headed toward his family's sleeping hollows at the side of the cave. His half brothers and sister, Falling Dusk, Morning Star, and Melting Ice, were already awake, wrestling together and trying to see who could jump the highest. Dewy Leaf sat beside her hollow, grooming herself and watching the kits play.

"Are you okay?" she asked as Sun Shadow approached. "Does your face still hurt?"

"No, it's fine," Sun Shadow replied, settling down beside her.

Dewy Leaf gave him a sideways glance. "You don't have to tell me how you got injured," she meowed after a few moments. "I just want you to be safe—do you understand?"

I don't want to be safe. But she'll only get angry if I tell her that. Sun Shadow didn't know how to reply, so he said nothing.

Dewy Leaf shifted uncomfortably, pausing as she drew her paw over one ear. "I'm sorry Sharp Hail is so hard on you sometimes," she went on. "It's just . . . oh, you really worry me, Sun Shadow! You're so much like your father! Sometimes I don't know what to do with you."

Sun Shadow pricked up his ears at the mention of Moon Shadow. "How am I like my father?" he asked, his voice cracking with his need for an answer.

Dewy Leaf gazed at him affectionately. "You're curious and brave," she replied. "And sometimes reckless and selfish. And smart and cunning . . . Maybe I'm afraid that you'll leave, like Moon Shadow did," she finished quietly. "Maybe that's why I hold you so close."

Sun Shadow felt an ache in his heart at his mother's words. He wanted to reassure her, but he couldn't. *Maybe she's right. Maybe someday I* will *leave.*

Suddenly he didn't want to go on talking about his father.

And there was something more urgent pressing on his mind. "Dewy Leaf," he began, "what would happen to us if Stone-teller died?"

Fear flashed into Dewy Leaf's eyes. "Why are you asking?" she meowed. "Is Stoneteller . . . ?"

"She's fine," Sun Shadow replied abruptly, staring at his paws, as if Dewy Leaf could read in his face his weird experience in Stoneteller's den. "But what if . . . ?"

Daring to look up, he saw confusion in his mother's face. "We'd go on as we always have," she told him. "Some other cat would step up to lead us."

She glanced toward the other side of the sleeping hollows. Sharp Hail had appeared and was teaching the young kits how to pounce.

Sun Shadow felt something shrivel inside him. *Sharp Hail could never be our leader. He just couldn't!*

"But none of the other cats have visions like Stoneteller," he objected.

"Not all leaders have visions," Dewy Leaf told him. "In fact, Stoneteller was the first. There are other ways to lead."

Sun Shadow nodded, aware that he knew exactly how Sharp Hail would lead. *Even the bit of freedom I've got would be taken away from me.*

"I should get back to Stoneteller," he meowed, rising to his paws and heading for the back of the cavern.

"Don't you want something to eat?" Dewy Leaf called after him, but Sun Shadow didn't reply, increasing his pace until he could plunge out of sight down the tunnel.

* * *

When Sun Shadow emerged into the old cat's den, he found Stoneteller awake, sitting beside one of the pools and watching the reflections of the clouds scudding across the sky. He padded up to her and dipped his head respectfully.

"Sharp Hail sent me to look after you," he meowed.

Stoneteller looked up to meet his gaze. In spite of her age, her green eyes were sharp and full of wisdom. "That was kind," she responded.

Kind? Sharp Hail? Sun Shadow bit back the words. "Is there anything I can do for you?" he asked.

Stoneteller thought for a moment. "You might freshen up the bedding in my sleeping hollow," she mewed.

"Of course." Sun Shadow padded over to the leader's nest and began to stir up the moss and feathers that lined the hollow, wondering whether he would need to go out and find more. He noticed that one of the hunters had brought prey for Stoneteller: a small bird whose limp body lay beside the nest. There was no sign that Stoneteller had even touched it.

A sharp cry from behind him made Sun Shadow whirl around, to see Stoneteller had moved a few paw steps away from the pool. She had collapsed on her side with a look of agony in her eyes.

Swiftly Sun Shadow ran to her. "What is it?" he asked, fear and anxiety swelling inside him. "How can I help?"

Stoneteller let out a long, shaken breath. "Please . . . bring me some water."

Sun Shadow grabbed a mouthful of moss from the nest and

went to soak it in the pool. It seemed so little that he could do for the old she-cat. *I'll do anything I can to protect her . . . but what can any cat do?* He wished he didn't have so much faith in Stoneteller's predictions. *If her visions tell her that she's going to die, then she'll die.*

"Thank you," Stoneteller murmured as Sun Shadow laid the soaking moss down beside her. She sighed as she stretched out her tongue to lap. "That tastes so good."

Sun Shadow watched her for a moment, then went back to the nest and fetched the bird. "Look, some cat has left this for you," he meowed.

Stoneteller shook her head. "I'm not hungry," she responded. "I haven't been able to keep food down for days."

Even more worried, Sun Shadow pushed the bird a little closer to her. "You should at least try," he coaxed her.

Once more Stoneteller raised her head and fixed him with her brilliant green gaze. "You cannot save me," she declared.

Sun Shadow felt his lower jaw beginning to tremble. "You— you *are* going to die, then," he stammered.

"Yes, it's my time." Stoneteller reached out her tail and laid it reassuringly on Sun Shadow's shoulder. "And my death will bring a time of great change for the mountain cats. But all will be well," she went on at Sun Shadow's gasp of apprehension. "A new leader will be chosen, and every cat will survive."

Sun Shadow nodded, feeling his fears recede a little.

"But you will not be part of the Tribe by the time the new leader is named," Stoneteller went on.

A bolt of understanding, fierce as lightning, passed through

Sun Shadow at Stoneteller's words. He stared at her in surprise.

"You knew that—didn't you?" Stoneteller asked gently.

Sun Shadow felt as if his throat was as dry as a sun-baked rock. "Where—where will I go?" he rasped.

"That is for you to decide," Stoneteller replied, though Sun Shadow sensed she could have said more if she had wished to.

"I could try to find my father," he mewed eagerly, his heart beginning to pound with excitement at the thought of meeting Moon Shadow.

Stoneteller didn't respond. Her jaws gaped wide in a yawn. "I'm tired," she murmured. "I need to sleep."

She staggered to her paws and Sun Shadow let her lean on his shoulder until she reached her nest. She sank down into the moss and feathers with a sigh and closed her eyes. Almost at once her regular breathing told Sun Shadow that she was asleep.

Once he was certain she was resting, Sun Shadow turned away and padded out of the cave. He tried not to think about how still and lifeless Stoneteller's small, curled form looked, sunk among the bedding.

It's too much like she's . . .

Sun Shadow cut off the thought. He bounded across the floor of the main cavern, then padded along the narrow path that led behind the waterfall, until he emerged onto the rocks that overlooked the pool. Finding a flat boulder to sit on, he gazed around him at the mountain peaks that surrounded his home.

At first he hoped that he could make out some kind of destination to aim for when he was ready to leave. But everything looked so vast and frightening: a huge expanse of gray rock and scree, with only the occasional scrubby bush to break the monotony, or narrow streams winding their way down steep valleys.

How will I ever find my father in such a big, wide—messy—world?

Before Sun Shadow could find an answer to his own question, he felt a shadow fall on him. Looking up, he felt claws of terror gripping his chest. A hawk was hovering over him, its wide wingspan blocking out the sunlight. Frozen by panic, Sun Shadow watched as the bird swooped down, its talons extended to clutch and tear.

No! A horrible realization swept over Sun Shadow. *Is this what Stoneteller meant? Is this why I won't be part of the Tribe any longer?*

Sharp Hail's contemptuous words came back into Sun Shadow's mind. *A scrawny thing like you would never stand a chance against a hawk.* Sun Shadow let out a whimper of fear. *Is this my end?* he wondered. *Why?*

The huge bird was almost upon him, letting out a harsh screech of triumph. The sound woke some deep instinct within Sun Shadow. *I have to try to fight it!*

He scrambled clear of the reaching talons, half jumping, half falling off the flat rock, and lashed out at the hawk with claws extended. But his blow missed the huge bird and instead he struck at the rock wall, letting out a yowl of pain.

There was no time to check if he had lost a claw. The hawk had mounted into the sky for a few wingbeats, then aimed for him again in a lethal dive.

Sun Shadow's heart was pounding, and his whole body shook from ears to tail-tip. He bunched his muscles against the tremors and reared up, bringing his forepaws together to strike out at the hawk again.

This time his blow landed, catching the hawk and slamming it down on the ground. He caught a glimpse of its yellow, glaring eyes as it tried to slash at him with its beak. Sun Shadow dug his claws in harder, but the bird tore itself away with a frightened shriek. Kicking and flapping, it struggled back into the sky and flew off; a few feathers drifted down onto the rock beside Sun Shadow.

Panting hard, Sun Shadow watched the hawk until it faded to a dot in the distance. Triumph was gushing through him. *I drove the hawk away!*

Feeling more confident, Sun Shadow surveyed the landscape again. But then he remembered that he was supposed to be looking after Stoneteller.

What if she wakes up and needs me, and I'm not there? What if . . . ?

Sun Shadow ran quickly back along the path behind the waterfall and bounded across the cave.

"Hey, Sun Shadow!" Melting Ice called out. "Come and play with me!"

"Later!" Sun Shadow called back, waving his tail at his young half sister. *I haven't got time to play now.*

He plunged into the tunnel that led to Stoneteller's den, and found her facing the entrance, sitting with her tail curled around her paws. She was watching him with a clear gaze, as if she had been expecting him to appear.

"You know now, don't you?" she mewed. "You're ready."

Sun Shadow instantly understood. "Yes, I'm ready to leave," he replied. "I drove off a hawk out there, and that means I've proved myself." Then sadness flooded over him as he realized where his paws were leading him. "I can't leave you, Stoneteller," he added. "Not like this!"

Stoneteller dipped her head gently. "Don't worry about me. I've lived a long life, and soon I'll be among friends. It's time for you to find your own life, your own friends who will greet you when at last you make the journey to the stars."

Sun Shadow blinked and dared to touch his nose to the old she-cat's. "Thank you," he purred.

That night, when his Tribemates had settled down to sleep and the cavern was quiet, Sun Shadow slid out of his sleeping hollow. He hesitated for a few heartbeats, looking down at his family. Sharp Hail, sleeping a little to one side. The three kits, nestled cozily within the curve of Dewy Leaf's body.

Dewy Leaf . . .

Sun Shadow's heart came near to breaking at the thought of leaving his mother. He knew how sad she would be when she realized that he was truly gone.

But I know her life is here, with Sharp Hail and my half brothers and half sister.

Sun Shadow bent over his sleeping mother and gently touched his nose to hers, not wanting to wake her. "I'll be okay," he promised in a whisper.

He drew back silently and padded across the cavern floor toward the waterfall. But before he reached the opening that led out onto the mountain, a meow sounded from behind him.

"Where are you going?"

Gulping, Sun Shadow whirled around to see Quiet Rain watching him from the top of a rock beside the cave wall, her eyes wide with alarm.

"Just—just out for some air," he stammered.

Quiet Rain blinked. "Please, Sun Shadow. I'm not stupid. You were saying good-bye back there."

Claws of desperation gripped Sun Shadow's heart. "Don't tell them!" he begged, padding up to Quiet Rain. "Don't try to stop me. I need to do this."

Quiet Rain jumped down from her perch, landing neatly on all four paws beside Sun Shadow. Though she didn't speak, there was determination in her gaze.

She's going to tell Sharp Hail! Sun Shadow thought, anguished.

He opened his jaws to beg Quiet Rain once more to let him go, but before he could speak a piercing cry came from the tunnel leading to Stoneteller's den. Quiet Rain turned toward the sound, and while she was distracted Sun Shadow slipped out onto the path that led behind the waterfall.

Stoneteller is dying!

His paws were tugging at him to go back and do what he could to ease the old cat's last moments, but he knew that if he did that, he would never get away.

I'm doing what she wanted. . . .

Sun Shadow emerged from the end of the path and began to scramble down the rocks, his paws sliding where the surface was slick from the spray of the waterfall. Down and down into the darkness . . . Sun Shadow's heart was pounding, and he had no idea where he was going, only that he had to get away from the cave as fast as he could. Sharp stones poked into his pads, and once he almost hurled himself over a precipice because he didn't see the curve in the path in time.

Sun Shadow drew back, shivering against the rock wall, trying to block out his glimpse of the dizzying depths. As he was gathering himself to go on, he heard paw steps approaching him from farther up the rocks.

Springing up, Sun Shadow tried to pick up the pace, to escape from the cat who was pursuing him.

"Wait!" a voice yowled from behind him.

Sun Shadow realized that the sound came from a she-cat. He halted in surprise and turned. *Has my mother followed me to say good-bye?* Then he spotted Quiet Rain only a few tail-lengths behind him on the path.

"I'm not going back!" he blurted out, his shoulder fur bristling.

"Of course you're not," Quiet Rain replied. "But we'd better hurry. Stoneteller has died, and Sharp Hail is waking all the cats."

Even though he had known what was happening, Sun Shadow felt a pain gripping at his heart when he heard the news of Stoneteller's death. Then as he fought with his grief, he realized what Quiet Rain had said.

"We?" he repeated.

"I'm coming with you," Quiet Rain hissed, squeezing past him on the narrow path. "Now let's hurry. The Sun Trail is long, and we don't know what dangers we'll face. . . ."

CHAPTER 1

Clear Sky yawned and stretched his forepaws until they trembled. He looked over the edge of his nest. A biting wind sliced beneath the arching root, which usually shielded him as he slept. It nipped his ears, and he narrowed his eyes against its sting as he gazed over the clearing.

Quick Water was crossing the camp, her fur fluffed up against the cold. A shriveled mouse hung from her jaws. Birch and Alder peeked out from beneath the low, spreading yew. Petal had made their nest beneath its dark green branches after she'd adopted them. Their own mother had been killed, and they hardly remembered her scent. Now Petal was dead too, taken by the sickness that had swept the forest before leaf-bare had come. Birch and Alder had nearly died, but the Blazing Star had saved them.

The Blazing Star. Clear Sky felt a pang of grief. If only Star Flower had told them about it sooner. It was the only healing herb that could cure the sickness. Now it shaped their future. He stood and shook out his fur as Alder and Birch hurried out to meet Quick Water.

"Is that for us?" Birch's eyes were hopeful.

His sister, Alder, dipped her head to Quick Water. "If you tell us where you found it, we could go and catch our own." The littermates were almost fully grown, lithe and fast and always eager to hunt. Clear Sky felt proud of the cats they'd become, and was pleased that he'd decided to let Petal take them in.

"Don't be squirrel-brained." Quick Water dropped the mouse at their paws. "We can share this one and hunt together later."

Alder and Birch blinked at her gratefully.

Clear Sky felt a prickle of worry as he watched them crouch close to Quick Water, taking turns to snatch a bite of the skinny prey. Prey was scarce. The sickness had killed much of it, and the forest was eerily silent, even for leaf-bare.

He shook the chill from his fur and hopped out of his nest. He'd wandered in the forest until dawn and had returned to rest, weary from the cold. The memory of the dream had followed him into sleep. Fluttering Bird wanted the cats to join together. They must be like the Blazing Star and gather like petals around the heart of a flower. He was sure of it. It made sense. If the cold had reached this deep into the forest, it would be bitter on the high moor. And with prey so scarce, the moor cats would surely freeze or starve if they stayed in their hollow. They'd be safer here, sheltered by the trees, hunting together, as Fluttering Bird had ordered.

He must tell them.

Perhaps they already know? For the first time he wondered what the spirit cats had shared with the others. Hope flickered in his belly. Perhaps they were ready to unite.

He slid out from beneath the root, its gnarled bark scraping his spine, and padded across the frozen earth.

Pink Eyes was crouching in the shelter of the spreading holly, squinting against the wind. Tiny flecks of snow swirled in the air and clung to his fur. Pink Eyes's tail twitched with annoyance and he drew his paws tighter under him.

Clear Sky nodded to him. "Where's Blossom?" he asked.

The old tom had arrived at the border with the tortoise-shell-and-white she-cat when the moon was only a scratch of silver in the sky, not long after the battle with One Eye.

"Still asleep," Pink Eyes answered, flicking his muzzle toward the holly bush. In the shadows beneath, Clear Sky could make out Blossom's pelt. When she was awake, the young she-cat hardly stood still. She was skittish and full of energy.

When Clear Sky had first met her, she'd been leaping for a dead leaf as it fluttered toward the forest floor while Pink Eyes sat a few tail-lengths away, his thin white tail curled neatly over two dead mice. He'd stood when Clear Sky had approached and had spoken before Clear Sky had a chance to challenge them for loitering near his border. "May we join your group?"

There had been a time when Clear Sky would have driven the two strays from his border—especially Pink Eyes, whose sight was so poor he couldn't see a bird in a tree—but these cats had respected his scent line and kept their hackles soft, and Clear Sky had learned that friends were better than enemies.

So they'd joined the group, and Clear Sky was soon glad that they had. Pink Eyes's weak eyesight had strengthened his other senses. The white tom could hear a mouse in the next glade and smell a rabbit through a patch of wild garlic.

Alder looked up from her meal, her splotchy gray-and-white pelt pricking where tiny snowflakes had settled along her spine. As she licked her lips, her gaze flashed toward Pink Eyes's twitching tail. Clear Sky saw mischief light up her eyes. She lunged and grabbed it, rolling onto her back. With a purr, she began pummeling it playfully with her hind legs.

"Hey!" Pink Eyes turned on her angrily. "Chase your own tail!"

"Why?" Alder froze, her paws in the air, and blinked at him innocently. "I'm not a dog!"

Pink Eyes glared at her. "And my tail isn't *prey*."

Birch padded to his sister's side, his ginger pelt bright in the weak morning light. "I just wish prey was so easy to catch," he said lightly.

The old tom snorted and marched away. He circled in a sheltered spot between the roots of an oak, then sat down and stared pointedly at Birch and Alder.

The brambles at the far end of the camp rattled. Nettle padded through the gap at one side. His thick gray pelt was damp. Acorn Fur followed him, a battered starling hanging from her jaws. Leaf padded after them, carrying a scrawny squirrel.

"I've never seen prey so scarce." Nettle padded past his campmates and stopped beside Clear Sky. "I don't know how we'll make it to newleaf."

Anxiety wormed in Clear Sky's belly. Alder and Birch were staring hungrily at Acorn Fur's starling. Quick Water's mouse clearly hadn't filled their bellies. *We must survive!* Clear Sky glanced through the trees. Was there more prey on the moor? Suddenly the boundaries he'd fought so hard to establish seemed to trap him. *We need to share what we have, not guard it.* Fluttering Bird must have known that.

"I'm going to Gray Wing's camp," he told Nettle.

Nettle's ear twitched. "Why?"

Clear Sky shifted his paws. Nettle had fought beside him to keep the boundaries they'd made. What would he say when he heard Clear Sky had suddenly decided that the cats should share their land and live as one group? He would understand once he knew that it was what the spirit cats wanted. But there wasn't time to explain now. "I want to see Jagged Peak's kits." This was true. He hadn't visited his brother's litter yet.

"The weather's closing in." Nettle glanced at the thick yellow clouds crowding the treetops. "There'll be heavy snow before the day's out, and if the wind picks up—"

Clear Sky interrupted. "I come from the mountains, remember? I'm used to getting snow in my whiskers."

Nettle shrugged. "It's your pelt." He glanced across the clearing as Blossom slid out from beneath the holly.

"Do I smell prey?" she asked brightly. Her gaze swiveled toward Acorn Fur.

Acorn Fur dropped her starling. "There's not much, but we can share."

Leaf laid his squirrel on the ground. "It'll do for now." His mew was cheerful, but Clear Sky could see worry darkening his gaze. The sooner he persuaded the cats they'd be safer working together, the better. He headed for the gap in the brambles. "Make sure Pink Eyes gets some food," he called over his shoulder. "His hungry belly is making him grouchy." He shot a teasing look at the white cat.

Pink Eyes stared stiffly ahead, as though deaf. Clear Sky knew his sharp hearing hadn't missed his jibe. Affection surged beneath his pelt. *Proud old fleabag!*

Blossom leaped onto a root beside Pink Eyes. "Do you want to share the starling or the squirrel?"

"I guess a bite of squirrel might be nice," the tom huffed grudgingly.

Purring, Clear Sky slipped through the bramble tunnel.

Outside camp, the wind was brisker. The branches above him swished in the breeze. He opened his mouth and tasted snow. It carried the stone tang of the mountains. Nettle had been right. A heavy snowfall was on its way. He hurried between the trees. The sooner he reached the moor cats' hollow, the better.

He followed the ridge until it dipped, then he leaped a fallen tree and climbed the slope beyond. Bare brambles snaked over the ground, and he had to watch where he put each paw. The ferns had withered long ago, but in their musty stumps Clear Sky could smell a hint of the forest's greenleaf lushness. Stiff bracken crowded the top of the slope. Clear Sky pushed through it, narrowing his eyes against the light as he neared the edge of the forest. He broke from the trees, ducking instinctively as he hit open country.

The icy wind streamed through his whiskers, and he flattened his ears. He glanced one way, then the other, tasting the air for danger. Dog scent clung to the grass, but it was stale, and he crossed the swath of withered ferns edging the woods and began to climb through the rough grass.

He paused as he neared a stunted thorn tree standing alone on the barren moorside. Beneath it, a mound of soil marked the grave where they had buried One Eye, the bloodthirsty rogue. The cats from moor, forest, and river had joined together to defeat him. Snow flecked the soil, and thrushes sang in the branches above.

He was a true ray of light.

Bitterness rose in Clear Sky's throat as he remembered Star Flower's words at the burial. How could she have been so deluded? One Eye might have been her father, but even she must have been shocked by his cruelty.

How could she have betrayed Thunder for him? Clear Sky snorted. He still couldn't believe that the treacherous she-cat had deceived his son.

The wind blew harder. Heather swayed ahead of him, and he hurried for its shelter, ducking among the brown bushes until he found a rabbit trail between the stems. He followed it, relieved to be out of the wind, zigzagging this way and that as he made his way up the winding path.

The heather gave way to a smooth grassy slope. In the open once more, Clear Sky spied the dip in the hillside where the moor cats' camp lay. He quickened his pace. Snowflakes streamed around him, falling thicker now.

Movement caught his eyes. A small flash of fur against the grass ahead made him freeze.

Prey.

A small rabbit was hopping toward the heather. Clear Sky dropped into a crouch and pricked his ears. Excitement surged through him as warm rabbit scent filled his nose. His tail twitched. He waggled his hindquarters, preparing to pounce.

Suddenly, the rabbit stopped and looked around, ears high. Clear Sky froze.

The rabbit blinked, then bolted for the heather.

Now! Clear Sky surged forward. His paws rang on the frozen earth.

The rabbit fled. Fear-scent trailed in its wake. Clear Sky was closing in. He pushed harder against the frosty grass, fixing his gaze on the space in front of it.

Then he leaped. Stretching his forepaws, he landed squarely on his prey. It struggled beneath him. He was surprised at its strength. Quickly, he dug in his claws and sank his teeth into its neck. The spine snapped cleanly and the rabbit fell limp.

Clear Sky's mouth watered as blood bathed his tongue. He sat up and licked his lips. Should he leave his catch to take back to his own cats? He glanced toward the hollow. The moor cats might have greater need. And it would make a generous offering to Jagged Peak and Holly, in honor of their first litter.

He grabbed the rabbit's scruff in his jaws and carried it up the slope.

As he neared the moor cats' camp, he scanned the top of its gorse wall. Where was Tall Shadow? She was usually watching from her rock, scanning the moor with her solemn, wary gaze. He slowed as he reached the camp entrance. There was no cat guarding it. He pricked his ears. Had the weather driven them into their tunnels?

"We should wait for the snow to pass before we send out a hunting patrol."

Clear Sky heard Thunder's mew beyond the camp wall. Pride swelled in his chest. His son had grown into a fine tom.

"What if it lasts for days?" Gray Wing's mew answered Thunder.

"Let's worry about that when it happens."

Clear Sky nosed through the gap in the gorse.

Gray Wing turned to meet him, eyes round with surprise. "Clear Sky? What are you doing here?"

Clear Sky dropped his catch. "I came to visit Jagged Peak's kits." He glanced around the camp, a purr rumbling in his throat as he spied three kits tumbling across the grass at the far end of the hollow.

Thunder didn't follow his gaze. He was staring at the rabbit on the ground in front of Clear Sky. "Did you catch that on our land?" His amber eyes narrowed.

Clear Sky blinked at him. Only a few moons ago, they'd begun to grow close. Now he felt further from his son than ever before. "I—I brought it for Jagged Peak and Holly."

One of the kits squeaked excitedly. "I'm the fastest!"

Clear Sky saw a brown tom-kit struggle from his littermate's grip and race toward Jagged Peak, who was watching from the long grass at the edge of the hollow.

"No, you're not!" A tabby she-kit raced after him. The splotches on her pelt were like Holly's. White tips on her nose and her tail made her look as though she'd been dipped in snow.

"Wait for me!" A third kit trailed behind. His thick gray pelt and lithe frame reminded Clear Sky of Jagged Peak before the accident that had crippled his hind leg.

"Eagle Feather!" Holly stepped from the shelter of the long grass, and the brown tom-kit bundled into her. She scooped him up by his scruff and dropped him into the grass behind her. "Storm Pelt! Dew Nose! Back into your nest, all of you! It's too cold to be out."

Jagged Peak swished his tail. "They'll be warm enough so long as they keep moving."

"Let them play!" Shattered Ice called across the clearing. "It'll make them strong." The gray-and-white tom looked thin.

Mud Paws and Lightning Tail sat a tail-length away, sharing an emaciated mouse. Clear Sky could see their bones jutting beneath their fur.

Mud Paws looked up, chewing. "Check their tail-tips," he advised. "If they're frozen, it's time to stop."

"Let them have fun!" Sparrow Fur padded out from beneath the arching broom at the end of the camp. The she-kit had grown, but she was skinny, and her pelt dull. "If there *is* a snowstorm on the way, it might be the last fun they have for days."

Gray Wing kneaded the ground with his paws. "We really should send out a hunting party now."

"They might get caught in the storm," Thunder argued. "And Clear Sky has brought this rabbit." He nudged it with his wide paw. "The kits won't go hungry."

Clear Sky blinked. "Are they eating prey already?"

"They were born the new moon before last," Gray Wing reminded him.

That long ago? Clear Sky's thoughts flitted back to the dream. *We grow tired of waiting.* They had promised to spread and grow like the Blazing Star. He caught Gray Wing's eye. "We have to talk about what we saw." He scanned the clearing. "Is Tall Shadow here?"

"Pebble Heart's treating a scratch on her paw." Thunder nodded toward a jutting stretch of gorse. "In Cloud Spots's den."

"I can get her if you like." A mew sounded behind Clear Sky.

He jerked around. It was Owl Eyes. The young tom had broadened across the shoulders. His forehead was nearly as wide as Gray Wing's. "You've grown!" Clear Sky exclaimed.

"So has Pebble Heart." Owl Eyes stalked away and called into the gorse. "Tall Shadow, Clear Sky is here."

"I know." The black she-cat's familiar mew sounded from the shadows. "I can smell his scent." The bush quivered as Tall Shadow slid out.

ERIN
HUNTER

is inspired by a love of cats and a
fascination with the ferocity of the
natural world. As well as having great
respect for nature in all its forms,
Erin enjoys creating rich mythical
explanations for animal behavior. She
is also the author of the bestselling
Seekers and Survivors series.

Download the free Warriors app and
chat on Warriors message boards at
www.warriorcats.com.

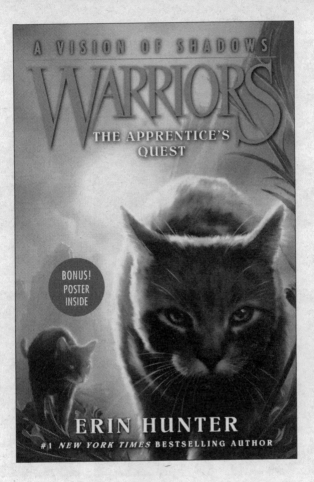

WARRIORS: POWER OF THREE

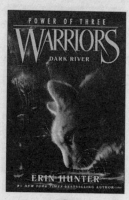

In the third series, Firestar's grandchildren begin their training as warrior cats. Prophecy foretells that they will hold more power than any cats before them.

HARPER
An Imprint of HarperCollins Publishers

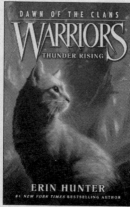

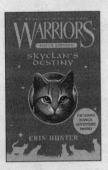

WARRIORS: BONUS STORIES

  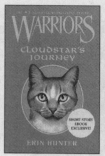 

Discover the untold stories of the warrior cats and Clans when you download the separate ebook novellas—or read them in two paperback bind-ups!

WARRIORS : FIELD GUIDES

FOR THE ULTIMATE FAN!

Delve deeper into the Clans with these Warriors field guides.

HARPER
An Imprint of HarperCollinsPublishers

www.warriorcats.com